THE
ARABIAN
PEARL

The Miss Danforth Mysteries:

The Punjat's Ruby
The Arabian Pearl
The Cat's Eye
Diamond Head
The Sunken Treasure

A MISS DANFORTH MYSTERY
THE ARABIAN PEARL

MARIAN J.A. JACKSON

Mystery Writers of America Presents
San Jose   New York   Lincoln   Shanghai

The Arabian Pearl
A Miss Danforth Mystery

All Rights Reserved © 1990, 2001 by Marian J. A. Jackson

Mystery Writers of America Presents
an imprint of iUniverse.com, Inc.

For information address:
iUniverse.com, Inc.
5220 S 16th, Ste. 200
Lincoln, NE 68512
www.iuniverse.com

Originally published by Pinnacle Books/Windsor Publishing Co.

ISBN: 0-595-19393-5

Printed in the United States of America

With Love For
Christy, Jim, Joshua, Kaleena
and
Rebecca

ACKNOWLEDGEMENTS

It is only by having free access to the treasures in the New York Public Library system that I was able to write this book. Thank you for being there.

I would also like to thank Trumbull Rogers for his generosity with his private collection of books on the American West.

CAST
(In order of appearance)

Abigail Patience Danforth	Ambitious to be the world's first female consulting detective
Maude Cunningham	Abigail's companion and chronicler of her adventures
Kinkade	Abigail's major domo
Jacqueline Bordeaux	Abigail's lady's maid
Charles Osgood	Friend of Marshal Tilghman
Polecat	Drifter, Mulehead's Friend
Mulehead	Drifter, Polecat's Friend
Billy Bub	Member of Baxter Gang
Boss	Maw Baxter's Son, and Leader of Baxter Gang
Maw Baxter	Mother of Boss
Sampson	Member of Baxter Gang
Hank	Member of Baxter Gang
Curly	Member of Baxter Gang
Crosspatches	Abigail's horse
The Arabian	Marshal Tilghman's Foundation Sire
Railroad Agent	Employee of the Atchison, Topeka & Santa Fe Railroad Company
Pinkerton Agent	Employee of the Pinkerton National Detective Agency
Jake	Citizen of Cameron Junction, and Leader of Posse
Marshal William Tilghman	Famous Lawman of the West
Mr. Dade	Owner of Fastest Horse in Kansas City
Morgan Dade	Mr. Dade's son
Ms. and Mrs. Dawson	Ranchers
Various Speaking Parts and Walk Ons	

Chapter One

"So this is private varnish!" Abigail exclaimed, tossing her squirrel muff onto a tufted-silk, golden-tasseled chair. Swiftly doffing her squirrel-trimmed cloak, she draped it carelessly over the back of the chair while turning full circle to survey the elegant appointments of the parlor of the private railroad car. "What a swell way to travel!"

"There is no need to resort to vulgarisms, Miss Danforth." Maude's reproach seemed automatic, much like the manner in which she unbuttoned her unadorned black woolen overcoat and dropped it on top of Abigail's.

"Ah, but Miss Cunningham." Abigail's smile was ironic. "Is it not vulgar to have an entire railroad car all to ourselves? Rather makes our overnight in a first-class Pullman from New York seem like steerage." Skirts arustle, she settled herself into an overstuffed, tasseled armchair by the lavishly curtained window. Ignoring the dreary February morning outside, she took advantage of the reflective qualities of the window glass to check that the angle of her elaborately befeathered hat had survived their change of trains and escorted tour through the car. "We must find a splendid gift for the Humbolts for lending it to us," she said, rearranging her skirts to fall gracefully before resting her gloved hands in her lap.

Maude sat in the chair opposite without comment and apparently without care for the flow of her skirts, or how her modest bonnet had fared on their trek between trains. As she faced the windows, her gaze was intent upon the people still milling about outside. "Well it's about time," she said after scanning the crowd. "Here come Kinkade and Jacqueline with the luggage." Shaking her head, she said, "They appear to be quarreling again." With a frown of disapproval, she turned to Abigail. "You really must speak to Jacqueline, Miss Danforth."

"I daresay I'd not know what to say." Abigail shrugged. "I fear Kinkade is smitten with her and for some reason she cares not a whit for him."

"She is your maid, not mine." Maude's tone was indifferent even as she said, "We cannot tolerate indelicate behavior from the servants. Especially while we are traveling."

"Ah, but think how convenient it would be if they should marry." Abigail smiled.

Maude's expression was suddenly as bleak as the weather outside. "Marriage should be more than a matter for convenience, Miss Danforth."

Abigail was immediately contrite. "Oh, I pray you, do forgive me for making light of the solemnity of matrimony." Her chin was as firm as a Gibson girl's portrait as she added earnestly, "I shall find the killer of your beloved Charlie, I promise." Her dark eyes were warm as she reached out a hand to touch Maude's. "Indeed, I am most grateful to you for providing me with the opportunity to practice the infant science of detection." She paused before continuing persuasively, "But we have the entire continent to cross before we reach San Francisco wherein the dastardly deed occurred. The trip threatens to be a dreadful bore. Can we not take some pleasure in the journey?"

"I'd warrant you already have enjoyed yourself overmuch, young lady." Maude withdrew her hand. She raised a disapproving eyebrow. "I saw you talking to that man."

"Don't you sound the gooseberry," Abigail said, sitting straight, hands once again folded in her lap, all sympathy for Maude's plight erased by her irritation at being scolded. "May I remind you that it is only my father, and possibly Kinkade, who believes you to be my chaperon? In truth you are to chronicle our adventures."

"Then you should know without my telling you that no true gentleman would presume to introduce himself to you." Although Maude's words were directed at Abigail, her gaze wandered about the interior of the car as if taking inventory of its luxurious contents, thereby lending a nonchalant quality to her lecture. "Just because that man found himself standing next to you at a fence while you were watching stablehands exercise your horses, however exclusive Chicago's Paddock Club may be, gave him no excuse for such impertinence."

"I had to see how Crosspatches had suffered his night in the horse Pullman, hadn't I?" As Abigail glanced at Maude's reflection in the window, a feeling of dismay began to dampen her enthusiasm for their impending journey. She had known Maude but a few months and had not seen this Mrs. Grundy side of her before. But she had not broken free from her father's domination only to be bullied by the chronicler of her adventures; therefore she did nothing to conceal her defiance as she said, "Furthermore, I mean to exercise Crosspatches myself, by myself, in the morning. We'll have an hour's wait while we hook up with the Union Pacific at Kansas City."

Maude glanced at Abigail. "I suppose you're going to wear those preposterous gentlemen's clothes and ride astride?"

"No, Miss Cunningham, I am not going to wear gentlemen's clothes," Abigail said haughtily. "I had a riding habit made with split skirts." She lifted her chin defiantly. "I shall, however, ride astride."

"Your reckless behavior on horseback will land you in serious difficulties one of these days," Maude said with a heavy sigh.

"May I remind you that it is 1900?" Abigail replied heatedly. "Women of the new century should no longer be bound by the ridiculous convention of riding sidesaddle. Especially in the West."

Several loud blasts from the engine's whistle announcing their departure overrode Maude's reply. As the car lurched into motion and echoes of the whistle abated, she said, "I should not have to caution you about talking to strange men."

"But how could I resist?" Abigail's natural enthusiasm returned at the memory. "Did you not see his magnificent horse?" Her eyes were alight with excitement. "He's brought it all the way from Arabia." She paused for the train's insistent whistle to subside again. "Oh, how I wish I could invite him to dinner," she continued when she could be heard. "He seemed such an interesting man."

"Why, your father would have a conniption." Maude gazed at her appraisingly. "He'd cancel all our arrangements and send you straight back to New York.''

"How would he find out, pray tell?'' Abigail responded with a conspiratorial glance. "And how else can we have adventures unless we dare a little?'' Her grin was wicked. "Kinkade would protect us. He could serve dinner.''

Maude gazed absently at the passing view. "That would be unseemly,'' she spoke at long last. "There are porters enough to do the serving. Kinkade should supervise. I daresay his fierce physiognomy would discourage any untoward advances from your Arabian.''

"Then you do not object?'' Amazed by Maude's sudden change in attitude, Abigail could but stare at her.

"I have merely been testing the strength of your thirst for adventure, Miss Danforth,'' Maude said with a rare smile. "As long as there is no delay in reaching our true destination, why should we not—as you say—enjoy our journey?''

Too relieved that Maude's chiding had been feigned to be vexed by being thus tested, Abigail stood and accustomed herself to the motion of the train before hurrying to the desk. "I shall pen an invitation for Mr. Osgood at once.''

"Mr. Osgood is it?'' Maude said in mock horror. "So he did introduce himself. What impudence!'' Maude stood also and went to the bellpull. As she rang for Kinkade, she added, "I suppose you told him your name as well?''

"Of course not!'' Abigail exclaimed, seating herself at the elaborately carved writing desk. "What do you take me for?'' Finding stationery in the drawer, she dipped the quilled pen in ink. "By the by,'' she said as she wrote, "Mr. Osgood is not Arabian; his horse is. From his looks and accent, I judge him to be American.''

''You may spare me the details, Miss Danforth,'' Maude said as she resumed her seat to gaze wistfully out of the window. ''I'll not upset your father by writing about Mr. Osgood, or our journey across the country. Our next adventure will not begin until we reach San Francisco.''

Kinkade staggered down the corridor of the private car, Abigail's note in one hand, grasping the brass trim at the windows to steady himself with the other.

Nimbly following him toward the pantry, Jacqueline smothered a giggle at his awkwardness. Erasing all trace of amusement from her expression when he closed the door behind them, she asked, ''What is so urgent, *Monsieur* Kinkade?''

Hoping to patch their latest quarrel by enlisting her aid, yet not daring to apologize again for fear of another rebuff, Kinkade thrust Mr. Osgood's invitation at her. Without preamble, he said, ''What do you think of this?''

Unwilling to admit she could read no English, Jacqueline suddenly began adjusting her apron strings. ''Read it to me,'' she said, haughty as any duchess.

Instantly realizing his tactlessness, Kinkade fumed at his unfortunate talent for upsetting her as he said, ''You know that man who had the crust to speak to Miss Danforth when she was looking after Crosspatches?''

''Oui.'' Jacqueline nodded with a puzzled frown.

''Well, she has invited him to dinner.'' Kinkade brandished the note.

''So?''

"What shall I do?" he asked, rubbing the lump on his nose. Badly reset after a childhood accident, it lent a pugilistic cast to his face that his benign nature did not deserve.

"I do not understand, *Monsieur.*" The frills on Jacqueline's cap were atremble from the motion of the train. "It is not your place to question the instructions of our mistress."

"But Mr. Danforth paid me handsomely to watch after his daughter!"

"Aha!" Jacqueline stood as tall as her diminutive stature would allow. "Is not Miss Danforth paying your wages?"

He nodded sheepishly.

"Well then—" Jacqueline threw up her hands— "deliver the invitation!"

"I cannot." Kinkade shook his head hopelessly. "Her father would not approve of her dining with anyone she'd not been properly introduced to. Why, the man probably doesn't have the correct dinner clothes."

"Impossible!" Jacqueline cried. "You cannot serve two masters!"

"What?"

"You must decide between them!"

"How can I? I was her father's valet before Miss Abigail was born. If Miss Cunningham will not act the proper chaperon, then I must protect her from harm."

"You were *Monsieur* Danforth's valet until the treacherous Samuel unseats you!" She shook her finger under his nose. "Miss Danforth saves you by giving you a position on this journey or "pouff!" out you go! Now it is the traitor you are!"

"But how can I allow her to ask for trouble?" Kinkade glared at the note in his hand.

"Did you not warn her?"

"I didn't know what was in the note until I was almost in first class and it—ah—fell open." He blushed. "And I came to seek your opinion." Gazing down at Jacqueline shyly, he said, "What if I just don't deliver it?"

"Imbecile! They will discover your trick when he does not appear."

"Wouldn't they just think him rude?"

Jacqueline looked at him as though he were simple. "And Miss Danforth says nothing when they meet again?"

"I must say you don't seem overly concerned about your mistress's behavior."

"Mais non, Monsieur Kinkade." Jacqueline glared at him. *"Our* mistress is perfection. She does not hand me the sack when I betray her to her brother. She—"

"Say no more, Miss Bordeaux," Kinkade interrupted, holding out his hand to stop her. "I have just thought of the perfect solution."

Suspicious, hands on hips, Jacqueline stared at him, waiting for him to continue.

"I shall deliver it, as you say." Kinkade smiled at his own cleverness as he added triumphantly, "But I'll also cable Mr. Danforth at the next stop."

"Fie on you!" Shaking her head in disgust, Jacqueline opened the pantry door. She turned to face him as she said with all the fierceness she could muster, "You . . . you . . . tattleteller!"

"He paid me for the information!" Kinkade shouted at her over the increased din.

"May the train forsake you at the station!" she said, slamming the pantry door behind her.

Tempted to rip the accursed invitation to bits, Kinkade waited until he was sure that Jacqueline would be out of sight before opening the door. As he struggled

14

toward first class, he bitterly regretted having consulted her, thereby widening the rift between them.

Terrence Osgood speared his last bluepoint and smiled with pleasure. "These are the best oysters I've had in ever so long, Miss Danforth." Deeply tanned, his blue eyes seemed all the brighter, and their expression bespoke his genuine delight at the sumptuous repast, flawlessly served by white-gloved porters.

"Oh, that's Kinkade's doing, none of my own," Abigail said, herself pleased with the fine damask napery ironed to crisp perfection, delicate crystal, and golden flatware. She had chosen a relatively plain, gold-rimmed Wedgewood china from the many patterns Kinkade had found in the pantry cupboards.

Osgood dabbed at the corners of his mouth with his napkin before lifting his goblet toward Kinkade. "Well done, my man!"

Kinkade acknowledged the toast with a curt nod. He'd had to admit that Osgood cut a fine figure in his impeccably correct white tie and tails, but he did not care for the intensity with which the man continually gazed at Miss Cunningham.

"And did Kinkade provide this superb champagne as well?" Osgood asked, placing his emptied glass by his plate. He hoped to ingratiate himself with Kinkade so that he would answer a few indiscreet questions concerning Miss Cunningham after dinner. While he found Miss Danforth charming, dressed in the latest fashion with sapphires at her ears and throat, the older woman's brusque manner intrigued him. She wore no jewels. Her honey-colored hair was severely dressed, and her unadorned black gown suggested recent widowhood.

Sensitive to Osgood's interest in Maude, Abigail wondered at Maude's reserve. She'd been friendly enough when their guest had arrived, but had since become increasingly withdrawn, almost rude, toward him. As Kinkade signaled to one porter to refill Osgood's glass and another to begin the next course, she found herself suddenly burdened with keeping the conversation going. "That is a splendid horse you have, Mr. Osgood." She glanced at Maude for corroboration, but Maude kept her gaze upon her plate. "An Arabian, you say?" Abigail added hurriedly to detract from Maude's lack of response.

"Actually he's a *Saglawi*, Miss Danforth." Although Osgood returned Abigail's smile, his gaze soon shifted to Maude as he spoke. "One of the five accepted pure strains, and quite rare. He is deserving of your admiration. The Arab traces the genealogy of his horse through the mare, not the stallion as the English and you Americans do, and will not breed a purebred mare to an unpure stallion, or *kadischi*, regardless of how perfect he may be."

"He must be worth a great deal of money for so small a horse," Abigail said when Maude quite deliberately forked a mushroom and ate it without responding.

"In a sense he is as priceless as a fabled pearl, Miss Danforth." Again, Osgood turned, but briefly, to smile at Abigail. "And do not let his small size fool you. Amazingly enough, even when mated with a small mare, his blood will increase the size of their get."

Abigail swiftly retrieved her fan from her lap. "Amazing, indeed," she said, fanning cheeks made scarlet by so close a brush with an unmentionable subject.

Maude stifled a yawn.

16

"I say, Kinkade," Osgood said expansively, trying not to allow Maude's all too obvious boredom with his conversation to unnerve him, "this capon is excellent."

Having had nothing to do with the food, Kinkade chaffed at the compliment. The train was due to stop soon at a station with a telegraph, but he dared not leave his post as long as Osgood was present.

"If I may say, Miss Danforth, your horse is as handsome a specimen of an English thoroughbred as I've seen." This time Osgood's gaze did not stray. "And he seems to travel well."

"Why, thank you, Mr. Osgood," Abigail said, observing Kinkade's silence. While he was much too well trained to speak unless spoken to, it was unlike him not to have some small riposte. She continued, "I plan to be away from home for some time and did not wish to leave him."

Maude pursed her lips and glared at Abigail for so indiscreet a comment upon their itinerary. Much to Abigail's relief, Osgood did not pursue the topic.

"Unfortunately," he said, "the Arabian is not mine. I'm on my way to deliver him to Bill Tilghman."

"Not the famous Marshal Tilghman?" Abigail was impressed.

"He resigned as lawman when his wife died, Miss Danforth. Devotes his time to his horse farm now. The Arabian will be his Foundation Sire and stud." Osgood turned directly to Maude in that interested fashion that had Kinkade on guard. "He plans to put Chandler on the map with his grand horses."

"And where is Chandler?" All but forced to respond, Maude withheld any expression of genuine interest from her gray eyes, which merely served to fascinate Osgood all the more.

"Indian Territory," Osgood replied. "A cyclone pretty near blew it away last year. I'll be switching to the Missouri, Kansas and Texas Railway at Kansas City to take me south."

"I've been out of the country for some time, Mr. Osgood," Abigail said. "Pray forgive my ignorance, but Indians are no longer a threat, are they?"

"Oh, no, ma'am, they're tame enough now, on their reservations. Territory should become the state of Oklahoma soon."

"Tame!" Maude exclaimed. "You make them sound like the United States domesticated the wild pony!" Her interest piqued at the possibility of a political discussion, Maude finally joined the conversation, but her tone was sarcastic as she continued, "What our brave Congress did, Mr. Osgood, was to order the buffalo decimated so that the Indian would have nothing to sustain him except the government's charity."

"Perhaps it is as well that there is no risk that the savages will try and stop this train as they did so many others, Miss Cunningham." Encouraged by her response, Osgood leaned toward her and lowered his voice so that the porters could not overhear. "On my way back from bedding down Mr. Tilghman's horse, I passed through the freight car as they were locking up a shipment of gold in the safe. I heard the station master say it was bound for San Francisco. So for your sakes, I'm glad the only danger of being stopped that you ladies face might be a blizzard."

"Gold?" Suspecting that she was being fobbed off by a pretense of intrigue, Maude glared at him. "I thought gold was shipped out of the West, Mr. Osgood, not into it. Are you sure you're not just trying to titillate us?"

"What does it matter, Miss Cunningham," Abigail said. Turning to Osgood, she continued before he could answer Maude. "I would simply adore meeting Mr. Tilghman, sir. I do not think it untoward to confess that I long to prove myself as the world's first female consulting detective."

Astonished, Osgood sat back in his chair. "How extraordinary!" he exclaimed. Not in the least certain that his words were smooth, yet eager for any excuse to see the mysterious Miss Cunningham again, he continued, "Mr. Tilghman would be honored to meet you, Miss Danforth." Facing Maude, he added sincerely, "And, of course, you too, Miss Cunningham. It would give me great pleasure to provide an introduction. Couldn't you have the station agent switch your car?"

"I am sorry, Mr. Osgood," Maude said, without a trace of regret in her voice. "That would be quite impossible." Her expressive glance toward Abigail said that she'd brook no disagreement as she continued, "We are scheduled straight through, gratis, and the correspondence necessary to reroute us would be impossible to accomplish on such short notice." Turning to Abigail, she added firmly, "Must I remind you we have urgent business in San Francisco?"

Mystified by Maude's refusal of Osgood's invitation, but not wishing to appear quarrelsome in front of him and spoil the pleasant evening, Abigail resolved to confront her later and change her mind. Forcing a smile, she feigned agreement with Maude and changed the subject to the theater.

This naturally led to gossip about the late Miss Lily Langtry and the colorful Judge Roy Bean, all of which entertained them until dessert had been cleared.

"I'll take my leave now, ladies, and have my cigar in the parlor car," Osgood said after observing the

19

amenities. "May I take the liberty of ordering Cross-patches saddled in the morning, Miss Danforth?"

"I'd be much obliged, Mr. Osgood," Abigail said with a smile.

He turned to Maude. "Will you join Miss Danforth and me?" he asked hopefully. "Perhaps I could persuade you to change your mind about coming to Chandler."

"I fear not, Mr. Osgood," Maude said. "I leave the exercising of her horse to Miss Danforth."

Holding his disappointment at bay, Osgood said, "Well, then, until morning, Miss Danforth."

Alas, none of them knew that the circumstances of their next meeting would be grievously different.

Chapter Two

As the train sped through the night, Jacqueline swayed slightly to maintain her balance while she stood behind her seated mistress, applying the ritual one hundred strokes of the hairbrush. She frowned, but not at the chore; she enjoyed dressing Abigail's luxuriant, waist-length hair and took extra care to banish all traces of the coal dust that seemed to settle everywhere. It was the threat of Kinkade's treachery that clouded her expression and had her chewing her lower lip.

Because the train had made no stops wherein he'd have had access to a telegraph, she was certain that Kinkade had had no opportunity to cable Abigail's father before dinner. Or during.

Like most servants, she was skilled at seeing without being seen and had been watching as he'd conversed with Osgood in the passageway afterward. She was certain she'd seen Osgood slip him some money. But that could have been innocent enough. Kinkade not only had a right to a gratuity, he deserved one for managing a flawless dinner in such cramped, albeit fancy, circumstances with only porters to assist. Or Osgood might have wanted him to tip the porters; they had proven to be trained surprisingly well.

She had to admit, for a man who'd spent so many of his years in service as valet, Kinkade was proving to have a flair for executing those unusual functions demanded of him with skill and aplomb. She'd been not a little surprised by how friendly he had seemed to become toward Osgood after the exchange of money. Was it possible he'd changed his mind about telling Abigail's father? If so, she didn't want to tattle to no purpose. But before she had been able to seek him out and ask his intentions, Abigail had summoned her.

Heavy draperies and thick carpet muffled the sound of the train's motion, but enough noise intruded into Abigail's quarters to conceal any murmuring that might have escaped Jacqueline's lips.

Nor had Abigail observed her maid's agitation in the tiny dressing-table mirror. Earlier in the day, she had planned to use this interval of their nightly routine to ask some delicate questions about Jacqueline's feelings for Kinkade, but distracted by pondering upon Maude's curious behavior at dinner, Abigail dismissed her maid without having noticed her distress.

Over the past few weeks while residing in her father's house, she and Maude had developed a pleasant ritual of discussing the day over a liqueur in Maude's quarters before bedtime, especially when they'd been to a party or dance, or met someone new at dinner. Abigail had learned to value Maude's assessment of people's character and disposition. Although she'd been surprised when Maude had first claimed that Mr. Danforth seldom reviewed his opinion of people once he'd made up his mind, afterward, she had carefully observed her father and discovered that Maude was correct. Maude's remarks might be tactless at times, which mattered little as long as they were alone, but nonetheless she had a most useful gift for seeing through a person's pretense. If she had a reason for not liking Osgood, Abigail wanted to hear it before meeting him in the morning. But this evening Maude had excused herself with nary a word the moment Osgood had departed. Considering Maude's reserved behavior toward their guest, it was singularly unlike her not to have had a private comment.

Further, there was the matter of Osgood's kind offer of an introduction to Marshal Tilghman. This serendipitous opportunity to talk with a famous lawman of the West was too good to pass by with the meek acquiescence she had feigned at dinner. The marshal could no doubt give her valuable advice upon the best way to pick up a cold trail, which would be her first task upon their arrival in San Francisco when she began the hunt for Charlie's killer. At the very least, he could add to her modest store of knowledge regarding the infant science of detection, and she had no intention of allowing the burden of good manners to prevent such a meeting. Although she did not relish a confrontation with Maude, she was too determined to grasp the opportunity to meet the marshal to shirk such an interview, however disagreeable it might prove to be.

Therefore, despite the hour, she donned her dressing gown and slippers and padded down the corridor to knock upon Maude's stateroom door. She heard no invitation to enter but blamed the noise of the train for her inability to hear Maude's voice and opened the door a crack.

Maude was asleep, a book open, facedown, by her side. Not caring if she awakened her, Abigail did not bother to tiptoe as she took the few steps to reach

Maude and extinguish the oil lamp. As she reached across the bed for the lamp, Maude stirred.

Leaving the lamp burning, Abigail withdrew her hand as she whispered, "Are you awake?"

"I am now," Maude grumbled, opening one eye to glare at Abigail. ·

Risking her companion's further displeasure, Abigail sat in the chair beside her and asked, "Are you feeling all right?"

"Yes, of course, I am," Maude replied testily. "What makes you ask?"

Abigail shrugged nonchalantly. "I was just wondering why you were so rude tonight."

"Rude? What do you mean, rude!" Maude propped herself up on an elbow. "Aren't you being unduly sensitive?" she asked, plumping up her pillows. "I did not know our after-dinner tête à tête was mandatory!"

Abigail rescued the book before it fell. "I did not mean to say that you were rude to me, Miss Cunningham," she said haughtily, stung more by Maude's patronizing tone than her words. "You may retire whenever you please as far as I am concerned."

"Did you rouse me to play conundrums, Miss Danforth?" Maude collapsed against the pillows.

"Very well, then, not rude," Abigail said as she retrieved the bookmark from the bedcovers. "Perhaps, unkind." Carefully preserving Maude's place in the book, she closed it and placed it upon the nightstand as she hastened to add, "Not to me, to Mr. Osgood, that is." Turning to face Maude, she paused a moment before asking cautiously. "Could you not tell that he was fond of you?"

"He was not very subtle, was he?" Maude replied, shielding her eyes from the light with her arms, thereby concealing the expression on her face.

"Were you not flattered by his attention?" Abigail asked. Having no desire to insult Maude, she was careful not to have her voice insinuate the astonishment she'd felt that a man would find Maude attractive. Indeed, upon having duly reflected upon Osgood's obvious affection for Maude during dinner, she'd realized that had she herself taken a liking to the gentleman, she might have had cause for a bit of jealousy. After all, there she'd been, expensively gowned, in the bloom of her youth, and at her most charming; and there had been Maude, in unadorned black, fast approaching the end of her twenties, if she had not already departed them forever, and her behavior bordering upon the rude. Yet Osgood had clearly preferred her. It would seem that the male sex was going to prove to be every bit as mysterious as any crime that might come within her purview.

They traversed at least a mile before Maude responded, "Have you never been irritated by an unwanted suitor when he presses his attention upon you?"

"Goodness gracious, yes, Miss Cunningham. Of course I have!" Abigail exclaimed. "Hasn't every girl?" It was her turn to be testy. "But you know perfectly well that it is our duty to make even the most dreadfully boring man believe he is utterly fascinating. Suitor or no." She paused, trying to peer into Maude's face. "Mr. Osgood was far from boring. That is why I was puzzled by your—"

"The difficulty lay not with Mr. Osgood, my dear child," Maude interrupted only to be overtaken by a yawn. She tried to stifle it, but it got the better of her.

Somewhat mollified by Maude's admission, Abigail waited for the spasm to pass.

"Any discomfort you or the kind Mr. Osgood may have suffered this evening was all my doing," Maude continued when the yawn had run its course. Still shielding her eyes with one arm, she lowered the other to reach out, seeking Abigail's hand.

Disarmed by Maude's admission, Abigail took Maude's hand in both of hers as she said gently, "Neither could I understand why you would deny me the opportunity to visit with Marshal Tilghman." Moved by Maude's rare gesture of affection, all trace of defiance had melted. Instead of demanding that Maude change her mind, she found herself saying, "Meeting the famous lawman would mean a great deal to me." She hesitated before adding, "It would take us out of our way by no more than a week. Won't you reconsider?"

Once again, they traversed somewhat more than a mile before Maude spoke. "I shall never forget your bursting into my room in those ridiculous gentlemen's clothes." Maude's smile was so fleeting, Abigail doubted she'd seen it. "I had almost gotten used to my life in your father's house," Maude continued. "I had my privacy to write." She patted Abigail's hand, and her voice grew tremulous as she added, "I had given up any hope of ever solving the mystery of Charlie's death."

Abigail murmured sympathetically.

Maude sighed heavily. "I do believe it is hope that is our most grievous source of torment."

"Oh, Miss Cunningham," Abigail said, appalled at the idea. "I could not disagree with you more heartily. Hope is what keeps us going. Why, had I no hope that I could pursue the infant science of detection, my life would not be worth—"

"Tosh and nonsense!" Maude interrupted. "You would marry and have many babies!" Lifting her arm from her eyes, she glared briefly at Abigail. "Don't you understand, Miss Danforth?'' she continued as she shielded her eyes with her arm once again. "When I had no hope, I cared not a fig where I was or how I passed my days. I was almost content."

Irritated by the cavalier manner in which Maude had brushed aside her ambitions, yet loathe to begin a quarrel, Abigail kept silent.

"But there again, how could you understand?" Maude continued. "I have not yet told you to what extent Charlie's reputation was besmirched. Or how my life was threatened and how I was forced to seek sanctuary in your father's house. It was only by abandoning all hope of clearing his name that I was finally able to begin a new life." Maude squeezed Abigail's hand. "And then you appeared."

"I—?"

"Pray do not play the innocent, Miss Danforth." Maude withdrew her hand. "Yes, it was you who restored my hope that I could clear Charlie's name. And, like a miracle, here we are, speeding across this vast country, and all of a sudden you seem ready to detour at the whim of a stranger—" Maude twisted away and hid her face in the pillows so that Abigail could not see the tears she could no longer hold at bay.

For the first time in her young life, Abigail understood why a gentleman dreaded a female's tears. She felt utterly helpless to press her own case in the face of Maude's distress. Disappointed at the opportunity she doomed by surrendering to Maude's entreaties, yet unable to behave otherwise without hating herself for a cad, she murmured soothingly, "There, now, pray do not fret so, Miss Cunningham."

When, at last, Maude's weeping had subsided, she turned her tear-streaked face toward Abigail. Again, her smile was so fleeting, Abigail doubted that she'd seen it. "Can you understand why I might have no patience with casual flirtations, or for side trips to meet strange lawmen however famous they might be?"

Abigail fished out a handkerchief from her dressing gown pocket and handed it to Maude.

"Hope, Miss Danforth," Maude said as she took the delicate square of linen and patted her face dry. "It is the hope that you yourself gave me that has me thus overwrought."

Knowing herself to be guilty of Maude's accusation, and feeling neatly skewered upon it, Abigail sighed heavily.

"But I must admit you are quite right about one thing, Miss Danforth." Maude yawned and stretched before continuing, "About being rude. Manners are our best defense if we are to survive in this man's world." She settled into her pillows. "I'll not soon misuse mine again." Maude gazed directly into Abigail's eyes. "But, I pray you," she said with an intensity seldom displayed. "No detours."

"I promise, Miss Cunningham," Abigail said solemnly, placing her hand upon her heart. "No detours."

"Good morning, Miss Danforth!" Osgood shouted to make himself heard over the noise in the freight car as he stepped away from the Arabian's stall to greet Abigail. Although his dinner clothes had been correct for any eastern dinner table, his riding habit included a hat with the exceptionally wide brim, as well as the tight-fitting, heeled boots in the western mode. "I am so glad you are early," he continued. "There seems to be a mix-up with your saddle."

Abigail steadied herself with a hand on the railing

28

that penned the horses. "Crosspatches has only been ridden with an English saddle, Mr. Osgood," she shouted also. "I suspect he might find adjusting to a western difficult, without practice."

"Ah, you mistake my meaning." Osgood blushed. "I don't know how to tell you this, but your sidesaddle seems to be lost. The agent claims you boarded with only a man's saddle."

"He is quite correct, Mr. Osgood," Abigail said, steeling herself against any untoward comments Osgood might make about her predilection for riding astride.

Osgood concealed his astonishment with a smile as he replied without hesitation, "In that case, may I help you saddle up? The agent had to return to the express car."

Much to her chagrin, Abigail discovered that she was beginning to like this agreeable young gentleman and regretted her promise to Maude anew.

The masked man planted his feet square in the middle of the railroad tracks. The very ground shook beneath him, setting his whole body atremble. His stomach knotted in fear. The lantern he was swinging suddenly felt as heavy as the railroad tie he was standing on. Sweat slid from his armpits in spite of the cold. Worry about this moment had cost him much sleep. Only the disgrace of being branded a coward by the six men who called him Boss, and who were watching his every move, kept him glued to the spot, along with the fear of his mother's sharp tongue should he fail to stop, and rob, the train.

Frantic now, he waved the lantern as the train continued to thunder toward him. Even though the wide brim of his hat was pulled low over his eyes, he had to squint against the glare of the monstrous, onrushing headlight. Why wasn't the engineer stopping? Was the damn fool blind? Or was the tiny red glow of the lantern he was swinging too puny to be seen in the growing light of dawn? Would he stop even if he saw it? Heart thumping wildly in his chest, thinking it better to be a coward than dead, Boss readied himself to jump aside when through an ear-splitting shriek of steel against steel, he heard the angry blast of the engine's whistle as the brakes caught hold. He leapt into the air and cheered.

The damn fool was stopping!

Abigail lurched forward when the brakes caught. Longing to clasp both hands to her ears against the screaming brakes and deafening blast from the train's whistle, she was forced instead to clutch the gate to Crosspatches' stall to keep from falling. Her plumed riding hat was knocked askew, but she remained on her feet.

The horses crashed against the fronts of their stalls. Neighing, wide-eyed with fright, they managed to stay upright.

Osgood was not so lucky. After a desperate lunge to keep his balance, he tripped and landed on his hip by the wall that separated the makeshift corral from the express car.

The instant the brakes finally stopped squealing, and Abigail could let go of the gate, she seized Crosspatches by the bridle and stroked his neck to soothe him.

Seeing that his companion was calming down, the Arabian did too.

"Are you all right?" Abigail called to Osgood when

the last blast from the whistle died down enough for her to be heard.

"Has that engineer gone daft?" Osgood cried as he staggered to his feet. He pulled his watch from his vest pocket. "It's too early for Cameron Junction."

"Could it be that we are being held up?" Abigail said, her eyes wide with excitement.

Fearing that her assessment was correct, but not wishing to alarm her, he teased, "You've not been reading the pulps, have you, Miss Danforth?" Smiling, he continued in as casual a tone as he could muster, "Now pray remain here with the horses while I go into the express car and find out what's going on."

"Oh, do be careful, Mr. Osgood!" Abigail cried. Suddenly, the possibility of an adventure unfolding was not so thrilling if it meant that he might be in real danger.

"Pray do not worry your pretty little head, Miss Danforth." He withdrew a .32 Smith & Wesson from the pocket of his jacket. "I have a gun."

The tiny pistol did little to reassure Abigail.

"Take the fireman, Hank!" Boss shouted as he dropped the lantern and picked up the sawed-off, double-barreled shotgun lying beside the tracks. Half blinded from the headlight, he staggered through the clouds of steam surrounding the engine. Aiming the shotgun in the general direction of the engineer, he shouted, "Climb down outta there!"

High in the cab, the engineer cursed himself for stopping. He'd been just a boy during The War, but he'd seen first hand the damage even a random piece of shot could do to a man. As he stared down at the large masked man pointing the shotgun at him, he tried to remain calm and calculate his chances of starting up the engine again before the man could pull the trigger.

"Hurry on outta there!" the man shouted again, waving the shotgun. "With your hands high!"

Still cursing to himself, knowing the moment for flight had passed, the engineer slowly descended from the cab. Praying that they didn't shake, he raised both hands over his head. "No need to be trigger happy, now," he said soothingly. "Train's all yours. Got lots of innocent people aboard. Don't want nobody hurt, ya hear?"

As the engineer climbed out of the cab, the man called Hank, also masked with hat pulled low, was on the other side of the engine. Brandishing a shotgun, he shouted at the fireman, "Get down outta there! Now! If you value your life!"

The fireman, grumbling under his breath, climbed down. Hank kept the shotgun pointed at his back and herded him around the cowcatcher to join his partner and the engineer.

"You can't do this!" the fireman cried. He could contain himself no longer as Hank circled in front of him to stand beside Boss. "Do something, Gene!" he shouted at the engineer.

"What the Sam Hill you expect me—"

"Shut up!" Boss shouted. Aiming his gun at the fireman's head, he said, "You better believe we can do whatever we want! Real quick!"

"I do!" The engineer scowled at the fireman, then turned to the bandits. "We do!" he amended. "I already said the train is yours. Please, just don't hurt nobody."

Disgusted with the engineer, but with hands still high, the fireman spat on the ground, narrowly missing Hank's boot.

Nerves already taut, the insult was too much. Hank cocked the shotgun.

"Whoa now, son," Boss said in a soothing voice, waving his free hand at Hank as though gentling a horse. He'd sworn on the Bible to his mother that there'd be no killing.

"Ain't no man gonna spit on me!" Hank growled.

"Jesus. Oh, sweet Jesus," the engineer cried, lowering his hands in supplication. "You ain't gonna kill a man on account of a little tobacco juice?"

"You shut up, I said!" Boss shouted, wishing he could yell at Hank. It was Curly, who was taking the express car with Sampson, who'd almost been left behind because of a quick trigger finger. He hadn't expected Hank to be so jumpy.

The engineer clamped his mouth shut as he swiftly raised his hands again.

Hank glared at the fireman. "You better swallow—hard—mister, next time you gotta spit."

Hands over his head, for one breathless moment the fireman held Hank's gaze. Then, slowly, still chewing his wad, he bowed his head.

Relieved that the tension had eased, Boss peered down the tracks to see what progress Sampson and Curly were making. There was no mistaking Sampson's huge bulk, with Curly no doubt nearby but still outside the express car. Wondering what was causing the delay, with a nod at Hank, Boss said to their prisoners, "I'm leavin' you with this here friend of mine. He's got one mean temper. You've already pushed him more'n most and got away with it."

The fireman glared at the engineer.

Hank grimaced under his mask. His temper at being spit upon had already cooled. Hoping he could live up to Boss's description, which suited Curly more'n him, he snarled, "Lie down!"

Before the fireman could protest, the engineer shoved him to his knees. "You heard the man," he said. Shivering from the cold, he slumped from his knees to lie facedown on the ground.

By the time the fireman eased himself the rest of the way to the ground, Boss had run past the coal tender and had reached the freight car, and Curly.

A slight, wiry man when compared to men the size of Boss and Sampson, his blond ringlets that nicknamed him covered by his wide-brimmed Stetson, Curly was crouched out of any line of fire from the car, a satchel of dynamite beside him. "This is your last chance!" he hollered. "Open up, or I'll blow you apart!"

Boss heard the glee in Curly's voice and was thankful anew that he'd not let the man carry a shotgun. It was highly unlikely that they would need dynamite, but just the chance that he could use it had satisfied Curly. Praying that whoever was inside would obey, Boss shouted, "Your engineer and fireman have been captured!" Mumbling came from inside the car, but no words, as Boss paused before adding, "They can't help you!"

"No, I won't!" came through the walls of the freight car.

"Give him a dose of your shotgun!" Curly shouted so that the express clerk could hear. "If that don't roust him, I'll use a stick of dynamite."

Boss took aim on the lock and fired.

The blast shattered the door. Dodging the flying splinters, Sampson hoisted himself up to examine the hole where the lock had been. "It worked!"

"Stand aside," Boss said.

Sampson jumped down from the car and ducked.

"I've got another shot like that last one for the belly of any man fool enough to try and stop us!" Boss shouted. "We're comin' in!"

There was no response.

Saddlebags over his shoulder and a six-shooter in hand, Sampson yanked the sliding door open just enough to walk through. He hung back while, shotgun at the ready, Boss climbed into the car first.

Curly followed, carrying the satchel of dynamite with great tenderness.

On the far side of the car, the express agent kept his hands high.

"You all alone?" Boss asked, peering into the shadows from where he stood by the door.

The agent nodded without speaking. After the train had stopped and he was certain that they were in the middle of a holdup, he had persuaded Osgood to remain in safety behind the door in the makeshift horse pens.

"Now this here is enough dynamite to blow this whole train to kingdom come." Boss pointed at Curly's satchel with the barrel of his gun. "We'll use it if'n you don't open that safe, nice and easy."

The agent stared at him, mute.

"Aw, come on." Sampson winked, towering over him. "Ain't you been hero enough for one day? Them Pinkertons will see without you tellin' 'em that we had to blast our way in here."

The agent dared not look at the face of the huge man. He gulped. "Can I put my hands down?"

"If'n you're gonna open that safe for us, you can," Sampson replied.

"I reckon I ain't got much choice," the agent muttered, reaching for a bunch of keys in his back pocket.

"Hold it!" Boss swung the shotgun so that it pointed at the agent's stomach.

The agent flung his hands in the air. "I was just goin' for my keys," he gasped.

"Nice and easy, I said." Boss lowered the shotgun so that it pointed at the agent's feet.

With an exaggerated slowness, the agent again reached for his keys. Keeping both hands in sight, he unlocked the cabinet that concealed the safe. Stooping, he dialed the combination, then swung the door open.

"Stand back!" Boss shouted at him.

The agent leapt away from the cabinet, his hands above his head.

Sampson holstered his gun and, depositing the saddlebags nearby, knelt before the safe and reached inside. "Jeez," he said, dragging out a sealed canvas sack covered with stenciled government stamps. "Gold is heavier than I thought." He laughed. "And there's a whole lot more of it than I thought."

Curly bent over to help.

"Heavy as lead," Sampson said as he shoved Curly aside and motioned for Boss to come closer. "You better help, else we'll be here till noon."

With the safe open and the need for shooting past, and before Curly could get insulted, Boss tossed him the shotgun. "Hold this," he said. "Keep him covered while I help load up."

"With all this gold, we got no need to wait for them two nitwits in private varnish!" Sampson exclaimed.

"The kid's got their horses," Curly said as he motioned with the shotgun for the agent to move away from the safe and stand in front of the door that concealed Osgood. "We can skedaddle soon as you're done."

Having no desire to get caught in the line of fire

should Osgood decide to play the hero, the agent pretended to be faint. Pointing to a stool in the opposite direction, he asked, "Can I sit down?"

"Move!" Curly snapped, keeping the shotgun aimed at the agent's midsection as the terrified man dashed to the stool and sat.

With Boss and Sampson working together, the saddlebags were soon bulging with the contents of the safe.

Sampson stood. "That kid better have them extra horses close by." He chuckled, hoisting two of the bags to his shoulders.

"Let's go!" Boss said, dragging the other bags toward the door.

From his limited view in the makeshift corral, Osgood had lost sight of the agent, nor could he see Curly with the shotgun. When two large men crossed his line of vision, he only saw that laden with sacks of gold, neither man had a weapon drawn. Seizing what he thought was his chance, he stepped from behind the door. "Stop where you are!" he cried, steadying his pistol with both hands. "Stop! Or I'll shoot!"

"No!" the agent screamed, diving to the floor. "Don't—"

Crouching, Curly spun toward Osgood. And pulled the trigger on the shotgun.

Chapter Three

The two bandits that Sampson had referred to with such contempt were breathless with the unaccustomed exertion of running on foot by the time they reached the observation deck of the private car and clambered up the stairs. A wide-brimmed hat pulled low on his forehead, and masked like the others, Polecat was not quite as short as Curly, but scrawnier. Mulehead was as tall as Boss, but his generous belly testified to years of eating Polecat's share rather than seeing it wasted. In all their time together, they had never before robbed a train.

Finding the door unlocked, guns drawn, they tiptoed down the corridor past Abigail's and Maude's closed stateroom doors and, after stealthily separating the velvet draperies at the end of the passageway, found themselves in the parlor.

Awed by the splendor of the car's appointments, Mulehead's voice was hushed. "Well, if'n this ain't the swellest place I ever did see, with or without no wheels." He waved his Remington at a covered candy dish on the table. "You reckon that's real gold?"

Unable to decide what to grab first, Polecat snarled

under his breath, "How am I supposed to know, you blunderpated dimwit! Heft it and see."

Mulehead transferred his gun to his left hand. Curling his right pinky, he used his thumb and forefinger to gingerly grasp the knob on the cover and lift it. "Naw," he said, "it's jes' colored glass." Discarding the top on the table, he exclaimed happily, "Lookit what's inside!" He stuffed a rum-chocolate bonbon in his mouth. "Lord-a-mercy," he said around the candy melting on his tongue, "I ain't never tasted anything so fine." He held out the dish. "Try one, Polecat."

"Judas H. C. Priest and heaven be spared, Mulehead, if'n you ain't misplaced your brains in your stomach!" Stamping his foot, Polecat waved his pistol in the air, his face red with the effort to keep from shouting. "We ain't here to eat!"

"Okay, okay, okay. Calm yourself," Mulehead muttered. "A man's gotta take his pleasure where he finds it," he said as he pocketed a handful of the delectable morsels. "Why don't you put some a them gimcracks and geegaws in the gunny sack?" he said, returning his gun to his right hand and using it to point at the many artifacts strewn about on the desk and tables.

"And jest how in the black shades of Hades am I supposed to know what ain't glass?" Polecat said, starting back toward the curtains they'd just come through. "Come on. Let's go see if we cain't find somebody what's got some money on 'em."

"Naw, we been thataways already," Mulehead said. "Let's go this way."

"Now hold your horses!" Polecat stiffened to his full height, which, even in his high-heeled boots, scarcely brought the brim of his hat up to Mulehead's chin.

"I'm trail boss here, and I say we go back the way we came."

Mulehead didn't budge.

"You gotta be the stubbornest, the most—" Polecat stopped, shook his head and sighed. "You sure 'nough deserve the name you got!"

Mulehead's grin was hidden by his kerchief, but Polecat knew it was there.

"Come on now," Polecat continued. "Dumb as you are, even you gotta see it's gonna be a dadblamed sight easier to git off the rump end of this train than if'n we git caught in the middle."

Turning his back on Mulehead, Polecat parted the curtains and tiptoed back down the corridor. Mulehead followed. Pausing in front of Maude's door, Polecat whispered, "You stay out here and guard the hall."

Mulehead glanced toward the exit, longing to keep right on going through it, but nodding in agreement, he stationed himself beside the door.

Polecat took a deep breath and burst into Maude's room. Aiming his gun at the sleeping form on the bunk, he hollered, "This is a stickup!"

A sleeping draught after Abigail had left had kept Maude dreaming of her beloved Charlie during the commotion of the train's sudden stop. Surfacing at Polecat's shout, she sat up, clutching the sheet to her breast.

"Jumpin' jehosaphat!" Polecat exclaimed, backing away. "It's a lady!"

Still under the influence of the laudanum, Maude was unaware of any danger. Thoroughly annoyed at having her favorite dream interrupted, she demanded, "What do you think you are doing in my room?"

* * *

After dressing Abigail in her riding habit, Jacqueline had assumed that her mistress would be occupied with her horse for the next few hours and had retired for a much deserved rest. The train's sudden stop awakened her. She rose at once, alarmed that she might have slept through their arrival in Kansas City. Tidying her bed, she donned her cap and a fresh apron and hurried toward Abigail's stateroom to lay out her morning clothes. Much to her amazement upon entering the parlor car, she spotted Kinkade eavesdropping at the draperies on the other side. She slowed her pace.

Hearing the rustle of her skirts, Kinkade whirled around, waving his arms frantically for her to return to her quarters.

Not about to be swayed from her duties without a proper explanation, Jacqueline ignored his strange gyrations and continued toward him.

Hand to his lips, he urged her to silence.

Reaching his side, she glared at him for an answer to his queer behavior.

"The train is being robbed," he whispered.

Eyes wide, Jacqueline gasped.

"Shhhhhh!" He motioned for her to peek through the crack in the curtain.

Though muffled, Jacqueline could hear Polecat's halfhearted demand, "Well then, ma'am, give me any money you have."

"Don't be ridiculous!" Maude yelled at him. "I have no money!"

"Your jewels then," Polecat said, backing toward the door.

"I will not!" Maude hollered. Grabbing the book that had fallen by her side, she threw it at him. "Get out of here!"

41

Polecat ducked. The missile grazed his shoulder as he fled to the corridor.

Mulehead saw him coming. He started for the exit.

"Stop them!" Jacqueline yanked on Kinkade's sleeve.

"Why?" Kinkade whispered. "They are leaving. They didn't take anything."

Jacqueline was appalled. "How can you just let them get away?" she cried.

"They have guns." He shrugged. "We do not."

Before Kinkade could stop her, Jacqueline dashed through the curtains and, shaking her fists, pursued Polecat and Mulehead down the corridor, yelling at them in French.

Polecat looked over his shoulder when he heard Jacqueline's first incomprehensible words. "Git!" he shouted at Mulehead. "Ain't there nothin' but wimmin on this here train?"

Mulehead needed no encouragement.

Flinging open the door from the observation deck, they ignored the steps and leapt to the ground, running.

From the safety beside Crosspatches' stall, Abigail watched, horrified, as Osgood drew his pistol. It looked like a toy. She thought the agent had dissuaded him from taking action, but before she could stop him, he stepped through the door.

She feared the worst when she heard the blast from the shotgun.

The horses reared again and needed settling, but she fell to the floor and remained there, listening. At long last, certain that the bandits had departed, she slowly opened the door to check on Osgood. Splattered bits of

42

him were still sliding down the wall. Although dawn had long ago vanquished the night, a merciful darkness enveloped her. Abigail swooned.

Those brave souls in the Pullman cars who had dared to open their windows when the commotion of departing horses had signaled that danger was past, closed them swiftly and pulled the shades at the sight of Polecat and Mulehead dashing alongside the train with pistols drawn.

The engineer and fireman had gotten to their knees but, seeing two more bandits heading straight for them, flung themselves on the ground again.

Nearing the express car, Polecat cried, "Where's our horses!"

"There he goes," Mulehead pointed at the kid in the distance, leading their mounts. "I told you so!"

Polecat stared at him, dumbfounded. In that moment's silence, they heard Crosspatches and the Arabian snorting.

Clambering onto the express car, Mulehead surprised the agent bending over the unconscious Abigail and pointed his gun at the man.

Shaking his head in disbelief, the agent sat down heavily beside Abigail and raised his hands.

"Oh, no!" Mulehead cried when he spotted Osgood's remains. "They promised nobody'd get hurt!"

"Cover that up!" Polecat shouted at the agent while pointing at Osgood. "Ain't you got no respect for the dead?"

Too unnerved to think of trying to stop the two men, the agent scrambled to his feet and went for a tarpaulin to cover Osgood's remains.

Polecat and Mulehead ran to the makeshift stalls.

"Ooeeee, if'n Lady Luck ain't smiled on us after all!" Polecat marveled at the two horses. "Lookee here, if'n they ain't all saddled 'n ready to go!" He opened the gate to the Arabian's pen. "You take the big one."

"How'm I gonna stay on a chicken-plaster of a saddle like that!" Mulehead complained, leading Crosspatches from his stall. "And look at them spindly legs!"

"Cain't you see I took the runt?" Polecat said. "Now mount up! And let's git outta here!"

Although skittish from the shotgun blasts and unaccustomed to strange handlers, the well-trained horses allowed the men to mount. They were bred for speed and eager to escape their tumultuous surroundings.

Almost in unison, Polecat and Mulehead shouted, "Giddyup!"

The horses obliged.

Feeling guilty at leaving Polecat and Mulehead behind to get caught, the kid looked back toward the train to see what was happening to them. His jaw dropped in wonderment. Ejected from the freight car as though shot from a cannon, Polecat and Mulehead flew into the distance on horses the likes of which he'd never before seen.

Abigail groaned. Whatever she was lying upon was too hard for a bed. It smelled of horse droppings and gun smoke. And blood. She knew that there was good reason for remaining still and not questioning why she found herself in such a disagreeable circumstance and, for the moment, was content to keep her eyes shut. But even thus blinded, the memory of Osgood foisted itself upon her. She moaned. A wave of nausea swept over her, and rather than humiliate herself further by throwing up, she took a deep breath through her mouth, thereby avoiding the oppressive odors, and opened her eyes.

"There, there, young lady," the express car agent said as he kneeled over Abigail. "You've had yourself a nasty shock." He patted her hand. "Where's your smelling salts?"

"I never use it," Abigail said disdainfully. Withdrawing her hand from his, she swallowed rapidly to subdue the nausea as she sat up. All of the normally healthy color had drained from her face.

"Sight made me a mite queasy, too, missus," the agent said with as much sympathy as he could spare in his haste. "I've covered what I could. Best not to look thataway." He scrambled to his feet. "Now if you'll 'scuse me. . . ." He hurried off to the open side of the car to speak with the engineer and fireman, who had come running up as soon as Polecat and Mulehead were out of sight.

Fearing she looked as frightful as she felt, Abigail brushed at her skirts to rid them of what straw and coal dust she could see as she slowly got to her feet. Her gloves were a mess, but there was nothing for it but to touch her hair and, with no mirror to guide her, trust by feel alone that her hat was secure at not too ridiculous an angle. Eager to hear the men's conversation, she took several more deep breaths through her mouth to clear her head before trusting herself to walk. She avoided looking at the blood-spattered wall, and a tarpaulin covered the rest of Osgood; but just knowing the awful sight it concealed made her knees wobble. Chiding herself for her weakness as she joined the men, she relished the cold air at the side of the car.

"We're overdue at Cameron Junction," the engineer said. He was standing at the side of the tracks and tipped his cap to Abigail as she joined them. "They gotta know there's been trouble."

"But you gave in so easy like!" the fireman sputtered. "I'm gonna get me a shotgun and shoot them—"

"Whoa!" the express agent interrupted, indicating Abigail. "There's a lady present!"

"How do you plan to go about catching the murdering bandits?" Abigail asked solemnly, this being no time for smiles or friendly introductions.

"We'll telegraph from the Junction," the engineer replied. "The Pinkertons can meet us in Kansas City." Tipping his cap again, he turned to leave just as the conductor came running toward them. "Get them people back on board," the engineer shouted, waving at the conductor to go back in the direction he'd just run from. "We're leavin', pronto!" Without further ado, he sped away toward the engine, with the fireman close behind.

The conductor reversed his course to coax back on board those few intrepid souls who had ventured off the train to find out why they'd been so rudely awakened.

Sliding the door half closed, the agent removed his cap. "Allow me to extend my condolences, Missus." He held out his hand to Abigail.

"Oh, I'm not married." Abigail ignored his hand. She remained by the opening; the chill air was restorative, and she wished to postpone passing the tarpaulin until her nausea was under control.

The agent shrugged and looked at her askance as he sauntered over to the table that served as his desk.

"I just met Mr. Osgood yesterday." She sighed heavily, saddened by the knowledge that she'd have no chance to know him better, and angry with the killer who had robbed her of the opportunity. More than anything else in the world at that moment, she wished she had Osgood's murderer before her. In that instant she came to truly appreciate the intensity of Maude's desire for haste. Would Maude rebel if she volunteered to deliver the marshal's horse? And join the hunt for Osgood's killer? "He seemed such a nice gentleman," she said earnestly. "We must find his killer as soon as possible."

"A mightly stubborn man, miss." The agent's tone had lost some of its respect, and he looked at her with a glint in his eye. If she'd been married, he mused, then it would have been on her husband's head that he'd allow her to ride astride. No decent girl would do such an outlandish thing, and only the knowledge that she came from the fancy car kept him from becoming more forward with her. "I told him not to—"

The blast from the train's whistle cut off the rest of his sentence, but not before Abigail had noted the shift in his demeanor. As the train jerked into motion, she steadied herself with a hand on the opened safe and raised her voice to be heard. "I really must look after the horses." She turned to go.

"Your horses ain't in there, miss," he called out to her.

"What?" Abigail threw open the door to the make-shift stalls and rushed inside. Hand on her heart, stunned and heartsick, she stared at the empty pens. When she had recovered sufficiently to trust herself to speak, she returned to face the agent. "Where are they?" she asked, her voice faint with shock.

He shrugged with a wordless smirk.

"Who took them?" she cried, grief-stricken at the loss of her beloved Crosspatches.

"Them robbers." He shrugged again.

"What do you mean?" she cried. "Before I fainted, I heard the bandits riding off." She pointed toward the corral. "My horse was in his stall!"

"I thought they was gone, too." He sauntered toward her. "Two more climbed in the car when I was tryin' to revive you. I liked to jump outta my skin." He pretended his hand was a gun and held his pointed finger at his head as he said, "Held a gun on me while they stole them two horses to escape on."

"Stop the train!" Abigail exclaimed. "You cannot let them just ride away. Those horses are valuable!"

"Now, don't get riled, miss," the agent said in his most patronizing tone. "You heard the engineer. We'll telegraph the Pinkertons. They'll take care of everything."

"But Kansas City is two hours away!" Abigail cried. "Can you not see that it is going to rain again?" Her heart sank as she indicated the half-opened door and the fast-moving landscape beyond. "There will be no trail left to follow by the time they return!"

Indifferent to her plight, the agent shrugged once more. "We got no horses to trail 'em with."

"Oh, fanny feathers!" Abigail exclaimed and turned to leave.

With a curt bow toward her retreating back, the agent went to his desk. He had just opened his notebook and begun his report when Abigail reappeared at his shoulder.

"What did they look like?" she asked.

"Now, what does a pretty little miss like you wanna know that for?" His grin twisted into a leer as he looked up at her without rising from his chair. "I told you the Pinkertons will take—"

Abigail had been so distraught at Osgood's death

and by the loss of her horse that she had chosen to ignore the agent's increasing show of disrespect. But she had finally had enough of his cheek, and with a fierce expression in her dark eyes, she assumed the intimidating manner of her father. "I would appreciate it, my good man," she said, drawing herself tall, her tone as imperious as any queen's, "if you would simply describe them to me."

Taken aback by the change in the young woman, the agent stood so swiftly, the stool he was sitting on nearly toppled. "One man was real big and the other, tall as him, but not so big," he replied as quickly as he could speak. "I reckon I didn't see the one with the shotgun too clear; I was too busy watchin' the barrel—"

"No, no!" she said impatiently. "Pray describe the two men who took the horses."

"The one what surprised me with the gun was kinda big, too." He had spent some time with the first gang, and so was able to describe them swiftly; but since he'd only glanced at Polecat and Mulehead before rushing off to find the tarpaulin, he had to think to remember them, and the effort slowed his speech. "Not as big or tall, mind, as the first two. But heavy in the middle like. The other was not as tall as me, and skinny. What with kerchiefs hidin' their faces and hats on, I couldn't see much else, ma'am."

"Did they say anything?" Abigail asked eagerly.

"Well, they was grousin' about the horses."

"Grousing?"

"Complainin', ma'am—"

"They complained about two of the finest—?" Shaking her head in puzzlement, Abigail returned to the point. "What did they say, exactly."

"Lemme think." The agent shoved his cap back and

49

scratched his forehead. "The big one allowed as how his horse's legs was spindly." He chuckled. "Couldn't figure how he was gonna sit such a little bitty saddle. The scrawny one had nerve enough to call his mount a runt."

"By any chance did they call one another by name?"

"Hey what is this?" he asked, squaring his cap. Abigail had dropped her imperious manner, and he no longer felt intimidated. "You sound like a Pinkerton, askin' all them questions," he said peevishly.

"Did you hear any names?" Abigail insisted.

"No, ma'am, nary a one." The agent turned his back on her and, shoving the stool closer to his desk, sat upon it. "Now, if you'll 'scuse me, I got things I gotta do 'fore we get to Cameron Junction."

Satisfied that the ill-mannered man had no further useful information, Abigail turned away without saying good-bye and started toward the Pullman cars, which she had to go through to reach the private varnish.

Chapter Four

Maude dressed herself in her usual black frock as swiftly as the required undergarments and innumerable buttons allowed. Lacing her boots only halfway, she ran to the observation platform.

By the time she got there, Kinkade was escorting Jacqueline up the steps, her elbow firmly in his hand.

"Unhand me, *Monsieur!*" Jacqueline wrenched her arm from Kinkade's grasp when they reached the platform. "Where is my mistress?"

"You should not have run after those robbers like that!" he cried. "You could have been shot!"

"You—you—*poltroon!*" she cried.

"Jacqueline!" Maude exclaimed. "You mustn't call Kinkade a coward. I chased the bandits away before he had need to rescue me." She glared at the two of them. "Now, where is Miss Danforth?"

"I ready Miss Danforth for the ride at dawn and she go," Jacqueline replied. She hesitated a moment before continuing, "Beg pardon, miss." Her gaze filled with admiration. "You have much courage, Miss Cunningham."

Ignoring the compliment, Maude said, "Did the thieves take anything from the rest of the car?"

"I do not know, miss," Jacqueline replied with a hard glance at Kinkade. "I did not know what was happening until I saw *Monsieur* Kinkade hiding behind the curtains—"

"I was not hiding!" Kinkade exclaimed, embarrassed by her accusation. He drew himself tall. "I had heard voices and was waiting for an opportunity—"

"Enough squabbling!" Maude interrupted impatiently. "Let us go inside and take a look."

Kinkade hastened to open the door for them and stood aside so that they could precede him. He longed for Jacqueline to look at him with admiration, but chin held high, she swept past him. Absorbed in watching Jacqueline's dignified carriage, he paid no attention to the blast from the train's whistle, and the sudden jerk of the car as it began to move caught him off guard. Staggering forward, he grasped for the railing at the window.

Jacqueline heard him stumble and smiled.

As they entered the parlor, Maude stopped. "I know they took nothing from my quarters," she said. "Check Miss Danforth's room, Jacqueline. You know her possessions best."

"Yes, ma'am," Jacqueline turned swiftly and was gone to do Maude's bidding.

"What a nuisance!" Maude exclaimed. "It wouldn't be so bad if we weren't using borrowed property." When Jacqueline had disappeared, Maude turned to Kinkade. "Go at once to the front part of the train and fetch Miss Danforth here, whether she wishes to come or not."

"Yes, ma'am." He paused in the doorway. "Beg pardon, Miss Cunningham," he said. "I don't think they got any farther than the parlor when they decided to turn back."

When Kinkade had departed, Maude opened the secret compartment in the desk to see if their cash supply was still there. It was.

Pullman car passengers, in various stages of dishabille, stuck their heads into the corridor from their bed/sleepers and shamelessly begged Abigail for news. But as the train gathered speed to continue its journey to Cameron Junction with its dreadful cargo, Abigail could only think that every turn of the wheel was taking her farther away from her beloved horse. Distraught, tight-lipped, she steeled herself against their importuning as she nimbly sped toward the private varnish. Bursting through the door to her car, she bumped into Kinkade, nearly knocking him down in her haste.

"So sorry," Kinkade apologized automatically, knowing only that it was a lady who had nearly knocked him off his unsteady feet. "Oh, Miss Danforth!" he exclaimed with his next breath, recognizing Abigail. "Thank goodness you are safe! I was just coming to look for—"

She brushed past him with a curt nod for him to follow.

Hastening to catch up and pass her, Kinkade reached the curtains to the parlor just before she did and was able to part them for her.

"Miss Danforth!" Maude turned in her chair at the desk to face Abigail as she entered, but did not rise. "I am pleased to see you safe and sound. We have had robbers on board."

Jacqueline rushed through the curtains from the opposite sides. "Miss Danforth!" she cried. Her voice expressed her relief.

Noticing Abigail's grim expression, Maude refrained from commenting upon her disheveled appearance. "Why, Miss Danforth," she said, alarmed. "Is something amiss?"

Kinkade pulled a chair from the table for Abigail so that she could sit facing Maude.

Abigail nodded her thanks to him as she sank into the chair. "I fear I am the bearer of sad news, Miss Cunningham," she said, her eyes filling with tears she refused to shed. "Not as sad perhaps if you'd taken a fancy to him."

"Has something untoward happened to Mr. Osgood?" Maude asked with a worried frown.

"He is, I am sad to say . . ." Abigail's voice became faint. She swallowed a few times to keep the waves of nausea at bay before continuing, "quite dead."

Jacqueline gasped and crossed herself.

Shocked himself by the news, Kinkade nonetheless hastened to Jacqueline's side to comfort her, but as he drew near, she moved away, closer to the window.

"Oh, dear," Maude said. "Poor man. That is a dreadful turn of events." She reached out a sympathetic hand toward Abigail. "How did it happen, my dear?"

Not wishing to burden them with the ghastly details of Osgood's demise, Abigail said merely, "To protect the gold, he went against a shotgun with a pocket pistol."

Maude winced. "Did they get the gold?" she asked.

Abigail nodded silently, color draining from her face as the horrid memory refused to subside.

"Some brandy, miss?" Kinkade asked, worried that

she might faint, yet knowing she disdained smelling salts.

"Yes, thank you, Kinkade."

While Kinkade went to the sideboard on the far side of the table for the decanter of Napoleon, Maude said, "We had an adventure of our own while you were gone."

Unable to contain her admiration, Jacqueline spoke without having been spoken to. "Miss Cunningham has much courage."

Ignoring Jacqueline's obvious adoration, Maude continued, "I was awakened from a sound sleep by a skinny masked man, scarcely larger than Jacqueline, waving a gun at me, demanding that I hand over my jewels or money. Some bandit, he was." She sniffed. "When I threw a book at him, he ran. Kinkade says there were two of them. They didn't take anything that we've discovered so far." She turned to Abigail's maid. "Is anything missing from Miss Danforth's room, Jacqueline?"

"No, ma'am."

Kinkade proffered a silver tray with a tot of brandy.

As she turned to take the snifter from the tray, for the first time Abigail noticed that the lid to the candy dish was off and lying on the table. "Been nibbling at the chocolates, Kinkade?" she asked, swirling the brandy in the glass.

"Oh, no, miss," Kinkade was horrified even though he knew she was teasing. "I filled it before I retired last night. I wouldn't—"

"Of course, I know you wouldn't," Abigail said, glancing swiftly in Jacqueline's direction. Jacqueline blushed and shook her head vehemently.

"Is any candy missing?" Abigail asked.

Kinkade peered into the dish. "Yes, ma'am," he said. "I'd say about half."

"So the horse thieves have a sweet tooth," Abigail said and downed the brandy as though taking a dose of medicine.

"Why are we just traveling on, prattling about candy as though nothing has happened?" Maude asked.

Abigail shut her eyes and shivered as the brandy burned its way down her throat. When she could finally speak, she said, "When we reach Cameron Junction, the engineer will telegraph the Pinkertons to meet us in Kansas City." Placing the empty snifter on the table, emboldened by the rush she felt as the liquor did its work, she continued, "I intend to ride with the posse."

Shocked, Kinkade spoke before he thought. "You cannot do such a thing, Miss Danforth! Your father would never allow it!"

"Must I remind you that you are working for me now?" Although Kinkade was a servant, he had been with the family since she'd been in diapers, and too many girlish memories prohibited Abigail from summoning the imperious manner that had intimidated the clerk. Indeed, without the aid of the brandy, she might not have been able to continue as haughtily as she did. "It is I who pay your wages," she said, her jaw firm, not knowing quite what she'd do if he remonstrated with her. "My father is far away in New York."

"Yes, miss," Kinkade said. He might have been in the family for many years, but he scarcely knew this young lady that Abigail had turned into, and Jacqueline's opinion to the contrary, he still felt his first loyalty was to her father. He turned to leave the room even though he had not been dismissed.

"Where are you going?" Abigail demanded. That he had not confronted her further bolstered her courage.

"Why, uh, to check on the porters for breakfast, miss," Kinkade stammered, turning to face her.

"Oh, no you don't," Abigail said. "I'll not have you telegraphing my father. You stay right here where I can watch you. We'll not breakfast until after we leave Cameron Junction."

Jacqueline glared at him, delight at his comeuppance agleam in her eyes.

"Yes, Miss Danforth." With a sheepish smile, Kinkade positioned himself at the window on the opposite side of the car, facing Jacqueline, the better to steal an occasional glance at her.

Although Maude agreed with Kinkade, she would never consider taking sides with a servant in his presence. "I'm surprised you aren't after them already on Crosspatches," she said instead.

"I've not had a chance to tell you that both horses are gone. The bandits who tried to rob you must be the ones who took them," Abigail said. "As long as you're at the desk, Miss Cunningham, you might as well take down the descriptions I have. We can compare—"

"Surely you jest!" Maude exclaimed. "I am not about to chronicle a frivolous tale over a missing horse! You know perfectly well I want to get to San Francisco as soon as possible," she said heatedly. "Besides, you know nothing whatever about the wilderness we are crossing. You'd get lost the moment you were out of sight of the posse."

"They killed Mr. Osgood," Abigail said with a puzzled frown. "Don't you care?"

57

"The only person's death I care to avenge is Charlie's!"

"But they took Crosspatches!" Abigail exclaimed. "He was a gift from the marchioness of Hunterswell!"

"He is only a horse!"

"How can you say that?" Hurt to the quick, Abigail stood.

"Because it is true." Maude spoke slowly, and clearly, as though Abigail might be daft. "However special he may be to you, Miss Danforth, Crosspatches was born a horse, and will stay a horse!"

"And Mr. Tilghman's Arabian?" Abigail was flabbergasted by Maude's shallow thinking. "I suppose you think a Foundation Sire is just another horse!"

"Let Mr. Tilghman worry about finding his horse!" Maude said emphatically. "He is a lawman. He knows this territory. You do not. Nothing Dr. Conan Doyle wrote about detection could possibly help you trail those bandits in a wild country such as this."

"Certain principals of detection will hold true wherever the science is practiced."

"Tosh and nonsense!" Maude exclaimed. "The marshal can recover Crosspatches, too, and return him to you." Maude shook her finger at Abigail for emphasis. "In San Francisco."

Abigail was furious at being thus ordered about. She was about to retort heatedly but in the same moment realized that she'd never dissuade Maude by arguing. She would need all of her persuasive powers, and time was growing short. "Really, Miss Cunningham," she said, controlling her temper, "we must not quarrel in front of the servants." She started for the curtains leading to her stateroom. "If you will excuse me, I must tidy up before we reach the Junction.''

Vastly relieved that Maude had dissuaded Abigail from her perilous course, Kinkade decided he need not trouble himself to cable Mr. Danforth.

As Jacqueline followed her mistress down the corridor, she wondered what to pack for a posse.

Chapter Five

Crosspatches tried his best to outrun the unfamiliar weight in his saddle. The terrifying noises and wild smells had stripped away the veneer of his domestication, and once free of the confines of the makeshift corral, his hooves scarcely touched the ground in his haste to escape.

Having been cooped up for weeks on his journey from Arabia, his small companion eagerly joined the race.

It was only when the grinding of their bits grew intolerably harsh that the two horses finally slowed to a prancing walk beside one another.

When he'd finally brought the Arabian under control, Polecat turned in his saddle to peer in what he thought was the direction of the train. "Now where in the name of the Almighty's eight-day, green creation do you suppose Billy Bub has got to?" A gray mass of formless cloud cover dimmed the new day's sun. The kid could've been as close as the dip in the next gully and not been seen.

"Good riddance, if you ask me!" Mulehead said, frowning. Blaming his difficulty in keeping his seat solely upon the small size of the saddle, he saw no reason to make any comment on their horses' extraordinary speed.

"I ain't heard nobody asking you, you noddle-noggin mush brain," Polecat said. He had too much on his mind to notice how short a time it had taken them to get so far away from the tracks. "We gotta git our saddles back," he added. "And our share of the loot."

"Ain't nobody wants his saddle more'n me, Polecat, but we'll git our share of a hangin' for murder, too! They didn't want us to follow 'em, else that kid wouldn't a run off with our horses like that."

"Billy had to hightail it outta there on account of the shootin'."

"He coulda left our horses so's we wouldn't a been stranded!" Mulehead insisted. "I say he meant to leave us behind. And we best stay left!"

"Maybe you cain't say boo to a goose, you quiverin' mountain of quail eggs, but I got me a thing or two in my saddlebags that I ain't lettin' nobody git till they shovel dirt on my face!" The Arabian responded instantly to Polecat's knee and pranced ahead.

Crosspatches caught up before Mulehead could prod him. "Aw, come on, Polecat, I ain't scairt. I jest think—"

"Trouble is, you're tryin' to think without enough brains to do any tolerable thinkin' with!"

"Okay, okay. But they're long gone, and we lost sight of Billy Bub. How do you reckon on findin' 'em?"

"Oh, I reckon they was gonna meet back at the Baxters' cabin. Anyways, that's as good a place as any to start lookin'," Polecat said. "Lemme see now. We better head back across them railroad tracks." Without consulting Mulehead about the direction, he turned the Arabian around in what he hoped was the way back,

The horses needed no urging to resume their race.

"Where's Billy Bub?" Maw shouted at Boss and his men as they rode into the yard. A shawl around her shoulders against the chill, hands on her ample hips, she stood on the front porch of the cabin, a barking, tail-wagging hound beside her.

The hound, still barking, its tail in a frenzy of greeting, scrambled down the steps when it recognized Boss.

"He'll be along directly," Boss called to her. The whole trip home he had worried that his mother was going to find out that Curly had killed a man, and blame him. He was the leader. He was supposed to be able to control his men. He'd given Curly a tongue lashing while they were packing the spare horse. When Sampson could get a word in, he'd pointed out that Maw didn't have to find out unless they told her, and while they'd been mounting their own horses, they had agreed to a man not to mention the incident to her.

As Boss dismounted, he scratched the dog on its head, transforming its bark to a whine. "He's layin' a false trail for Polecat and Mulehead," he said as he hurried over to help Curly.

"Yeah." Curly laughed, untying the sacks on the packhorse. "If'n they got sense enough to git off the train."

Boss pretended to stagger cross-legged under the weight of one of the saddlebags as he headed for the porch.

Sampson laughed at Boss's antics as he casually hefted one of the saddlebags to his shoulder and walked toward the cabin.

Curly and Hank carried the rest of the gold between them.

"What's so heavy in them sacks, boys?" Maw could scarcely contain her excitement as she held the door wide.

"Gold!" they cried in unison.

"Well, bring it on in and let's celebrate!" she cried, happier than Boss had ever known her to be. He prayed the gold would keep her that way.

The door on the porch opened directly into the kitchen, which was dominated by a large round wooden table with chairs of mismatched wood surrounding it. Pegs near the door held hats and jackets. On the far side of the room, a wood stove with its ubiquitous coffeepot provided both heat for the cabin and food.

While the men heaved the saddlebags onto the middle of the table and hung up their hats and jackets, Maw hurried to the cupboard to fetch a bottle of whiskey and, with a flourish, placed it at the head of the kitchen table by the tin cups.

Boss kept a careful eye on the men as they pulled the bags of gold out of the saddlebags. Each thick canvas sack was pulled to a tight knot at one end with wire rope, with a lock running through. Boss poured whiskey, and Maw topped it off with hot coffee. They passed the cups, and standing around the table laden with treasure beyond their wildest dreams, the men and Maw saluted one another and drank deeply.

"Would you look at all them government stamps!" Maw laughed. "Reckon that gold is as legal as you can git, huh, boys?"

They all laughed in appreciation of her rare witticism as boss examined the lock on one of the sacks. Pulling out his pocket knife, he began to saw at the rope that the lock secured.

"Well, now, tell me. How'd it go?" Maw asked, pulling out a chair at the foot of the table. "Have any trouble?"

Suddenly, all the men seemed too engrossed with watching Boss to answer her. No one had planned what to say if she asked a direct question.

In the lengthening silence, Boss went to fetch a butcher knife when his pocket knife failed to penetrate the heavy canvas.

"You're not lyin' to me about Billy Bub?" she demanded, looking at them each in turn.

"No, Maw," Boss stammered, standing by the cupboard. "It—"

Curly squared his shoulders. "Why beat around the bush," he said with a smirk, unable to hide his contempt for Boss's cowardice before a woman, especially his old mother. "That man pulled a gun on me! I had to shoot him," he said righteously. "You'd a done the same!"

"You shot a man?" Maw slammed down her cup as she stood.

Boss's mouth went dry.

The men edged away from the table.

"Did you kill him?" she demanded.

"It was self-defense!" Curly cried, glancing at the others for corroboration. "He had the drop on Boss!"

"I told you plain and clear there was to be no killin'!" Hands on hips, Maw glared at Curly. She had never trusted him and was glad to discover she'd been right. "Lawmen will soon fergit a little gold; but you go shootin' one of their own, and they start huntin' you down real serious."

"But he wasn't the agent—"

"I don't care who he was!" She pointed at the door,

64

only too happy to have a reason for getting rid of him. "You git on outta here!"

Curly planted his feet. His eyes were slits, his voice a growl. "I ain't goin' nowhere without my share!"

"They all look the same." Maw waved impatiently at the heavily laden table. "You take one sack," she said. "And git!"

"I should git more'n one sack!" Curly protested.

"The trouble you're causin' us, you shouldn't even git a whole sack! But I don't want you around here long enough to open one and split it. You take what I say right now. Or nothin'!"

Curly's gun hand twitched.

Sampson and Hank had their hands on their holsters before he could reach, only too happy to split part of Curly's share.

Realizing at last that his mother was not going to blame him, Boss found his voice. "You better do as she says, Curly," he said, resting his hand on his gun.

His face twisted with hate, Curly glared at them silently, each in turn. With his hard-eyed gaze on Boss's face, doing his best not to show the effort it took, he grabbed one of the sacks and heaved it onto his shoulder. Without a word, he stalked to the door, rammed his hat on his head, grabbed his jacket, and slammed the door on his way out.

Hank went over to the door and, opening it a crack made sure Curly rode off.

"You don't suppose he'll circle back?" Sampson asked.

"Naw," Boss said, returning to the table to saw at a bag with the butcher knife. "Soon as he sees the yellow of all that gold he's got, he'll keep right on goin'."

Hank joined the others at the table to watch Boss. "Must be wire mesh," he said when the knife failed to cut the heavy fabric. "Why don't you jest shoot the lock off?"

Boss flung the knife on the table and went for his gun.

"Have you gone daft?" Maw cried. "Not in the house! Take it to the woodpile and axe the lock off!"

Amongst much good-natured, back-slapping grumbling, they put on their hats and jackets and did as they were told.

Out in the yard with the men surrounding the stump and Maw at his side, Boss was about to swing the axe when the dog began barking. Billy Bub rode up, trailing Polecat's and Mulehead's mounts. Maw waved at him to ride over to the woodpile.

Boss took aim and, with one clean swing, chopped the lock off. They all cheered as he reached inside, grasped a heavy bar, and hoisted it overhead.

"Lemme see that!" Sampson cried, holding out both hands.

Boss tossed it to him.

Sampson fondled the bar. As he peered at it closely, he gasped with dismay. "This ain't gold!" he cried. "I knew it! I jest knew it!"

"Give it to me!" Maw said, snatching it from Sampson. She sniffed it. "Why, it's jest a brick!" she exclaimed, disgusted.

"You sure?" Hank got out his pocket knife and, while Maw held it firmly, scratched the gilded surface.

It was, indeed, a brick.

The men were too stunned to speak.

"Open the rest!" Maw ordered, her expression grim. "And be quick about it!"

Muttering that he'd known it was bricks all along, Sampson dumped the first sack on the ground. As fast as Boss could chop the locks from the others, he and Hank dumped them, too. Soon there was a heap of empty sacks around the stump. And a lot of bricks. But no gold.

"Damn the hide off that agent!" Sampson spat. "He deserved what Curly gave him!"

"You hesh your mouth, Sampson!" Maw said. "I don't take to blaspheming." She shook her head. "Though I gotta say, this time, I allow as how your temptation is great."

"You don't suppose Polecat and Mulehead coulda stolen the gold?" Billy Bub asked.

"Them two is probably still on that fancy car, trying to explain themselves," Boss said with disgust.

"Oh, no." Billy slid from his horse. "I saw 'em flyin' outta that express car—on horses!"

"What horses!" the men cried in unison.

Suddenly noticing that he had everyone's attention, Billy stood erect. "Why, when I turned to see if I was being followed, I watched 'em disappear over into that gully."

"Where was they headed?" Boss asked.

Billy grinned at the memory. "They was so busy stayin' on them horses, they was goin' where they was took."

"Do you think they spotted you ridin' off with their horses?" Maw asked.

Billy Bub shrugged.

"Well, for sure they know you're gone now," Sampson said.

"They ain't likely to come lookin' for us, so I reckon we better go lookin' for them." Boss sighed wearily.

He knew all too well from the look on her face that his mother was storing up an explosion of temper, and although he was exhausted, he preferred being out of her range till she cooled.

"Cain't we git some grub first?" Sampson asked.

"Now wait a minute," Maw said. "They're bound to want their saddles. They're gonna have to come here and git 'em." As she headed for the porch, she said, "Billy, you bed them horses in back of the barn real quick and bring them saddles into the house. You stay here with me in case they come to call afore they're found."

Too hungry to protest missing out on riding with the men, Billy hurried to do her bidding.

"Well don't jest stand around stirrin' up steam, boys," Maw called from the screen door. "Git goin' and find them two scatterbrains!"

Grumbling at missing their meal, but not so loud as Maw could hear them, the men mounted up. As soon as they were out of sight of the cabin, Sampson said, "I don't care what your maw says, Boss, if I lay eyes on 'em, I'm gonna shoot them two first and ask 'em questions second."

"You get no argument from me," Boss said. Sampson and Hank hadn't blamed him, out loud, for the gold being bricks, but he could tell they did. He was feeling about two feet tall, and it was okay by him if they wanted to take revenge on Polecat and Mulehead

"Hey!" Hank called after them as Boss and Sampson pulled ahead. "Do you think Curly got any gold in his sack?"

"Naw," Boss said. "They was all alike."

Hank drew alongside them. "What do you reckon he's gonna do when he finds out?"

68

Each man looked at the other. None spoke.
They knew full well what Curly was gonna do.

Abigail could scarcely believe her ears. "Are you saying, sir, there was no gold?" She shouted so that the well-dressed man in the derby could hear her. The fancy Union Pacific ticket office, with its two-story map of the West dominating the far wall, was filled to overflowing with fellow travelers and those citizens of Kansas City who were not supervising the removal of Osgood's remains.

"Now, now, Miss—uh—Danforth? is it?" The Pinkerton agent tipped his derby at the obviously rich young lady. Noting that her elaborate hat alone was worth a month's wages, he smiled unctuously. "I'd a thought you'd be right pleased that the bandits got nothing for their trouble."

Abigail pointed an accusing finger at the express car agent standing beside him. "Why didn't you tell Mr. Osgood the truth?"

"It was supposed to be a secret!" Insulted at being challenged in public by this upstart of a girl who rode horses astride, the agent continued angrily, "How'd I know he wasn't in cahoots with the robbers?"

Abigail was outraged. "But if he had known they were only stealing bricks, he would not have tried to stop them!" she cried.

"I done told you he was stubborn!"

Onlookers took sides in the debate. The ruckus they raised drowned out any possibility of Abigail's being heard.

Furious with the express car agent, and disappointed in the Pinkerton representative, she threaded her way through the crowd to rejoin Maude, who had saved her place on the wooden bench.

The coal stove had overheated the crowded room, and while the Pinkerton agent attempted to restore order, Abigail unbuttoned her fashionable fur-trimmed cape and handed it to Jacqueline, who stood behind her. No detail of her stylish dress or of Maude's widow's weeds went unnoticed, or without comment, by the few women present.

Kinkade frowned. Alarmed by the blatant admiration in every man's eye who was ogling his charges, his expression increased the menace of his already stern visage. He hovered as near to Jacqueline as she would allow.

Waving his derby in the air, the Pinkerton agent threatened to clear the room. When some semblance of order was finally restored, he shouted, "We seeded that car because a real shipment is on its way through."

"If you planted the false gold, why did you not have agents on board?" Abigail called out.

"Hear! Hear!" shouted a man standing beside her.

Holding up his hand for quiet, the Pinkerton answered, "Because they're ridin' with the real gold shipment. We don't have enough men to go around. In fact, I won't be able to go after your robbers myself."

"Are you going to let Mr. Osgood's killers get away?" Much to Maude's dismay, Abigail stood and made her way toward him again.

" 'Tisn't my jurisdiction, miss," the Pinkerton man said, smiling again. "They didn't take any gold, and that's what I'm contracted to protect—the gold."

"Did the engineer not telegraph you that one of the horses that was stolen belonged to none other than Marshal William Tilghman?" Abigail asked.

"No, ma'am, he didn't," the Pinkerton said. "But

70

it don't matter much to me whose horses were stole. Or who got killed. My job is to catch gold thieves.''

"But you said so yourself they didn't take any gold!" Abigail exclaimed.

"That's right, little lady. And that's why Jake here is gonna lead the posse to chase down Mr. Osgood's killer." The Pinkerton held out his arm for Jake to come forward.

The moment Maude heard the Pinkerton announce that a posse was forming, she rose and started toward Abigail.

Trying not to look as important as he felt, Jake shoved his wide-brimmed hat back and, with a shy grin that was invisible beneath his bushy moustache, stepped forward to join the Pinkerton agent.

The crowd murmured its approval.

Abigail saw Maude approach, and before her scowling companion could reach her, she turned to Jake. Smiling most winsomely, she said, "I'd very much appreciate your allowing me to join you."

Jake doffed his hat. "Sorry, ma'am," he said, his apology hollow. "I ain't never rode with no woman afore, and I ain't startin' now."

"See, Miss Danforth," Maude said triumphantly as she reached Abigail's side in time to hear Jake's refusal. "I told you so."

Kinkade hurried forward to maneuver Abigail and Maude away from the press of men clamoring to volunteer, and steered them toward the exit. Jacqueline met them at the doorway and, pausing, held Abigail's cape for her.

Furious at being so summarily rejected, Abigail played for time by fumbling her way into the cape and fingering the last buttons at her throat. Even had she been invited to join them, she might have considered refusing, leaving Jake and his posse to capture Osgood's killers so that Maude would not be delayed. But to desert her beloved Crosspatches in the wilderness at the mercy of murdering thieves was unthinkable. Furthermore, there was Tilghman. Surely the lawman would want to pursue the killer of his friend as well as search for his horse.

If he only knew.

And if he did know, perhaps she could join forces with him.

By the time they gained the sidewalk, she had a plan. Although it entailed deceiving Maude, she did not hesitate. Certain that Maude would refuse, she asked, "As long as we have to wait for our car to be connected, would you like to see some of Kansas City, Miss Cunningham?"

"I should say not!" Maude responded, looking askance at the wooden sidewalks and muddy streets. "You may, although I cannot imagine why you'd care to. As long as Kinkade and Jacqueline stay with you, I daresay you'll be safe enough."

"If you don't mind, I think I shall have a look around," Abigail said innocently. "I may never be this way again. Would you like to have Kinkade escort you back to the car?"

"That won't be necessary." Maude lifted her skirts free of the mud and started for the train.

The moment Maude was out of earshot, Abigail turned to Kinkade. "Go at once and arrange with the station master to have our car placed on a siding."

Kinkade was appalled. "Oh, Miss Danforth, I couldn't—"

Jacqueline put a hand to her mouth, her eyes wide.

Abigail grasped Kinkade's hand and placed a gold coin in his palm. "Keep this for your personal use," she said. "Just don't let Miss Cunningham know until after our Union Pacific connection has left the station."

Kinkade was about to protest again, but Jacqueline touched his arm, a silent plea in her eyes. He could not resist. With Jacqueline's adoring gaze upon him, he shrugged, pocketed the coin, and disappeared into the station.

Jacqueline hurried to catch up to Abigail, who was striding briskly toward the telegraph office.

Chapter Six

Curly gouged his spurs deeper into his nearly spent horse. Cursing at the hapless animal to keep at the gallop, he promised himself that the first thing he'd buy when he cashed in his gold was the fastest horse in the West. Determined to reach Leavenworth, and Sally, before nightfall, knowing that he was running this one into the ground bothered him not at all. Nor did the icy wind blowing through his hair.

Curly's blond ringlets had been an irresistible target for merciless teasing by older boys when he'd been growing up. "Girly-headed Curly," they had taunted. Enraged anew at every insult, and desperate to prove his manhood, he had challenged them all to fist fights. Being a slight boy, he'd lost every one. The name had stuck.

He'd reached his mid-teens when he finally realized he was never going to grow big enough to whip anyone with his bare fists, so he had dry-gulched two of his worst tormentors. There'd been talk aplenty connecting him with their deaths. Nothing had been proven, but from then on his name had been spoken with a tinge of fear. And that made him proud.

As his adolescence had progressed, he'd made the amazing discovery that fancy women also found his hair irresistible. Far from an object of scorn, they loved to wash it and, brushing it dry, run their fingers through it. And feet. All of which would inevitably lead to the incredible delights of the ultimate intimacy. No longer doubting his manhood, he no longer hated his name.

He'd been celebrating his quarter-century mark at Nelson's Saloon in Leavenworth just a few months past when Sally had danced into his life. With eyes black as midnight and skin fair as milk, she was the prettiest girl he'd ever seen. Fresh from the East, she too had been attracted to his hair. She liked rubbing more than just her feet in it and had taught him new pleasures that inspired him to spur his horse to greater effort. Sally was ambitious, and their plans to marry and move to California hinged on the amount of his share of gold. Although disappointed that he'd not gotten more, he was certain from the heft of the sack that he had more than enough to build her a grand house and start some kind of business. Not wanting to arouse any suspicions by toting any unusually heavy baggage into town, he had buried it, unopened, in a graveyard a few miles back.

The sun, weakened by the cloud cover, was high overhead by the time Mulehead pulled Crosspatches to a halt. "I ain't budgin' one more step till we rest a spell!" he shouted at Polecat's scrawny back. "And that is that!"

Polecat reined in the Arabian and turned him around to face Mulehead. "Aw, come on," he wheedled as Mulehead drew close. "We cain't be far now. And when we git there, you can have some a Maw's good cookin'.''

"We ain't no closer to the Baxters' place than we was two hours ago." Mulehead gestured at the horizon with a large sweep of his free hand. "All we've been doin' is chasin' our tails."

Polecat swiveled in his saddle. "If only we could find that dad-blasted rocky overhang we was under this morning."

"I'm so turned around now, we could be halfway to Leavenworth for all I know," Mulehead cried. "And you too, Polecat." He shook his finger at his partner. "Admit it. We're lost."

"I ain't gonna admit no such thing you beetle-headed, flap-ear'd excuse for fish bait!"

"Aw, save your tongue oil fer the cussin' bee in Dodge!" Mulehead pointed to a hillock a few yards away. "I'm gonna ride this here horse over to that there hunk of scrub and git off."

"You better pray we got our saddlebags back 'fore I'm due in Dodge, you rattle-headed nincompoop, 'cause you'll be spider bait by the time I'm through with you if'n we ain't'!"

Mulehead urged Crosspatches into a walk. "You comin', or not?"

Polecat just glared at him. The Arabian awaited orders.

"Aw, come on, Polecat," Mulehead called over his shoulder. "Your horse has got a bedroll on it. Maybe there's some grub in there." When Polecat just stayed put, staring at him, he added, "Maybe there's some money in it."

With a weary shrug, Polecat nudged the Arabian to follow Crosspatches to the indentation made by a small stand of bushes on a slight rise, which would afford them some shelter from the wind. Dismounting, they draped their reins in the brambles. While Polecat relieved his aching bladder downwind, Mulehead removed a blanket roll from the Arabian and spread it on the ground.

"Oooee, lookee here, Polecat!" Mulehead exclaimed as he dug into the saddlebags.

"What is it?" Polecat hurried back, buttoning his fly. "You find some money?"

"A good sight better'n that considerin' the hole we're in."

"You try and tell me what's better'n money, you donkey's behind!"

"When it's past supper time and you ain't et since dawn?" Mulehead held a roasted chicken aloft. "Food!"

Just in case he and Abigail had experienced some unforeseen delay, Osgood had provided a generous repast of biscuits, jam, cold chicken, and a fine Puligny-Montrachet wrapped in linen napkins to preserve the chill.

"Whatta you reckon this is?" Mulehead asked, unwrapping the bottle of wine.

"Whatta I care?" Polecat shrugged. "Looks wet."

As delighted as a child with his first toy, his mouth full of roasted chicken, Mulehead figured out how the corkscrew worked. When at last the wine was open, he took a taste. Rolling the clear liquid on his tongue, a beatific expression crossed his face.

"Gimme that!" Polecat grabbed the bottle and took a swig. "Lord-a-mercy," he said, wincing with disgust. "You could pickle a buffalo in that stuff!" He shoved the bottle back at Mulehead.

"It ain't all that bad, Polecat." With great tenderness, Mulehead placed the bottle between some rocks to safeguard it against tipping. "If'n you don't like it, I'll drink the rest."

Polecat contented himself with a chicken breast and one biscuit slathered with jam. He tried one more pull on the wine bottle, then willingly relinquished the rest.

Mulehead did not stop until he'd gnawed every bone, sought and devoured every biscuit crumb, wiped the jam jar clean with his finger, and licked his moustache. Neither man spoke till Mulehead had rolled and lit up his cigarette. He'd saved the last quarter-inch of wine for this moment and finished it off after the first deep drag.

Polecat sighed. "Lordy, what I'd give for a cup a coffee right now."

His hunger pangs stilled, and belly aglow from the wine, Mulehead was content. "See what I mean about some things bein' more important than money?"

Nothing upset him more than to have his partner get the better of him, and Polecat nearly blistered his tongue inventing new ways to call Mulehead self-important as well as dumb.

Mulehead ignored his tirade. "Did you see that telegraph pole a while back?" he asked. "There's gotta be a town near by."

"We ain't lookin' for no town," Polecat said with contempt. "We're lookin' for the Baxters'!"

"If'n we was to go to Cameron Junction again, I could find our way from there." Mulehead squinted against the smoke curling into his eyes.

"But that's jest up the tracks from the robbery," Polecat said. "They'd be sure to be lookin' for us there."

"Nobody knows it was us, Polecat."

"And what about them spindle-legged, runty horses we're stuck with?"

"Reckon anybody'd trouble to be lookin' for 'em?"

Polecat thought a minute before answering. "We

sure 'nough got ourselves turned around 'cause they's so all-fired fast.''

"What are you sayin'?" Mulehead took the cigarette out of his mouth and examined the tip.

"I'm sayin' maybe somebody is on the look-out for them horses, hollow head!"

"Then we better git shed of 'em pretty quick," Mulehead said, putting the cigarette back in his mouth. "And that means find a livery!" He took a drag. "And that means find a town," he said around the smoke.

"I want my saddle back!" Polecat cried, sticking his jaw out.

"You can get your saddle back on another horse jest as well as these two, Polecat."

Polecat thought another minute before he spoke. "Reckon we could trade for another horse and git some money left over?" His tone was hopeful.

Mulehead shrugged. "You jest said they was fast."

"And you think a horse trader's gonna jest take a look at that half-growed pony you're ridin' and know it is fast?"

Again, Mulehead shrugged, this time without speaking, as he scraped the bits of tobacco that hadn't burned back into the pouch. Tidying Osgood's bedroll, he handed it to Polecat.

They mounted wearily and rode in silence until, dead ahead in the distance, Mulehead spotted a telegraph pole. "Which direction you think we oughtta go in for Cameron Junction, Polecat?" he asked with exaggerated innocence.

"How in blazing blue thunder and lightning strike the devil's red tail do I know!"

Mulehead's moustache concealed his gratified smile.

* * *

Facedown in a gulley, Boss motioned for Hank and Sampson to stay put out of sight on their horses. Removing his hat so that it wouldn't be spotted over the rise, he watched five horsemen in the distance. As soon as they turned north, he replaced his hat and scrambled back to his horse.

"Ain't it too soon for a posse?" Hank asked as Boss mounted.

"It's comin' on dark," Boss said. He was bone-tired, hungry, and cold. And even though a terrible tongue lashing from his mother was as certain as tomorrow's dawn, he was more than ready to head home. But nobody else had complained, and as the leader, he could not be the first. "You wanna take a chance and cross them tracks?" he asked impatiently. "They'll spot us, sure, and come back and start askin' all kinds a questions."

"They ain't missin' no gold," Sampson protested, but with little heat.

"It's not from want of trying," Boss said. "And have you forgot Curly killed a man?"

"Boss is right," Hank said. He was ready to pack it in, but didn't want to admit it. "Besides," he added, hoping to supply a good enough reason to quit, "if Polecat and Mulehead are on the other side, they's good as gone anyhow, ain't they?"

"Okay, okay," Sampson said. "Then let's head back to the cabin, huh, Boss? My belly thinks my throat is slit."

"I could eat," Hank agreed eagerly.

Grumbling, pretending to give in to them with great reluctance, Boss gratefully turned his horse in the direction of home.

* * *

Seated in her favorite chair in the parlor of the private railroad car, Maude peered out of the window. Once again she consulted the watch pinned to the bosom of her black tea gown. "It is almost five o'clock and our car has not yet been coupled with Union Pacific's Number Eight yet," she said with a worried frown. She turned to Kinkade, who was standing nearby. "Do go and find out what is causing the delay, Kinkade."

"Yes, miss," Kinkade replied with a questioning glance at Abigail, who was seated in the overstuffed chair opposite Maude, apparently engrossed with the *Kansas Weekly Herald.*

"That won't be necessary, Kinkade," Abigail said without looking up from the paper.

Mystified, Maude glanced from Abigail to Kinkade and back again. "Explain yourself, Miss Danforth!" she exclaimed.

"We'll be spending the night on this siding," Abigail replied casually, turning the page.

"How can that be?" Maude asked, suddenly concerned that she might have made an error. "I, myself, arranged our schedule. "I am certain I received a confirmation note from the stationmaster—"

"I instructed Kinkade to cancel your arrangements." Abigail folded the paper so that it lay neatly in her lap and held her breath. The inevitable moment when she needs must tell Maude what she'd done was at hand. She prayed that her nervousness did not show.

"You did what!" Maude exclaimed. Anger put color in her cheeks. "Why?"

Wishing she had a sip of water to moisten her suddenly dry mouth, Abigail said, "Since that Pinkerton person has not seen fit to inform Marshal Tilgham about the death of his friend, or the theft of his Foundation Sire, I thought it not untoward that I should do so. When I received a return wire from Mr. Tilghman saying that he was leaving Guthrie on Santa Fe's 408 and would be here at seven tomorrow morning, I felt the least we could do was wait just long enough to breakfast with him.''

''How dare you change our plans without consulting me!'' Maude cried.

''Would you have agreed to it?''

''Of course not!''

''Then you understand why I did not consult you,'' Abigail replied. With a conspiratorial grin, she continued, ''Do forgive me, Miss Cunningham, but when I received Mr. Tilghman's reply, it seemed such a short time to wait to meet the great man personally that I could not resist. Furthermore, I was there when it happened. I may be able to supply him with some valuable clues that perhaps I am not even aware of until he brings them to my attention.''

Realizing that their connection was long gone by now, and that there was nothing she could do about it, Maude could not help but admire Abigail's audacity. ''I might have known that your desire to meet this lawman would lead you into devious behavior,'' she said with mock severity. ''You are to merely discuss arrangements for the recovery of Crosspatches and his return to you in San Francisco,'' she added more seriously. ''You must not even consider joining the marshal. I will brook no further delay. Is that agreed?''

''Agreed.'' Abigail crossed her fingers underneath the newspaper.

Maude glared at Kinkade. ''I'll hold you personally responsible if anything goes amiss,'' she said, sitting back in her chair. "Imagine!" she exclaimed, a bemused expression on her face. "I've been shanghaied!"

"Just a moment, Kinkade, if you please," Abigail said as he started to leave for the galley. "Did either bandit use a name, per chance?" she asked.

"No, ma'am."

"Very well." Disappointed, Abigail sighed. "Thank you, Kinkade," she continued. "We'll have our tea now."

Parting the curtains, Kinkade hesitated. He stood there for a moment, not even feeling the velvet of the heavily fringed drapery, before returning to stand before Abigail. "There was something, miss," he said when Abigail looked up from the newspaper. "I don't know if it will help."

"I'll decide that," Abigail said. "Tell me the particulars."

"The shorter man said something about the big one deserving his name because he was stubborn."

"The larger man was stubborn?"

"Yes, ma'am. He didn't want to follow the little fellow. When he insisted on going his own way, the short one started to call him the stubbornest—something—but he stopped before saying the actual name. Then he said that the large man deserved the name he had."

"So the larger man has a name that means or implies stubbornness?"

"Yes, ma'am."

"Thank you very much, Kinkade." She dismissed him with a wave of her hand. "Now it's getting on past tea time."

As soon as Kinkade closed the curtains, Maude said,

"I assume you will pester me to guess at names while we wait for tea?"

"You know me well, Miss Cunningham." Abigail smiled with pleasure, delighted that Maude was being so agreeable.

Maude faced the window so that Abigail could not see her wry smile. "I know a name that is perfectly synonymous with stubbornness."

"Do tell!" Abigail cried, her eyes alight with excitement.

Turning to rake Abigail with a ferocious glance, Maude exclaimed, "Miss Abigail Patience Danforth!"

Circling Leavenworth so that he'd enter from the direction opposite the robbery, Curly traded his spent horse for a fresh one in a livery on the outskirts of town. Tying up in front of Nelson's, he entered, searched the crowded saloon where Sally was working and, spotting her at a distance, gave her the high sign to meet him upstairs.

Up in the small bedroom they shared, he poured water from the pitcher into the bowl and washed his face. While drying his hands, he took a few steps to the window and peered through the curtains to make sure he'd recognize his new mount below.

When he heard the gentle knock, he flung the towel at the washstand. "Who is it?"

Reassured by Sally's voice, he swiftly opened the door, then yanked her inside and into his arms. Leaning his back into the door to close it, he held her tightly and kissed her.

Twisting her face away, she looked at him. "Well?" Her black eyes searched his face.

"Well, what?" He opened his eyes wide in puzzlement as if he didn't know perfectly well what she meant.

"Did you get it?" she asked, worried.

"Get what?"

"Oh, stop teasing me, Curly!" She stomped her foot in a flash of temper she knew he liked. "Did you get the gold?"

"Yep."

"Well, where is it?" She looked toward the chair on the far side of the bed where he usually put his things.

"In a safe place." He grabbed her hand and drew her toward the bed.

"Then what are we doing here?" She tried to pull away, but he held her fast.

Still holding her hand, he sat on the side of the bed and pulled her onto his lap. "What are you in such a hurry for, sugar?"

"The sooner I get outta this dump, the better I'll like it." Twisting a ringlet around her finger, she smiled the smile that never failed to melt his heart. "I'm all packed and ready to go." She pouted. "I was just waiting for you."

Pushing her down on the bed so that her head landed on the pillow, Curly bent over her. "I've had me a real tryin' couple a days," he said, stroking her hair, his voice gruff with anticipation. "I want some lovin' from you, a hot meal, and some sleep. In that order. Then we'll leave. Unless it's too late. In that case, we'll spend the night here and leave in the morning."

"But Curly—"

Smothering her protests with a kiss, he treated her struggles as he'd done in the past—as enticements to his pleasure. He had removed her dress and was fumbling with the buttons on his pants when the door burst open.

Sally screamed, pulling the bedspread to her chin.

Slamming the door shut with the heel of his boot, a bewhiskered man pointed his gun at the bed.

"Don't shoot!" Sally cried as Curly flung himself on the floor, using the bed as a shield.

The man fired.

The bullet missed Curly by an inch. He scrambled under the bed. His gun was in its holster hanging from a chair on the far side. Praying the man wouldn't kneel down and shoot him like a trapped dog, desperate, he snaked himself under the bed as fast as he could until he was near enough to the other side to see his gun. His heart was thumping so loud in his chest he could scarcely hear anything else.

"You darn fool!" Sally shouted. "Don't kill him!"

Under the bed, Curly wondered how much smarts Sally had if she thought he'd let some villain shoot at him, and live. He peered out from under the dangling bedcovers to see if he could reach his gun.

"But he was puttin' his hands on you," a deep voice replied.

Sally tried to whisper so that Curly couldn't hear her, but her anger got the best of her as she said, "You was supposed to wait outside and follow us till we had the gold, you idiot!"

"But I don't let nobody fool around with my girl," the man answered.

"I don't belong to you!" she shouted, beside herself with fury. "I don't belong to nobody!"

As their words sunk in, all feeling drained from Curly. He concentrated on easing himself from under the bed. The man's attention was on Sally. Slowly, still on his back, Curly squirmed closer to the chair and reached for his holster. He eased it from the chair.

"But I love you," the man said. "I—"

The bullet hit the man square between the eyes, knocking him into the washstand. It crashed to the floor under his weight. Curly scrambled to his feet and, seeing that the man was dead, turned to Sally, gun in hand.

Bedspread to chin, eyes wide, her mouth was working, but no words would come.

Curly stared at the prettiest woman he'd ever known. Without the slightest hesitation, he pulled the trigger.

Completely numb, he calmly restored his appearance in the bureau mirror. Climbing out of the window, he navigated the few feet of shingles, then dropped to the street. As if in a trance, he aimed his new mount toward the graveyard to retrieve his gold.

Chapter Seven

Tilghman relinquished his uncreased, white ten-gallon hat to Kinkade when they reached the parlor, whereupon Kinkade introduced the marshal to Abigail. Taking Abigail's outstretched hand in his, Tilghman admired her morning costume in various shadings of brown, which enhanced her chestnut hair and dark eyes. "Your invitation for breakfast was most welcome, Miss Danforth," he said, completing his many compliments gracefully.

Maude struggled for composure. Seated by the window, she had watched the lawman as he had approached the train, and had been stricken by his resemblance to her beloved Charles. Tilghman was older, and she could see that his size and moustache were the only physical similarities now that he was close, but his resonant voice and gentle yet manly demeanor so reminded her of her departed lover that she could not speak. She extended her hand when Abigail introduced him, but kept her eyes downcast.

To smooth the awkward moment, Abigail said, "I thought you might be hungry after your hurried trip, Mr. Tilghman." Believing Maude simply to be miffed by the delay, Abigail looked forward to monopolizing the handsome lawman's attention and gleaning some valuable tips on the art of detection. "And before you begin another journey," she continued, "I took the liberty of ordering chicken crepes with raisin sauce after the melon to start. I wasn't certain whether you'd prefer a T-bone or sirloin for your steak and eggs. Or perhaps a filet?"

"Why, a T-bone would suit me just fine, Miss Danforth," he said, offering his arm to escort her the few steps to the elegantly set table. Helping her into her chair, he waited until Kinkade had seated Maude opposite her before taking his place between. "Mighty thoughtful of you to telegraph me, ma'am." Completely at ease in the elegant surroundings, he removed the napkin from his service plate and unfolded it leisurely while including both ladies in his smile.

Their small-talk of his trip from Guthrie and a more serious discussion of the details of Osgood's demise floated around Maude as she sought to recover herself while the porters served.

After seating Maude, Kinkade had hurried out of the parlor to the galley. Spotting Jacqueline farther down the corridor, he raced after her. As he drew close, feeling quite daring, he teased, "Eavesdropping, eh?"

She turned and grinned up at him, kissing her fingertips. "Ooh la la!" she said, her eyes asparkle. "What fun to posse with *Monsieur* Tilghman!"

Wishing he had the nerve to ask the chef to scorch the handsome lawman's steak, Kinkade stormed into the galley. By the time he returned to the parlor car, Maude had finished her melon, without having said a word.

But as the steward ladled a spoonful of raisin sauce

on Tilghman's crepe, Maude cast a shy glance at the marshal and said, "I was saddened to hear of the death of your wife."

Flabbergasted by the personal nature of Maude's remark, especially after her prolonged silence, Abigail nearly choked on her first bite of chicken.

"Why, thank you, Miss Cunningham," Tilghman replied as though Maude had been taking part in the conversation all along. "I didn't realize she had the consumption until it was too late." He sighed. "I'm afraid I added to her misery by being gone too much."

"You mustn't blame yourself, Mr. Tilghman," Maude said, her gray eyes sympathetic. "Now that you are a widower and retired, how do you pass the time?"

Abigail disguised her astonishment with a suddenly lusty appetite.

Not in the least put off by the prying nature of Maude's question, Tilghman spoke in his easy-going manner of picnics when the weather was fine, of cock fights in a specially designed pit and, more animatedly, of his track for quarter-horse races. He regaled them with tales of a few of the more exciting contests.

Abigail was as fascinated by Maude's sudden attentiveness toward Tilghman as she was impressed by his story-telling.

When he spoke of his trips to Kentucky for stock because the men there kept better records of bloodlines, Abigail asked, "Is that why Mr. Osgood had to journey all the way to Arabia? That is to say, couldn't a person find a fast horse here in Kansas City?"

"Why surely, ma'am," Tilghman replied. "The Dades have one of the most fleet-footed stallions ever bred to a mare. They're probably going to be my biggest competitor."

"Mr. Osgood, may he rest in peace, said that the Arabian was to have been your Foundation Sire," Maude said.

Tilghman nodded. "He was a mighty fine man, Osgood. There's not many men a body could trust like I trusted him. I'm mighty sorry to lose him."

"And will you join Jake's posse?" Abigail asked.

"Oh, no, ma'am," Tilghman said with disdain. "After a few days in the cold, those men will get fed up and head back home. Osgood was a stranger in these parts, and they will soon lose interest. I'll pursue the killers on my own, using the same method that worked in capturing Bill Doolin."

"And what method was that?" Abigail asked eagerly, delighted that the subject of detection had come about so naturally.

With two such charming and attentive ladies for an audience, Tilghman could scarcely resist embellishing the tale somewhat as he recounted how he had trekked across the countryside garnering information until, by a clever ruse, he'd tricked a friend of Doolin's wife into telling him where he could be found.

The porters were serving the excellent coffee at the end of the meal by the time he said, "So when I got off the train in Eureka Springs, Arkansas, I was disguised as a preacher."

"How clever of you," Abigail said as he sipped his coffee, disguising her growing impatience with his monologue, which had precluded any questions. "Dr. Conan Doyle sometimes portrays Sherlock Holmes using a disguise."

"With all due respect to the doctor and his pulp fiction," Tilghman said huffily, "the disguise was my own idea."

Having hung on his every word, Maude was eager

for more. "Have you always ridden alone?" she asked. "Have you ever ridden with Wyatt Earp or Doc Holliday?"

"Not regular, ma'am," Tilghman's good humor returned. "It's been twenty years since I rode with Earp to catch the killer of Dora Hand. Earp and Holliday were a bit flashy for my taste. I'd rather keep my gun holstered. Now Heck Thomas and Chris Madsen are men of a different stripe. We've ridden many a mile together." He paused to take another sip of coffee.

"Are you going to look for your Arabian?" Abigail asked before he launched into another rambling, uninterruptible story.

"When I find Osgood's killers, our horses will probably be nearby, seeing as they are all part of the same gang."

"If I may say so, Marshal Tilghman, I am not so certain as you, sir," Abigail responded cautiously. While she might have become the least bit weary of his boorish story-telling wherein she had learned little that was new about the art of detection, she still respected him as a lawman. Further, she was loathe to breach the dictates of good manners by becoming quarrelsome with a guest, especially one of the male sex, who tended to dislike contradiction from females, a trait she found difficult to understand, but nonetheless respected. "I think that it is more than likely that the robbers who took the gold intentionally abandoned the two men who tried to rob Miss Cunningham."

"With all due respect, ma'am, I do not agree." Tilghman's grin and conspiratorial wink at Maude was intended to soften his words, but the gesture merely served to infuriate Abigail.

"Then why didn't they leave their horses behind?"

Abigail blurted out the question before she could stop herself.

"Now, you're much too pretty to trouble yourself with such matters, Miss Danforth." Reaching across the table, he patted her hand. "You were unconscious for some considerable time, making it impossible for you to recall exactly what was going on. For all you know, our horses were simply more convenient. Am I not right?"

Even though the memory of Osgood could still make her feel queasy, Abigail blushed with fury that Tilghman would take advantage of her one moment of weakness to dismiss all of her opinions out of hand. Rather than precipitate what could develop into an unseemly quarrel by defending her opinion, she retrieved her fan from her lap. Swallowing her ire with a smile, fanning her burning cheeks, she decided to withhold what she considered clues of the stolen candy and stubborn name.

As taken in by Abigail's flawless manners as was Tilghman, Maude said, "Pray, do prevail upon Mr. Tilghman to allow us join him, Miss Danforth."

Abigail was having difficulty enough controlling her temper to be surprised by Maude's request. Her tone was dangerously close to sarcasm as she spoke. "Anyone who can capture a Bill Doolin all by himself does not need the assistance of two helpless females, Miss Cunningham." Turning to Tilghman she asked sweetly, "And just how long did it take you, good sir?"

"Four years to capture the whole gang."

Maude gasped, impressed with his tenacity.

Stunned that it had taken him such an immoderate length of time, Abigail could but stare at him, her fan stilled, her open-mouthed expression fortunately mistaken by Tilghman for one of awe.

"I knew you'd understand about my not needing any help, Miss Danforth." Feeling expansive in the light of such open admiration, he added, "It's a big country out there. Dangerous for a tenderfoot. You'd take a lot of looking after so's you wouldn't get lost, or hurt. And you'd get no pampering like you ladies are used to."

Not trusting herself to speak without losing her temper, Abigail busied herself with drinking her coffee and allowed Maude to carry the burden of conversation.

When, at last, Maude stood, Tilghman was on his feet in an instant to stand by her at the writing desk while she penned the address of the Palace Hotel in San Francisco so that he could have Crosspatches delivered in the event that he was able to recover the horse.

Standing between the two overstuffed chairs by the window, Abigail forced herself to graciously perform the amenities of departure while Kinkade retrieved Tilghman's hat. Maude accompanied the lawman to the platform.

Paying not the slightest attention to the porters as they cleared the table, Abigail remained standing, staring out of the window. She cared not a fig whether the marshal's insults had been intentional or not, they still rankled. But she had to admit that he'd been right about one thing. The country beyond her gaze was a trackless wilderness about which she knew nothing. Crosspatches could be anywhere. Bound by her promise to Maude to proceed to San Francisco with all due speed, she'd have to leave him behind. Her eyes filled with tears. Whether they were from grief at the loss of her horse, anger at being so summarily excluded from the efforts to find him, or frustration at being trapped by her own word, she could not have said.

Tiptoeing so as not to disrupt the lady's reverie, the last of the porters placed a fresh bouquet of flowers on the cleared table and silently vanished just as Maude returned. With a bemused expression on her face, she took her chair by the window.

Determined not to use the emotional blackmail of tears to influence her companion, Abigail took a deep breath and, blinking rapidly to disperse the last bit of telltale moisture, turned slowly to face Maude. "I must say I dread what will happen to Crosspatches if I abandon him to his fate, Miss Cunningham."

"But Marshal Tilghman is going to find your horse for you, Miss Danforth," Maude said in an assured tone as if the lawman had all but completed the task.

"I beg to differ, Miss Cunningham." Abigail said with a wan smile. "The marshal is going to search for Mr. Osgood's killer."

"I suppose you would like to pursue him as well," Maude said, raking Abigail with a suspicious glance.

Abigail shook her head as she took the chair opposite Maude. "There are more than enough people on that trail." Automatically rearranging her skirts to fall more gracefully, she was relieved that Maude had not become agitated at the mention of her concern. "If I were free to do so," she said casually, as if the matter held little import for her, "I would concentrate upon finding my horse." Bracing herself for Maude's reaction, she continued, "Perhaps you could take this car on to San Francisco? I could meet you there." She paused before adding emphatically, "With Crosspatches."

"And just how do you propose to find your horse?" In spite of herself, Maude was not a little impressed by Abigail's perseverance in the face of all the rejection she had suffered. "If Jake and the marshal would not allow a woman to ride with them, I should think it would be impossible to gather a group of men to ride with you."

"Quite true, Miss Cunningham. And at this moment, I am not entirely certain how I would proceed. To hear Marshal Tilghman tell, one has a choice between a posse, or laborious tracking by a determined individual, as the only methods available." With an impatient rustling of skirts, she stood. "But these are modern times," she said as she paced to the table. She turned to face Maude. "There must be a better way." With a sweep of her hand, she included the outdoors as she continued, "Why, we have the telegraph with the Morse code to reach all corners of the country with the touch of a button."

Maude cast a sly glance at Abigail. "If you were to remain behind, would you also try to find the marshal's Arabian?" she asked in a fashion even more casual than Abigail's had been.

"If I were very lucky." Abigail's eyes clouded with dread. "If the bandits do not sell them before—" She shuddered, leaving the rest of the sentence unsaid, fully aware that more than enough time had already passed for the worst to have happened.

With her gaze focused upon her demurely folded hands resting in her lap, Maude asked, "Might I presume that you would return his horse to the marshal?" Maude paused briefly before swiftly adding, "In person, that is?"

"Oh, with the greatest of pleasure, Miss Cunningham," Abigail said, her eyes suddenly agleam with delight at the prospect. "I'd give a great deal to see his face as I handed him the reins to his precious pearl from Arabia." Her smile was triumphant. "He'd not call me tenderfoot again!"

"I say, Miss Danforth." Maude gazed up at Abigail, clearing her throat unnecessarily. "Since it is you who are the detective, it would benefit me not at all to precede you to San Francisco. I'd only get there and have to wait upon your arrival." She shrugged. "In that case, I might as well stay on."

"Then you do not object to the delay?" Astonished by Maude's easy acquiescence without even having been asked, Abigail returned to her chair and slowly sank into it.

"While I fail to understand your emotional attachment to a mere horse, Miss Danforth, I most certainly can appreciate the value of a Foundation Sire." She glanced swiftly at Abigail before turning her head to gaze out of the window. "It would be a tragedy of no small proportion to have so priceless a horse ruined by bandits who knew not what they had."

Abigail glanced at Maude with raised eyebrow, stifling a knowing grin as she accepted Maude's capitulation without questioning it, although how Maude could be attracted to such a patronizing bore as Marshal Tilghman was beyond her. "Whatever your reasons might be, Miss Cunningham," Abigail said, her tone ironic, "I am most grateful that you have released me from my vow."

"Do you think it will take years?" Maude asked anxiously.

"It must not take years," Abigail said firmly, realizing that Crosspatches had no chance to survive the next few weeks if the weather turned bitter. "But I do believe that you must cancel our more immediate commitments in San Francisco."

Maude rose to go to the writing desk. "If I remember correctly, aside from the reception upon our arrival, there is the Clayborne's ball celebrating Washington's Birthday on the twenty-second," she said as she withdrew a date book from the drawer.

"You must cancel that, of course," Abigail said, distracted. Now that she was committed to stay, she sorely needed a plan, and had none.

"Ambrose Bierce was to have been there," Maude said, not a little disappointed. Maude's detailing of their engagements out loud, some of which Abigail herself had insisted upon in order to pick up the threads of Charlie's activities, fell upon deaf ears. Unaware that Abigail had not been listening, Maude finished her recital and proceeded to pen their regrets to the Claybornes.

Although Abigail's gaze was focused somewhere outside the window, her thoughts were inward, examining the few clues she had and how she might use them to advantage. Just as Maude's quill scratched her signature upon her completed note, several ideas that had been clamoring for attention came together in what might pass for a feasible plan. Delighted that she had the makings of a workable outline, Abigail exclaimed, "Aha!" In contrast to the preceding silence, her outburst was quite loud.

Concentrating upon her task, Maude was startled by Abigail's exclamation. "Pray, do not 'Aha!' me, Miss Danforth," she said indignantly, drawing herself tall. "Explain yourself!"

"One can trap many more flies with honey than by chasing them about with swatters, Miss Cunningham." Abigail had merely to rise and approach the bell pull to ring for Kinkade and Jacqueline, before they both appeared quietly at the curtained doorway. Although Abigail knew that their too-swift appearance implied that they had probably been eavesdropping, she felt too pressed for time to inquire, much less issue a reprimand. "My gray tweed, please, Jacqueline," she said briskly, waving at her maid to be gone.

"Yes, ma'am." With a discreet, slightly flirtatious glance at Kinkade, Jacqueline sped away to do her mistress's bidding.

"Kinkade," Abigail continued without interruption, "go at once and hire the finest rig in Kansas City and have it here by the time I am dressed. We are going to pay a call on the Dades."

Only too relieved that they would not be joining Tilghman, Kinkade hurried to obey without a thought of protest.

Upon his departure, Maude spoke at last, annoyed by not having the slightest idea what Abigail was up to. "What do you mean honey, Miss Danforth! May I remind you that it is desperate criminals we are after, not insects!"

Ignoring Maude's protestations, Abigail pulled a chair away from the dining table so that she could sit facing Maude, who was still at the desk. "I am most pleased that you have decided to stay, Miss Cunningham," she said, leaning forward eagerly. "I can put the PV to good use. And you as well," she added swiftly. "In fact, I would ask you to arrange at once to have the outside railings gilded, or the window frames painted a different color. Anything to change the appearance of the car."

"Miss Danforth!" Shocked, Maude stood. "That I cannot do! The Humbolts would—"

"Pray, do not be tiresome, Miss Cunningham," Abigail said with an airy wave of her hand. "We will have the car restored long before we reach San Francisco. The Humbolts will be none the wiser." Paying not the slightest attention to Maude's forbidding scowl, Abigail continued, "Now, as soon as the painting is under way, take some cash and have the station master reroute us. Make certain that our connection has a proper facility to carry a fine horse."

"Now I do rebel, Miss Danforth." Maude put both hands on her hips defiantly. "It is a matter of the Humbolts' honor to have their private varnish carried gratis. A permanent stain would blemish the car's record if we were to pay."

"Very well," Abigail relented. "Then use the telegraph to seek the permission it takes to book us through to Wichita."

"Wichita!" Maude exclaimed. "Why Wichita?"

"We must seem to have abandoned the horses," Abigail said impatiently, loathe to take the time to explain more fully. "Wichita is far enough away without going too far."

"How on earth do you intend to track them down by going to Wichita?" Maude's exasperation knew no bounds. "And with honey?"

"Actually with chocolate, to be more precise, Miss Cunningham."

"Enough of your conundrums, Miss Danforth!" Maude exclaimed. "Explain yourself!"

"I shall over dinner, but now I must change." Abigail hurried toward the exit that led to her room. Pausing at the curtains, she turned to face Maude. "Do not despair, Miss Cunningham." Her smile was ironic. "Marshal Tilghman's and my methods differ. With much luck, if my plan works, I should have them in hand upon George Washington's Birthday."

100

Maude stared at Abigail in open-mouthed amazement.

Thoroughly enjoying Maude's reaction, Abigail
could not resist adding, "It would no doubt be more
manly to take four years, but I am just a know-nothing,
pampered tenderfoot. Three weeks should just about
do it for the likes of me!"

Chapter Eight

Seated in the Dades' parlor, Abigail waited for Mr.
Dade to freshen up before joining her. Until this moment, wherein she was suddenly terribly nervous, everything had gone remarkably well. Kinkade had not
only secured a fine rig and a matched pair, but easy-
to-follow directions to the Dades' place, which had
proven to be correct as well. Their good fortune had
continued when she had found that gentleman at home
and willing to receive her. She had taken pains to wear
a modestly trimmed, high-necked frock of gray tweed
with a single strand of pearls, hoping that the simplicity
of her costume would bespeak maturity. She concealed
further evidence of her youth behind the French net-
ting of an elaborately feathered hat.

Holding Abigail's sable-trimmed cloak, Jacqueline
stood behind her, still with her own overcoat on, trying
not to show her disdain for the rough plainness of the
furnishings in the parlor. The horsehair couch facing
Abigail had suspicious hollows in the seat wherein
springs had probably gone lax, and while the rug was
obviously of good quality, it was worn threadbare in

spots as was the upholstery on the overstuffed chairs. Curtains hung limp in windows none too clean.

Kinkade had been allowed to wait in the kitchen where, presumably, he was being treated to refreshments.

When a white-haired man finally appeared and approached Abigail, his hand extended in greeting, she resisted the impulse to stand as she'd been taught to do when one of her elders came into a room. If she were to be treated as full-grown, she must act it.

"Forgive my humble abode, Miss Danforth," he said in a deep-chested, rumbling voice that belied his slender physique. "It hasn't known the gracious touch of a woman since my wife died eight years ago. My only daughter followed her soon after. I fear my sons and I don't have much knack for civilization." He glanced at Jacqueline to include her. "May I offer you some refreshment?"

Jacqueline lowered her head, blushing to the roots of her hair at the idea of taking tea, or that American drink coffee, on equal terms with her mistress in a gentleman's parlor, no matter how plain that room might be.

"Thank you, no, Mr. Dade," Abigail replied. "I have little time." Determined to be taken seriously after so many rebuffs, she came to the purpose of her visit in what she thought was a most crisp, businesslike manner. "I hear tell you have the fastest horse in these parts," she said, without her normal, pleasant smile.

"And who might I ask told you this?" he asked warily. While there was no man alive who could intimidate him, this female creature, dressed in clothes costly enough to pay for horse feed for a year, who appeared in his parlor unannounced, had him flummoxed.

"Marshal Tilghman—"

"Ah, Bill Tilghman!" Relaxing his guard somewhat, Dade overrode Abigail expansively. "And how did you come to meet our famous marshal?" He paused by the sofa, but did not sit down since Jacqueline remained standing. "He's retired now." His suspicions aroused again, he added with raised eyebrow, "Living in Chandler, quite some distance south of here."

Suddenly realizing how strange she must appear to this man who probably had not traveled overmuch, Abigail softened her brusque manner with her most winsome smile as she replied, "I was on the same train as his friend Mr. Osgood, who was escorting an Arabian to the marshal to serve as his Foundation Sire."

Her smile was not lost on Dade. Wishing to hear more, but desiring to sit to do so, he indicated the sofa facing Abigail's chair. Glancing at Jacqueline again, he said, "Wouldn't you be more comfortable sitting down?"

Her cheeks pink once again at the very idea, Jacqueline shook her head vehemently.

Although she was unable to see her maid standing behind her, Abigail could well imagine her discomfort. "Why don't you join Kinkade in the kitchen, Jacqueline?" she suggested, seeking Mr. Dade's approval with a smile and nod in his direction.

Unwilling to abandon her duty as chaperon, Jacqueline looked askance at the suggestion. "I'm fine, miss," she said.

"I insist," Abigail said firmly.

Puzzled by the fuss, European-trained lady's maids being beyond his ken, Dade showed Jacqueline to the arched doorway that led to the rest of the house. "Down the hall to your left," he said, pointing the way.

Jacqueline's spine was stiff with disapproval as she followed his direction, but she nonetheless obeyed.

Dade returned to seat himself on the sofa, his blue-eyed gaze warm with interest. "I'd appreciate hearing some more about the nature of your errand so that I could understand it a mite better, if you please, Miss Danforth." He settled back into the stiff couch with its sprung seating as though it were filled with the softest of feathers.

Thus encouraged, Abigail told him such details as she knew of the train robbery, the theft of Crosspatches and Tilghman's Arabian, and of the subsequent rebuffs from the Pinkerton agent and Tilghman upon her offering her assistance in their recovery.

"And what is it you want from me?" he asked, not a little impressed by her swift, efficient manner in recounting a complicated tale and her singular lack of self-pity.

"I need a fast horse, Mr. Dade," Abigail said eagerly, leaning forward in her chair. "I have come to ask if I might buy yours."

Taken aback, Dade replied, "Belvedere is not for sale, my child."

More dismayed by his referring to her as a child than by his rejection, which she had anticipated, Abigail continued, "Then perhaps I can prevail upon you to lend Belvedere to me." She glanced at him appraisingly. "For a good price?"

"You intrigue me, Miss Danforth," he said. And, indeed, that a girl so young could be so full of bustle and whip-crack delighted him. Had his daughter lived, he would have wished her to have the same mettle. "However, may I point out that if you intend to track Osgood's killer, you'd need a hardy cow pony with lots of endurance for the long haul, not a horse that's been bred for speed."

"You mistake my intention, sir." Once again, Abigail leaned forward eagerly, her eyes alight with excitement. "Both Crosspatches and the Arabian have been bred for speed, Mr. Dade." She paused briefly to consider how best to persuade him.

Wondering what she was driving at, he waited for her to continue.

Finally, she asked, "Would you say that racing horses is a popular sport in these parts?"

"No question!" He shrugged. "A close race still tops baseball for enthusiastic wagering."

"Sooner or later, whoever stole Crosspatches and the Arabian is going to discover just how fast they are. If they haven't already. Is it not logical that men desperate enough for money to rob a train might desire to reap a profit from those extraordinary horses' swiftness and engage in a race?"

Dade smiled. "I do believe I am beginning to cotton on to your plan, Miss Danforth."

"Then you understand why I need a very fast horse to put up against the finest that Kansas and the surrounding territory has to offer."

Even as he nodded in agreement, he frowned. "Ah, but my best three-year-old already has a reputation in these parts and is easily recognized."

"I've thought of that. There are some devious ways to disguise a horse, Mr. Dade. I suspect that the thieves who have Crosspatches and the Arabian in hand will resort to disguising them also. My only hope is that they will not be too cruel in their methods."

"Marshal Tilghman has done much to settle this territory, Miss Danforth. I had looked forward to competing with him on friendly terms for the best horseflesh—''

''Then you agree?'' Abigail pressed before he could digress any further.

Dade looked at her squarely. ''Who would ride him?''

She blinked, not until this moment having thought about it. ''Why, I would,'' she said with an assurance she was far from feeling.

''Never!'' he exclaimed, more harshly than he had intended. Standing, hands deep in his pockets, he paced to the doorway whence Jacqueline had disappeared. Turning to face her, he said, ''You'll be in need of a rider familiar with the skullduggery that is sometimes practiced in small-town horse races.''

''Well, then perhaps Kinkade, if you insist.'' Abigail waved her hand toward the back of the house.

''That your factotum in the kitchen?'' he asked with a disparaging smile and raised brow.

Abigail drew herself tall. ''Kinkade is much more than just a handyman, Mr. Dade—''

''Now, now, miss, don't get your dander up.'' Dade gestured with his hand that he meant no offense. ''While I've no doubt your man can ride, he'd be no match for the likes of those who don't feel right lest they're astride a horse.''

Abigail's heart sank. Knowing his answer before she spoke, she said, ''I could hire someone—''

''No, my dear.'' Shaking his head, both hands jammed in his pockets once more, he returned to the couch before turning to look down at Abigail. ''I will lend you my horse with the proviso that you take my son Morgan with you.''

It was all Abigail could do to restrain herself from jumping up and hugging him around the neck. ''Oh,

Mr. Dade, thank you!" she exclaimed with a broad smile.

"Unfortunately, Morgan is not here at the moment, or I would introduce you." Dade smiled. "My son will not be as easy to disguise as his mount."

"Never fear, sir," Abigail said. "Jacqueline and I are quite skilled at disguise." She held out her hand before he could change his mind. "Then we have a bargain?"

"We have but to strike a guarantee price if something untoward should happen to him," Dade said, shaking her hand. "Though I must say, Miss Danforth—" releasing her hand, he returned to the sofa— "if your plan comes to fruition, it is not going to set well with Marshal Tilghman that a mere girl-child managed to outsmart him in the manner of getting his horse back."

Abigail blushed, even though her grin was wicked. "As long as we only have the details to settle," she said quickly, "I would enjoy a cup of tea now, if you please."

Maw Baxter may have disapproved of blaspheming, but her words were hot enough to redden the ears of Boss, Sampson, and Hank when they returned empty-handed. Fortunately for them, she did not consider that her temper excused her from a duty to feed her men well, though the pots took a mighty beating from the spoon-thwacking and lid-slamming that accompanied her scolding.

Boss signaled to Sampson and Hank to muzzle themselves, that to interrupt would only prolong her tongue-lashing. They ate in silence.

No longer yelling, but still grumbling under her breath, Maw finally joined them.

Boss waited till she'd eaten a few mouthfuls and was sopping some gravy with bread to ask, "Do we really need to find them two?"

"What have we got if you don't?" She glared at him, but the heat had gone out of her voice. "They're our only hope of gettin' some money outta the mess you made."

"You thinkin' they took the gold, ma'am?" Sampson ventured.

"How do I know!" Maw scowled at him.

Sampson was about to apologize for asking when he saw Boss's sign to keep quiet.

Maw smeared another piece of bread around, but before she ate it, she said, "Maybe we could hold them horses they stole for ransom. Billy Bub said they was fast." Putting the dripping bread in her mouth, she spoke around it. "They gotta be worth somethin'."

"Say, where is that boy?" Hank asked. "Sleepin' it off?"

"In the other room with the ague so bad I had to dose him with a mustard plaster." Maw's face softened.

Boss sat back in his chair, tilting it so that it balanced on two legs. "I don't know about you boys, but I'm ready to try me another train." He stretched his arms wide. "I stopped that one right easy like."

Maw stood, her cleaned plate in her hand. "You tell me what good it's gonna do for you to hold up another train!" Towering over her son, she laughed scornfully. "You don't even know the difference between a brick and gold!"

"Aw, Maw—"

"Don't you 'Aw, Maw,' me, son." Her voice was

109

full of contempt. "Right now, I'm sorry I borned you. There ain't no point at all in you holdin' up trains when you caint's git nothin' but chased after for murder for your pains!"

"So what do you think we oughta do?" Boss asked, squaring his chair with a thump.

"At dawn's first light, you and Sampson go lookin' for Polecat and Mulehead," Maw replied, returning to the table with the coffeepot.

"What about me?" Hank asked.

"You stay here."

Hank gave Boss a pleading glance.

Boss laughed. "Since when do you need protection from them two, Maw?"

Maw paused after filling Hank's cup and looked at each in turn. "You forgot about Curly? He's soon enough gonna find out he don't have no gold neither."

Sampson shook his head. "He's gonna be madder than a stomped rattlesnake."

"Then you boys understand why I don't want to be alone if and when he shows up," she said, her expression grim. "Billy Bub's worse'n no help." She refilled her own cup. "I cain't watch in every direction by myself." Placing the pot on the stove, she continued, "There's plenty chores to keep you busy, Hank, till somethin' happens."

Putting both hands around his cup, Hank hid his face while pretending to drink. He didn't dare protest out loud and didn't want his feelings to show. He hadn't joined Boss to become a handyman. Heck, he'd left a job mending fences so that he could have some excitement with maybe some money at the end of it. It wasn't his fault they hadn't come back with the real thing, but Maw had made out like he was the dumbest critter she'd ever met. She really must think he was a lackwit if she thought he'd stick around to protect a snotty kid and an old biddy against the likes of Curly. Yesterday, he might have just been a drifter, but at least nobody had been hunting him down for murder. He decided to let the others get to sleep, then he'd just mosey on down into the Oklahoma Territory. Nobody would find him there. Least of all Curly.

"They may not be all that bright," Maw continued. "But if Polecat and Mulehead do show up, there's two of them. Billy Bub's no use at all, shape he's in."

"I'm kinda surprised they ain't showed up already—what with us havin' their saddles and all," Sampson said.

Hank forced himself to sound relaxed. "Cain't nobody be that stupid they cain't find this place after they's been here once! Maybe they don't wanna come."

"Yeah," Sampson agreed. "Maybe they knew they was left behind on purpose and don't dare to show their faces."

"It ain't no accident they cain't find this place." Maw looked at Boss, her eyes full of pride. "Why do you think his Paw picked it?"

Sampson stood. "Well, if I gotta git up afore daylight agin, I'm gonna start gittin' my shut-eye right now." His yawn was huge.

"I want all of you out in the barn tonight." Maw shook her finger at her son. "And you take turns awatchin' the place."

"Aw, Maw," Boss protested. "If Polecat and Mulehead couldn't find the place in daylight, they sure ain't gonna find it in the dark."

Hands on hips, she replied as if to a simpleton, "You tryin' to tell me Curly'd wait till daylight if he could catch you by surprise when you're sleepin'?"

"Okay, okay, I'll take the first watch," Boss said, reaching for his jacket. "Since you're stayin' behind, Hank, you take the middle. That way Sampson and me'll get eight hours straight."

"You guys get all the breaks," Hank groused, but only because it was expected of him. It suited him just fine to get a nap on a full stomach before he took to the trail again.

Having pointed his new mount in the vague direction of the graveyard where he'd hidden the gold, Curly sat listlessly in the saddle, allowing the horse to plod along. No need to founder this one. No need to hurry. No need at all. It would be hours before Sally's body was discovered—with the stranger's. Since he no longer had her to fetch the gold for, it no longer mattered how fast he got to the graveyard. Or if he got there at all.

Suddenly aware that he had a mighty thirst, he reined in his mount to get his bearings. He had to think real hard about which direction he'd taken out of Leavenworth before he placed himself within a short ride to Williamstown. Little more than a tent city, it did boast a general store and a couple of saloons, which he'd scorned in the past for the finer accommodations in the city, but at this moment he was not particular.

Congratulating himself that he'd come to his senses before trying to find his gold in the dark, he rode into Williamstown and, leaving his horse at a livery, found the saloon.

Intent on their cards, or the serious business of getting drunk, none of the patrons noticed his entrance. Flickering gas-lamps lit a haze of smoke shrouding the cramped room in a mysterious envelope of fog, which might have been romantic had it not been for the stench of unwashed male bodies, stale liquor and even staler vomit. The piano in the corner was silent, the player sleeping off his afternoon bender before the evening's festivities began. The bartender, a hard man with a toothy smile who made extra money by shortchanging his customers once they became drunk, took one look at this newcomer's expression and decided to be real honest with him.

Curly bought a bottle. One foot on the rail, he stood at the bar and paced himself. With the precision of a hammer hitting nails, he poured and downed one shot at a time, allowing a good long time for it to spread throughout his whole body before taking another. The piano player had come and gone by the time his upper lip became numb and he was no longer certain that he could stand without the support of the bar under his elbows. Ever so carefully, he graped the bottle by the neck in one hand, took his shot glass in the other and, without staggering, made his way to a table and sat. The table's lone occupant had seen him coming and vacated without a word of protest.

He continued drinking, slowly, one shot at a time, until along about dawn when he put his head down on the table and passed out.

"Aw, come on, Paw, have a heart!" Morgan Dade exclaimed as he sat down heavily at the kitchen table. Grasping the pitcher of milk, he poured himself a glassful. "Why me?"

The others had finished their meal and left for afternoon chores. Having asked his youngest to stay behind so that he could talk to him alone, Mr. Dade stood on the other side of the table, watching with pride as his son drained the glass. He repeated himself patiently, "Because I need you to accompany Belvedere and ride him while he is on loan to Miss Danforth."

"But I don't want to spend weeks wet-nursing some green-horn girl." Morgan put the empty glass down with a thump and wiped his mouth with his napkin.

"I assure you, nobody's asking you to be a wet nurse, son." Mr. Dade smiled to himself, recalling Miss Danforth's self-assured demeanor. "You are to race Belvedere for her."

As Morgan ran a hand through his generous shock of dark hair, a lock strayed to his forehead. Dark brows shielded intelligent blue eyes that sparkled like his father's. Like his mother, he had a small cleft in his chin. "Why not make Tim go?"

"You're a better rider."

Morgan looked askance at his father. "That's not true," he said flatly.

"Well . . ." Mr. Dade shrugged. "Tim is engaged."

"What's that supposed to mean?" Morgan frowned.

"Miss Danforth's a mighty pretty girl, son—"

"And you're afraid Tim would—"

"You know your brother." Mr. Dade sighed. "The date is set. It would break Jessica's heart if she thought Tim would so much as look at another girl. She'd never forgive me."

Morgan stood and stretched to his full height. "You can be darn sure you won't find me mooning over a flibbertigibbit city girl." He shook his head disgustedly. "She probably can't even ride."

Amazed anew at how tall his youngest had become in this his twentieth year, Mr. Dade said, "She's mighty rich, son."

"We ain't exactly poor, Paw," Morgan said disdainfully. "Seems to me she's mighty uppity on top of it all, thinking she can outsmart Marshal Tilghman."

"Morgan, I'm done arguing with you." Mr. Dade shook his finger at the young man towering over him. "I want you to accompany Belvedere and race him as often as Miss Danforth asks you to."

"Yes, sir," Morgan muttered under his breath, his mouth a grim line of disgust.

As Mr. Dade moved quickly toward the kitchen door, he said, "She's invited you to dinner tonight on her private varnish to talk over plans." Opening the door, he turned to glance up at his son. "Mind you shave again, and wash behind your ears before you go," he said, slamming the door behind him before Morgan could protest any further.

Chapter Nine

Dinner had been awkward. Morgan had arrived late, muddied from a misadventure with his horse. But even after Kinkade had brushed him clean, there had remained his impossible clothes.

When he had tripped over his own feet while being introduced to Maude, she had stifled a smile and, with a not so subtle glance at Abigail, proclaimed herself victor of that afternoon's discussion of whether it was proper to ask the hired help to dine. Worried that Abigail was becoming much too democratic in her selection of dinner guests, and having made no secret that she'd thought Abigail's invitation preposterous, she'd been pleased to have her opinion so swiftly, and obviously, vindicated. She did, however, admit that the tall, well-muscled young man was strikingly handsome. Except for his ghastly clothes.

Abigail had ignored Maude's triumphant glance. Morgan's father had treated her with courtesy, and while he was probably not a millionaire, he was certainly far from poor. She had been prepared to consider Morgan part of the family, even though she was paying his father for the use of his horse. Quick to realize that westerners probably did not dress for dinner, she had immediately forgiven his clothes. However, she was not prepared for his singular lack of conversation, a highly prized skill in her social circle. While she certainly would not have cared to have him monopolize the evening in the manner of a Tilghman, his continued silence despite her most earnest efforts to draw him out had doomed the meal to a tedious ordeal.

From time to time, Maude had come to her rescue, but despite both their efforts, he had remained mute.

When even her banal comments upon the weather had failed to elicit a response, Abigail had come to the end of her tether. Then Morgan had asked for a glass of milk. With a smothered giggle and sly glance at Maude, which would have been missed by him in any case since his eyes were focused resolutely upon his plate, Abigail had conceded defeat. She placed her knife and fork across her plate as a signal to the porters that she was finished with the meat course, even though she had scarcely touched her pheasant, which had dried out from awaiting the arrival of their guest.

Morgan felt as out of place as a colt let loose in the parlor. That he'd all but ruined his Sunday best, bought less than a week before to accommodate his latest growth, bothered him not at all. But the high, new linen collar was proving a size too tight, and every time he moved his head, it rubbed a raw place in his neck. While Miss Cunningham was dressed properly in high-necked black, Miss Danforth's shiny gown with its huge leg-o'-mutton sleeves and low-cut neckline was more fitting for a fancy dress ball than supper.

He also felt bedazzled by the sheer number of candles that burned so wastefully in their splendid candelabra, their flickering light showering stars on the jewels at Miss Danforth's throat and on more crystal and silver than he'd ever before seen in one place. The overbearing room was too bright for comfort.

And too soft. His boots had sunk so deeply into the carpet, he'd nearly tripped when turning to meet Miss Cunningham, and his body had sunk a good two inches lower than he'd expected when he'd seated himself in the high-backed dinner chair.

Furthermore, when the folks he knew sat down for a meal, they ate. They didn't jabber at you and expect you to answer pointless questions when your belly was empty and your mouth full.

And further still, only men drank. And they drank whiskey. And they drank to get drunk, to kill pain, to drown sorrows, or to kick up a little sand. Or why bother? Ladies used whiskey for medicinal purposes only. The opportunity to enjoy a glass of wine to enhance the flavors of a meal and aid digestion had never before been offered to him. He'd naturally chosen milk.

When at long last the table had been crumbed, dessert, fruit and cheese, coffee and tea had been served, then cleared away, Abigail suggested that they move to the overstuffed chairs by the windows so that they could get to the business of the evening while the porters restored the table to order.

Much to the ladies' surprise, although Morgan still did not say much, he proved adept at helping Kinkade assist them from the table and into their new seating arrangement.

As Maude settled herself in her favorite chair, she spoke of her tribulations in arranging to have the private varnish painted. At Carlsbad's General Store where she'd gone to purchase the carriage paint, she'd discovered that skilled house painters were nonexistent. However, the generosity of her reward had spread so swiftly that before she'd paid for the paint, two sign painters had appeared who were willing to give it a try. She had questioned their sobriety, but they had seemed able-bodied enough. She'd been in no position to be particular and, giving them specific instructions, had hired them. "But it took an interminable length of time in the telegraph office to reroute us," she added. "Before I could check on the job they were doing—" She gestured toward the windows. "Well, you saw it!"

"We look not unlike a circus wagon." Abigail laughed, arranging her skirts. "At least we'll be attracting attention, which is all to the good."

"Perhaps we should hire a calliope!" Satisfied that it was unlikely that Abigail would invite the mummified young man to dinner again, Maude deigned to smile. "Now will you tell me why we've disguised the car?"

"What's your rush to leave Kansas City?" Morgan asked as he stuck a finger into the offending collar in a futile effort to loosen it.

The ladies were so startled by the sound of his voice that both turned to stare at him.

Abigail recovered first. "It is important that we disassociate ourselves from the Chicago, Rock Island and Pacific Railroad where we were robbed," she said. "The thieves must not remember us as their victims." She glanced from Morgan to Kinkade, who was about to usher out the last of the porters. "Fetch Jacqueline, will you please, Kinkade?" she called to him. "And come back yourself. I want you both to hear this, and I prefer not to repeat myself."

Kinkade had not far to go since Jacqueline had been waiting for this moment behind the curtains.

Their faces bland, innocent of the resentment they felt at Morgan Dade's exalted position as guest, hands at their sides, Jacqueline and Kinkade stood before Abigail as she said, "As you have probably surmised, I intend to recover the horses."

They nodded solemnly, in unison.

"To do so, I must swiftly build a reputation as an heiress." Abigail gazed directly at Jacqueline. "I need your help especially."

"*Mademoiselle?*"

"English!"

"Yes, miss." Although it was Abigail's habit to correct her, Jacqueline's face blazed with fury at being so corrected in front of the seated boy.

"When you accompany me as we stop along our route, you must begin rumors about how wealthy, and dotty, I am," Abigail said.

Morgan nearly strangled. That this rich, empty-headed, blabber-mouth would tell her servants to *pretend* she was rich, and scatterbrained, was more than he could bear. He knew he must not laugh, but the effort not to do so almost cost him his new linen collar, and pre-tied cravat. Swiftly covering his mouth with a handkerchief, he prayed the noises he made sounded like sneezing.

Abigail glared at him suspiciously as she continued, "I am to be touted as traveling with a horse that I feel can beat all comers." She paused until his spasms passed. "That is where you come in, Mr. Dade."

Wiping his eyes with his handkerchief, Morgan nodded wordlessly, wondering how soon he could decently escape, with Belvedere, without jeopardizing his father's honor.

"You must make it clear that I am willing to pay to prove it," Abigail said solemnly. "I want to be considered easy pickings, wagering a large purse in every town."

"Yes, miss," Jacqueline replied with a solemnity that matched Abigail's.

"But this will take years, Miss Danforth!" Maude wailed.

"Not with the modern advantages of the Morse telegraph and the printing press, Miss Cunningham." Abigail leaned forward eagerly. "I shall ask you to help me design a poster. As soon as we reach Wichita, I will telegraph the information to every printing press in every small town within a fifty mile radius. Free food should be featured prominently on the poster." She turned to Kinkade. "You must arrange for it, Kinkade."

"Beg pardon, miss?" Kinkade said. His frown endowed his face with an even more pugnacious quality.

"Arrange for cakes and fancy pastries to be available at every race. Chocolates especially."

"Why on earth are you going to provide food?" Maude asked. "Isn't this expedition already expensive enough?"

"You have forgotten our most important clue, Miss Cunningham," Abigail said impatiently. "Our bandits took bonbons from the candy dish. It is obvious to me that anyone who would stop in the middle of a robbery to steal candy is extraordinarily attracted to sweets," she continued. "And I'll wager it was the larger, stubborn one who did it."

"Ah, I see," Maude responded thoughtfully. "You believe the horse thieves will be lured by the sweets, even if they do not care to race."

"You have hit upon my method precisely, Miss Cunningham!" Abigail exclaimed. "Let Marshal Tilghman take four years." She smiled happily. "With any luck at all, we shall recover Crosspatches, and his Arabian friend, before the month is out!"

Morgan could stand no more. "I'll ask you not to compare yourself with Marshal Tilghman, Miss Danforth," he said, his blue eyes suddenly cold. "He is a hero in these parts."

"It is not my intention to compare myself to your splendid marshall, Mr. Dade." Lifting her chin defiantly, Abigail looked directly into his eyes with a cool glint in her own. "Rather, my plan is to recover his horse, and mine, in the most expeditious manner possible."

Disconcerted by her unflinching resolve, and wanting to bring her down a peg or two, he said, "Well, there is just one gigantic flaw in your plan, Miss Danforth."

"What might that be, Mr. Dade?" she asked, still holding his gaze.

"What if the robbers who stole your horses sell them?"

Abigail's gaze faltered, then strayed to her hands folded demurely in her lap, but not before Morgan saw the brown of her eyes deepen with an inconsolable sorrow.

With a change of heart so swift that it left him breathless, he wished he'd torn his tongue out before causing her such distress.

His watch complete, Boss entered the barn and shook Hank by the shoulder, awakening him.

Hank stumbled to his feet. Before he could knuckle the sleep from his eyes, Boss had taken his place in the straw and was snoring.

Stealthily, Hank led his horse outside and had readied him to ride when it occurred to him that he didn't have a whole lot to show for his time with the Baxter gang. Polecat's and Mulehead's saddles would fetch some pocket change, and they were just lying there for the taking in the kitchen.

Tiptoeing as quietly as the old porch timbers would permit, he opened the door slowly so that it wouldn't creak. The dog knew him and didn't get up from its rags to bark, but thumped its tail on the floorboards so loud, Hank came close to bashing the animal's head with his gun.

A soft glow from the banked coal in the stove cast just enough light to show him the outline of his prize. Darkness concealed the chair in between, and as he tiptoed across the room, he stumbled into it, cracking his shin. He bit his lip to keep from crying out, but the chair spun and hit the floor with a crash.

"Who's that!" Maw shouted from behind the door where she and Billy Bub were sleeping. "I have a gun! Don't you come one step closer!"

With his shin smarting enough to show him stars, and his heart about to jump out of his chest, Hank couldn't speak.

"Who's that, I say!" Maw shouted. "Speak up or you're a dead man!"

"It's just me, Miz Baxter, Hank!" he managed to croak at last. "I was jest fetchin' me some coffee to stay awake by. Chair kinda got in the way."

While Maw told him her opinion of men who scared old ladies half to death in the middle of the night he grabbed the saddles and waited by the door. When he was certain that she would finish bawling him out without coming into the kitchen, he left.

He almost had to leave Mulehead's saddle behind when his horse turned skittish at so much baggage, but finally managed to rope it on. Leading the animal well

123

away from the cabin before he mounted, he bid them all a silent good-riddance and rode away.

Curly opened his eyes and then shut them real quick. His head hurt so bad, he couldn't lift it. While he waited for the pounding to subside, he surmised that his face lay on a table and the rest of him was slumped in a chair.

When he'd become accustomed to the ache, he tried opening his eyes again. This time he saw his arm, which was numb, and traced it to his fingers where he spotted the shot glass. Slowly, so that his skull would not shatter and expose his pulsating brains, he raised his head and, with the aid of both hands, pushed himself upright in the chair. Trembling from the pain, and not at all sure he was going to be able to keep the contents of his guts in place, he sat, blinking.

Although it was dark in the corner where he sat, sun streamed through the door in a streak that nearly blinded him when his gaze hit it. Shutting his eyes against this new source of agony, he groped for the bottle he knew must be there. Turning his body so that he'd be facing the shadows, he fumbled it to his lips before tilting it, and then his head, to drain the last trickle. The result was not worth the pain it caused. Knowing his only hope for survival was sleep, he held his breath against the additional pounding his head took as he lowered it back down onto his cradling arms.

When he awoke again, sun no longer streamed through the door. His head still ached, but it was bearable, even when he sat upright. He was feeling well enough to test whether he could stand when Sally's face appeared in the place the pain had filled. He shook his head to erase the vision, and the pounding accommodated him by returning full force.

When he could stand, the grinding in his stomach caught his attention, and he resolved to head for the general store and get some soda crackers.

Out in the street, his hat brim shaded his eyes from the afternoon sun, but nothing could shield his ears from the noise of the tent city transforming itself into a substantial town. Ignoring the racket as best he could, not caring about muddying his boots when he had to leave the timbered sidewalk to cross the street, he made his way to the shebang. Besides crackers, he bought two bottles of whiskey. Back out on the sidewalk, he scanned the signs on the wooden facades until he spotted what would pass just fine for a hotel.

Paying in advance, he holed up to treat himself to a few days' amnesia.

Mulehead could not sleep. Worry gnawed at his mind like ants after cake. The stars were still high, with dawn hours away, but he could wait no longer. Shoving his blanket back, he hoisted himself up on his elbow, reached over, and shook Polecat by the shoulder.

Polecat grunted and buried himself deeper into his blanket. "What in the name of all that is holy do you want at this hour?" he snarled.

"Let's sell the horses."

"You wake me up to ask me that?"

"Somebody might be lookin' for 'em."

Although he could not see his companion in the dark, Polecat twisted his head in the general direction of Mulehead's voice. "You think some city slicker's gonna stop in the middle of his trip on a train to look for some horse?" His tone was filled with disgust.

"But what if they did," Mulehead said earnestly. "They could git us for murder."

"How do you figure that, when we didn't do it, dimwit?"

" 'Cause we got the horses."

"Having the horses don't have nothin' to do with killin' somebody!" Polecat shouted, thoroughly put out.

"Well, there's some men around who'll hang you first, and find out if'n you did it after," Mulehead responded softly. "And you know that for a fact."

Polecat buried himself in his blanket without speaking.

Mulehead waited a few minutes before calling out, "Polecat?"

"Okay, okay, okay," Polecat muttered. "We'll sell 'em soon as we git to Dodge for the cussin' bee."

Chapter Ten

Maw Baxter was so mad she could scarcely contain herself. "It's way past daylight!" she shrieked as she hiked her skirts and kicked at the sleeping figures in the straw. Excited by her yelling, the dog began barking and lunging at Boss and Sampson as they stirred. "You was supposed to be up and gone!"

"But, Maw—" Wakened from a sound sleep, Boss automatically shielded his head with his hands.

"Don't you 'but, Maw,' me, boy!" She grabbed the stable broom and swung it at Boss's head. "Better for you if you was gone!"

"Aw, come on, Maw." Boss easily rolled out of reach. "What's your hurry?" He yawned mightily and, sitting up, caught the straw end of the broom as she swung again. "What difference does it make if'n we start after them two past first light?"

Yanking the broom from Boss's grasp, she swung it at Sampson. "Polecat and Mulehead come and took their saddles, that's what!" she cried. "And you two good-for-naught sluggards slept right through it!"

"What?" Dodging her blows, Sampson got to his

knees. Playfully mauling the dog's head with his huge hands, he rose to his full height.

"It was supposed to be your watch, Sampson," Boss growled.

"What happened, you big oaf?" Slinging the broom into a corner of the barn, Maw put her hands on her hips and glared up at Sampson as the dog begged him for more attention.

Sampson stretched. "Hank never woke me up," he whined.

"Where is Hank?" Boss asked, looking around.

"I ain't seen him," Maw said. "Scared me half to death when he got up for his watch. Said he was gittin' a cup a coffee. Them two nitwits musta snuck in after that."

Sampson walked over to the stalls to check on his horse. "You don't think maybe they done something to Hank, do you?" he called out over his shoulder.

"Nah," Boss said, relieved that Polecat and Mulehead hadn't snuck in on his watch. "Hey," he said, brushing straw from his pants. "I didn't hear the dog bark. He don't know them two, and he'd a started up for sure."

"What makes you think the hound would of woke you when you sleep like the dead?" Maw said.

"Now, Maw—!"

"Hey, Miz Baxter! Boss!" Sampson shouted. "Come see! Hank's horse is gone."

Maw hurried to Sampson's side. "You reckon Hank took wing?" she asked.

"Wouldn't surprise me none." Disgusted, Boss shook his head.

"You better hightail it outta here and bring them saddles back!" Maw said.

"And leave you here alone with Curly on the loose?" Sampson asked.

Suddenly unsure whether to trust Sampson to stay with her, or allow him to get out of sight so he could desert too, Maw cast him a speculative glance. "I reckon we need to do some tall thinkin'." She slapped straw from her skirts. "Wash up and come on inside, boys. I'll git some biscuits and bacon on the table while we figure out what to do."

"Oh, fanny feathers!" Abigail exclaimed in dismay as Morgan galloped Belvedere over the finish line well ahead of the others.

"But we won, Miss Danforth!" Maude clapped enthusiastically as she shouted over the thunder of horses' hooves and the cheers of the crowd lining Main Street. "Are you not pleased?"

Ignoring the local gentry who had paid extra to stand beside her, Abigail stepped down from the small wooden platform that had been nailed together to her specifications so that she and Maude might have an unimpeded view of the race. When Maude joined her on the wooden sidewalk, Abigail leaned close so that others could not hear as she said, "Must I remind you that we held this contest for the sole purpose of catching a thief?"

Maude gazed heavenward as though asking for help in pleasing her demanding young companion.

Lifting their skirts to clear the mud as they stepped off the plank sidewalk into the street, Abigail and Maude maneuvered their way through the milling bystanders toward the private varnish, which had been left on the siding behind the wooden shack that served as the railroad station.

Buggies and horses had been forbidden to tie up at the hitching posts that lined Main Street so that the race could be accommodated. The overflow was parked helter skelter near the tracks, and Abigail's gaze probed the mass of vehicles for the lost horses. Satisfied that neither Crosspatches nor the Arabian were among them, she headed for their car. "A sorry lot," she muttered, shaking her head.

"The best were presumably in the race," Maude said, as she hurried a few steps to catch up.

Upon reaching the observation deck, Abigail turned to watch the people as they followed the still mounted winner in his fancy silks. Abigail had insisted that he dress as a bona fide jockey in colors that suited the outlandishly painted railroad car, and the handsome young man was obviously enjoying his victory in spite of the gaudy costume he had protested so vigorously against wearing. Together with his moustache, the colors were an excellent disguise since people were more apt to stare at unusual clothes than the person who wore them. She had also hoped it would serve to keep people talking about her eccentricities, and from the crowd he was attracting, that seemed to be working.

Thinking him handsome, but dismissing him as dull witted after his poor performance at dinner, Abigail had not asked Morgan to join her and Maude for any further meals. He had not seemed to notice. A fundamentally decent sort, and by nature friendly, he had begun to ingratiate himself with Kinkade the following day when he'd arrived with Belvedere in tow. Indeed, unbeknownst to Abigail, he had been enjoying himself hugely and been eating extremely well in the pantry with Kinkade and Jacqueline.

Only too grateful that he had not been pressed into

130

service as jockey, and soon mollified by Morgan's un-assuming charm, Kinkade had even introduced him to some vintage reds with his steak—with unfortunate re-sults on the first attempt. Refusing to believe that any-thing so delicious could have a kick, Morgan had consumed almost an entire bottle by himself. And, in-deed, he had remained quite sober, until he'd tried to stand up. Kinkade had learned much new French, which Jacqueline had refused to translate, as they had struggled to put the unconscious young man to bed without waking the ladies.

Smiling with pride as he watched Morgan go by, Kinkade stood at the long table he'd had set up in the nearby field. He'd had it, and their private varnish, draped with bunting. The table was laden with fanci-fully arranged platters of cakes and pastries. Jacqueline stood by, ready to pour gallons of coffee, filled with pride at her handiwork as she overheard comments from the ladies about Morgan's costume.

In keeping with her supposed eccentricity, Abigail remained aloof on the car's platform with Maude. Crowned by her most elaborate hat, swathed in furs, with a great show of nonchalance and jewels, she scanned the crowd and listened to the exclamations of delight from the womenfolk as they admired the feast of delicacies.

Morgan continued to the horse car hitched to the PV and, dismounting, led the horse up the ramp and into its sheltered stall where its dye job could be re-stored with no one the wiser.

Back at the long table, the stake holder sought out Kinkade and handed him a fat purse. Every eye was upon him as Kinkade mounted the steps to the plat-form and handed it to Abigail. She accepted it, dis-

131

missing him with an airy wave of her hand that she'd seen Queen Victoria use.

The murmuring from below sounded good-natured. Once the race was over, there seemed to be no resentment on the part of the losers. A fast horse was respected in these parts, as was an ostentatious display of wealth. The harvest had been bountiful for the past few years. With ready and accessible markets eager for their produce, people had some hard cash to spend. It was a rare man who would begrudge a wager on a fine horse.

"Goodness gracious!" Maude exclaimed as Abigail handed her the purse. "I'll warrant this will meet our expenses and then some."

Abigail glared at her. "Must I also remind you that we are not in this for the money?" she said testily.

Annoyed by Abigail's ill humor, Maude glared back. "I need no further reminding of why we are here, Miss Danforth. And I meant no offense. I merely wished to point out that your plan has had a most serendipitous effect." Maude jingled the purse in Abigail's ear.

"If my plan is so excellent"—Abigail brushed Maude's hand away and indicated the crowd—"where is Crosspatches?"

"We are building the reputation you spoke of. I think you have worked a miracle with such a large turnout." Maude swept her arm wide. "Everyone for miles around is here, and it has only been one week since the robbery."

"It has been eight days, Miss Cunningham," Abigail corrected her. "Eight days and freezing cold nights that Crosspatches has been in the hands of those bar-

132

barians—" She withdrew a handkerchief and dabbed at her eyes.

"Come, come, Miss Danforth." Maude wished she might reach out and comfort Abigail, but it would have been an unseemly gesture in sight of their avid audience. She had no confidence that the horses had survived, yet she had no wish to add to Abigail's rare display of emotion by agreeing with her distress. "We have one more race tomorrow," she said with overmuch enthusiasm. "And then we've only to wait until this Thursday in Wichita to see your plan come to fruition."

The hollowness of Maude's jocular manner was not lost on Abigail, and it depressed her more than an expression of honest concern might have. It also served to strengthen her resolve and dry her tears. "You're quite right, Miss Cunningham," she replied as she pocketed her handkerchief. "I trust we shall then have more than Washington's Birthday to celebrate." Her smile was grim as she added, "And all in less than three weeks!"

"Okay, boys." Jake turned his horse around and spoke loud enough to be heard by the five mounted men who remained of his posse. "What's your complaint? Speak up, now, so's I can hear you. I'm plain wore out hearin' bits and pieces of gripes."

No one spoke. Jake held his ground and glared at them each in turn. "Jason?" His stare landed on a man young enough for the moustache he was sporting to be his first.

"I don't mean to be complainin', Jake." The young man touched the brim of his hat in respect. "We been out a week now, but I never thought we'd be on the trail for more'n a day or two. My wife didn't want me to come at all—''

The men interrupted him with laughter, passing around the old jokes about the trouble a man has when he allows himself to get hen-pecked.

"Now, you stop that!" the young man said. When the men had had their fill of sniggering, he continued, "We're expecting our first baby any day now. I don't want my wife to be by herself when he comes."

"So I suppose that means you want to desert the posse, too?" Jake said.

"Now, don't go makin' it sound like somethin' bad, Jake," Jason said plaintively. "I don't want to desert. I just think I ought to be home with my wife when her pains start. So's I can go for the midwife. It's our first—''

"And you?" Jake interrupted him to glare at the man he knew to be the troublemaker. Jake hadn't wanted Thaddeus to be part of the posse in the first place, but there'd been no way to refuse him. Member of the Town Council and Kansas City's oldest dentist, Thaddeus considered himself a lawman on the order of Bill Hickock and volunteered for every posse. Mostly he was as vexatious to have around as a rock in your boot.

Everyone knew he drank, but desiring to uphold the dignity of his profession, Thaddeus thought he kept his dipsomania a secret. However, Thaddeus also figured that while hunting for a man, a nip against the cold (or heat) and mud (or dust) was excusable. Only trouble was, the few nips from his flask of brandy inevitably led to his having some kind of accident. Disgruntled and uncomfortable, and not a little hung over, he'd not be willing to admit that he wanted to call it quits

134

after a few days. Instead, he'd use his considerable talent for getting the other men so peeved that they'd be ready to go home just to get shed of him. Witness the men who'd already left.

This morning, Thaddeus had slid off his horse as it drank from the creek, wrenching his knee. Jake knew the jig was up when he had to concede the validity of Jason's excuse before the rest of the men had had an opportunity to make one up. But, for once, he wanted Thaddeus to admit that he was the cause of a posse's disbanding before it had caught its man.

"Well?" He glared at the dentist.

"You heard the kid." Thaddeus shrugged.

"What about you?" Jake pressed. "How's your knee? You want to head home and see Doc?"

"Not I!" Thaddeus proclaimed in his rich baritone, nearly unseating himself with a sweeping gesture of his arm. "I am ready to ride after that dastardly murderer as long as any man here has breath." Scanning his audience with a bleary eye, he continued, "Course if, as I and a few others among us suspect, you've lost the way and have run out of ideas of where to pursue this heinous criminal—"

"Oh, good grief," Jake said, kneeing his mount to a walk. "Let's head home."

"Din't I tell you I could find this place?" Mulehead was full of glee as he climbed off his horse. Wrapping the reins around a bush, he clambered into an outcropping of rocks where he and Polecat had sat out a wind-driven rain the first time they had found their way to the Baxters'.

"So whadda ya want me to do?" Polecat said. "Give you a prize?"

135

"This means we cain't be all that far from the Baxters' place, Polecat."

"You think I don't know that?" Polecat grumbled as he dismounted.

Mulehead shrugged and turned to the business of making a pot of coffee. Things had not been going too well of late. Polecat had won the cussin' bee in Dodge, hands down. But Old Brimstone, his toughest competitor, had died. Pneumonia had taken him near Christmas. They hadn't heard the news until the contest had already started and he hadn't shown up. It had taken the wind out of Polecat to hear so sudden like.

With Brimstone's passing, there weren't many men left with talent at airin' the lungs, or the desire to learn. Truth be told, he hadn't been too proud of Polecat's competition this year. His victory had been kind of shallow.

Used to be, young boys hung around Polecat after a match, hoping he'd give them some hints. If they were properly serious, Polecat would coach them for a while. This year, nary a one had lingered to ask him a single question. Soon as the applause had died down, everybody had just drifted away.

After they'd replenished some supplies with the prize money, they'd gotten drunk. Something rare for Polecat. While he liked his nip now and again, he wasn't a hard drinking man.

Rolling himself a cigarette, Mulehead hunkered down to wait for the coffee to boil. He halfway agreed with Polecat about going back after their saddles. Lord knows he was tired using that chicken-plaster that he'd been left with from the robbery. But he knew in his bones that askin' Maw Baxter for gold was as useless as trying to fly.

Dragging deep, he tongued his cigarette to the corner of his mouth and fetched the flyer from his back pocket. He sure wished he had his old mount back. Or, better yet, that fast one he'd traded for the nag he rode now, which wheezed like a train engine if he pushed it past a walk. Especially now that there were these horse races advertised on posters hanging everywhere.

He had taken one of the flyers from a kid who was passing them out on the street in Dodge, and he had it unfolded, poring over the remaining dates and places, when Polecat strolled over.

"Still moonin' 'bout them horse races?" Polecat asked.

"You saw the money we could win," Mulehead said without looking up.

"Humph." Polecat sat on his heels beside him. "You're jest after them fancy desserts."

" 'Tain't so!" Mulehead said with all the vehemence of a man denying the truth.

" 'Sides"—Polecat pointed at their mounts—"them two is fit for nothin' but the glue factory."

"We left two mighty fast ones behind at that livery." Mulehead sighed heavily.

"You changin' your mind agin, chucklehead?" Polecat said listlessly. "What about hangin' for murder?"

Mulehead gazed longingly at the poster. "Them horses was sure enough fast."

Polecat nearly blistered his tongue in a contest-winning tirade that fulsomely described Mulehead's changeable nature when he wasn't being stubborn, and the stupidity of retracing their steps to retrieve horses that might not be there even if they tried.

Relieved that his friend was showing some of his old

juice, when Polecat finally simmered down, Mulehead replied softly, "We gotta git us a stake from somewheres if'n we're gonna settle land 'fore we end up in the bone orchard."

The coffee had boiled, and Mulehead had poured him a cup before Polecat spoke again. "Which one you reckon we ought to trade back for?" he asked.

Mulehead shrugged. "Whichever one ain't gone."

Chapter Eleven

"You don't really 'spect me to believe you're Marshal Tilghman, do you?" Hugging her shawl close against the cold, the old woman stood at the railing on the porch of the clapboard house and squinted suspiciously at the man who'd pushed open their gate and ridden up to the house. When she stopped speaking, her toothless jaws moved as though she might be chewing on something.

Remaining on his horse, Marshal Tilghman tipped his hat. Talking to folks in an ever widening circle from the robbery had brought him to this isolated farmhouse. The Baxters' name had been mentioned more than once, and their place was thought to be in this vicinity. He smiled his relief at finding somebody at home. Most folks this far from town would have started in for tomorrow's celebration of Washington's Birthday.

"Mr. Dawson!" The old woman turned from her inspection to shout at her husband in the house. "I'm needin' your presence here, if you please."

"What say, Mrs. Dawson?" was the faint response.

The old woman cupped her hands to her mouth.

"Come here!" she shouted. "There's a man out here claimin' to be Marshal Bill Tilghman."

"Far as I know, the marshal's retired." In his haste to reach his wife's side, Mr. Dawson slammed the screen door while shrugging himself into a heavy sweater. Placing his arm around Mrs. Dawson's shoulders, he peered through his glasses at the mounted man. What hair he had left was as gray as his wife's, but he still had his teeth.

"My recollection, exactly." She looked up at her husband. "But he does have a moustache like the marshal's pictures in the newspapers."

"Half the men in the territory has the marshal's moustache, Mrs. Dawson." Turning to the mounted man, he said, "What brings you to these parts, Marshal?"

"I'm lookin' for the men who robbed the train near Cameron Junction some ten days back," Tilghman said.

"I heard tell they didn't git no gold," the old woman said. "How come you'd be lookin' for them?"

"Then maybe you also heard they killed a man?"

The man and woman looked at one another then back at Tilghman without speaking.

"They also took my horse," Tilghman continued. "The man they killed was bringing him to me to improve my stock."

The old woman shrugged her shoulders, loosening her husband's embrace, spat over the railing, and started for the door. The man continued to face Tilghman. "Well, come in, Marshal," he said, turning to follow his wife. "Come on in. It's a mite chilly to be standin' out here."

"I'd be much obliged if I could tend to my horse first," Tilghman said.

140

"Why, sure," the man said, shutting the door behind his wife and returning to the steps to point the way. "Round back thataway. Boys'll water him for you and put on the feedbag; you tell 'em what you want.'

"I thank you mightily," Tilghman said, kneeing his mount into a walk.

"Come back 'round in the front door; we'll meet you in the parlor," Dawson said, before hurrying to join his wife inside.

Mrs. Dawson was waiting anxiously for her husband just inside the door. "Not one word about Henry!" she said, her empty jaws working.

"What if he wants to search the house?" Dawson asked with a worried frown.

"He ain't got no right!" Her lips all but disappeared as she tightened her mouth in a firm line of righteousness.

"How do you know Henry didn't have nothing to do with that killin'?" Even though he knew that the lawman was well out of earshot, Dawson found himself whispering.

"How do you know he did?" she whispered also. Sighing deeply, her chin trembled, and a faraway look came in her eye. "Don't he call me Maw?"

The old man hung his sweater on the clothes tree. "He's clear outta his head when he says that, Mrs. Dawson." His gaze was tender.

"Don't matter to me none," she said. "He looks at me square when he says it. Ain't nobody called me that since—"

The man placed his arm around her shoulders and squeezed her gently. "Mrs. Dawson, you know our Henry's been buried lo these ten years."

She patted the hand on her shoulder and looked up

141

at him with tears in her eyes. " 'Twas like a miracle, me findin' him."

He pulled away. "I still say somethin's not right." He shook his head in puzzlement.

"Of course somethin's not right, Mr. Dawson." She was indignant. "He was hurt bad. But he's gettin' better."

"That's not my meaning, woman."

She glared at him through her tears.

His gaze remained tender as he whispered, "One man. One horse. Three saddles?" His eyebrows expressed his suspicions.

"That's what musta happened, Mr. Dawson." Brushing a tear aside, she didn't quite look him in the eye. "One of them saddles slid off and hobbled his horse."

"I know how the man got hurt," he said patiently. "Wasn't I the one what had to shoot his horse?" He looked guiltily toward the front door. "But you heard Marshal Tilghman. One of the train robbers stole his horse. Them extra saddles look mighty queer to me."

"I'm sure Henry will have a good explanation as soon as he can talk," she said, as determined as ever.

Mr. Dawson looked at his wife's sunken face with great tenderness and shook his head.

"You ain't tellin' the marshal, are you?" She stared at her gnarled hands.

"You got your heart set on nursin' him, don't you?"

"Never had no chance to nurse our Henry—"

"Hush, woman, here he is." Mr. Dawson interrupted her as Tilghman knocked on the door. "Skedaddle and git the marshal a cup of coffee." Waiting until she'd disappeared to the kitchen, he opened the door.

Marshal Tilghman hung his uncreased white Stetson

on top of his jacket on the clothes tree and followed Mr. Dawson into the parlor. Every chair as well as the sofa, which faced the fireplace, had its antimacassar on back and arm; and every table top, its doily, all crocheted by Mrs. Dawson.

Tilghman had sensed the old couple's reluctance. Although The War had ended thirty-five years before, sympathies for the vanquished Confederate guerrillas still ran high, and their attitude toward a lawman was not unusual. He was grateful to them for providing the hospitality of their parlor. It had been a while since he'd been on the trail, and he was finding it a mite wearisome.

That morning, he'd wired Kansas City and received the news that Jake's posse had turned in. His first reaction had been satisfaction at being right. But now, the thought of mounting up again and spending the night under the stars on the frozen ground because he was the only person interested in bringing a criminal to justice had lost its appeal.

Mr. Dawson had settled himself into his favorite armchair, and the lawman was warming his hands at the fire when Mrs. Dawson returned bearing a tray. While Tilghman settled himself on the sofa, she served her husband. Placing the tray on the doily-bedecked coffee table, she sat on the edge of the sofa beside Tilghman and handed him a steaming cup.

As he took the coffee from her, he said, "I wonder if I might ask you a mighty big favor, Mrs. Dawson, before I get on with my questions?"

"What might that be, Marshal?" She glanced nervously at her husband.

"I wonder if I might prevail upon your hospitality further to put me up for the night?"

Concentrating on not dribbling too much coffee into

his saucer as he stirred in the sugar, Tilghman missed the Dawsons' silent, horrified reaction.

"And how are you and Kinkade getting on with Mr. Dade?" Abigail's toilette complete for the afternoon ritual of tea, she turned to Jacqueline, intending to pay Mr. Dade a compliment upon his riding prowess. While she had already thanked him, Maude had felt her expression perfunctory. Knowing that kind words could mean more when confirmed from a second source, and unwilling to appear to fawn over the young man by thanking him again personally, Abigail had planned to ask Jacqueline to convey her sentiments. "It is well that his skills upon a horse are not as dull as his wits," she continued.

"Oh, Miss Danforth," Jacqueline replied, her blue eyes asparkle with delight. "Mr. Dade is the—how you say?—charming. He gives *Monsieur* Kinkade much laughter. They recite the poetry and try to out-funny the other. I do not understand them always—"

"Poetry!" Abigail exclaimed, looking askance at her maid. "Mr. Dade?" She returned her attention to the mirror. "Surely you jest."

Jacqueline's shrug was eloquent. "The words, they rhyme. The meanings I do not know, but they understand each other and have much merriment."

"Well, well, well, well," Abigail muttered to herself as she leaned forward to gaze into the tiny mirror while patting an errant tendril into place. Pinching her cheeks to bring her color high, she said, "Perhaps we should give Mr. Dade another chance at the dinner table."

"Oh, no, miss!" Jacqueline exclaimed before she could stop herself, heartily sorry that she had revealed the young man's conversational ability.

"I beg your pardon?" Abigail glared at her maid with the fierce, dominating expression of her father.

Blushing to the roots of her hair at the terrible gaffe of presuming to tell her mistress what to do, Jacqueline could but gaze at the floor, hoping it would open and swallow her.

Hank moaned. Surfacing from a deep sleep, he opened his eyes and looked at the now familiar ceiling. Surprised that the toothless old lady's face did not immediately appear above his, he closed his eyes again and stilled his breathing, the better to listen. When he could detect no page-turn of book, creak of chair, or snore, he shifted his position in his best imitation of a man asleep and nuzzled his head in the pillow to face the direction of the rocking chair. When his movements brought no calling of his name, he was sure he was alone.

Cautiously, he opened one eye. The chair was empty. Both eyes open, he sat up on one elbow and examined the room. Fresh-starched, ruffled curtains hung at the window, a washstand held the usual bowl and pitcher, and the night tables, dresser, rocking chair and bedside straight chair were all decorated with crocheted doilies. Certain of his solitude, he pushed himself to a sitting position. Shoving the covers down, he carefully lifted the poultice from his shin to examine his wound.

The old crone knew what she was doing. Still purple as ink near the center, yellow streaks radiated toward his knee and toe where the angry red of infection had been.

He'd had no need to fake delirium in the beginning. During those moments he'd been conscious before

145

she'd found him, tangled in the ropes and helpless, he had prayed for death to put him and his horse out of their misery. He still couldn't recall what he'd babbled that first time she'd bent over him. He did remember thinking that it was Maw Baxter who had found him. The next thing he knew, he was waking up in this incredibly soft bed, alive. That's when he must've called her "Maw" for the first time, thinkin' to follow it with "Baxter" until he pretty quickly saw his mistake. Seeing how much pleasure it gave the old lady, he'd taken to calling her Maw when she called him Henry.

Nor could he remember telling her his given name. It must've come from a deep place inside because he'd been called Hank for more years than he cared to admit. It sounded so homey when she said it that the last two days he'd been pretending to be sicker than he was. Also, he'd wanted to figure out just how safe he was while he gained his strength.

In the stillness, when he'd completed the examination of his leg, he could hear talking in the next room and longed to go to the door to find out if it was about him. Figuring he could claim a trip to the thunder mug, which had been left by the door, if caught standing in the middle of the room, he swung his legs over the side of the bed. His injured limb immediately sent shocks of protest, which he ignored. Until he stood. Then he nearly fainted from the pain. Had the bed not caught him, he would have landed on the floor. When it subsided and he was sure he was not going to vomit, he gently pulled the covers up. Fighting the tears, he called, "Maw!"

Morgan groaned as he splashed his face with water. Wine sure made a man sleep hard. Even just a glass

146

or two of white. At first, it had tasted sour, but as he'd sipped it to wash down the fresh trout, he'd had to agree with Kinkade that it transcended milk.

But he had overslept. He liked to exercise Belvedere before daybreak, and the sun was already up. Tying his kerchief as he dashed down the steps of the observation deck, he rushed up the ramp into the horse car hitched behind, whistling his morning's greeting. Still involved with the kerchief, he hadn't noticed that there'd been no answering neigh or snort from Belvedere's stall, and he was badly shocked to discover it empty.

When he'd overcome his disbelief, foolishly looking in corners much too small to contain so large an animal and relieved that there'd been no witness to his futile search, he swiftly retraced his steps to the PV. Calling out to Kinkade, he found him in the pantry, starting coffee.

They agreed that Abigail must be roused and told; so Kinkade hurried off to wake Jacqueline while Morgan ran to the observation deck to see if he could spot the horse.

A white-faced Jacqueline, joined Morgan almost immediately, with Kinkade not far behind. So swiftly had Jacqueline dressed that she lacked her apron. Her mistress was not in her stateroom. Nor had she readied Abigail for the morning. Each looked helplessly at the other. Could Miss Danforth have been kidnapped? And Belvedere? Could they have slept so soundly as not to hear? Morgan knew he had.

The three hurried to Miss Cunningham's stateroom and, with not a little pounding upon her door, roused Maude from her laudanum-induced sleep.

Jacqueline tiptoed to the bed while the men re-

147

mained in the corridor, out of any line of sight that might embarrass Maude, but not out of earshot.

Annoyed at being awakened, Maude made it quite clear that if both horse and Miss Danforth were missing, then there could be no doubt that she was riding it.

Morgan expressed his disbelief, since Belvedere would not let just anyone ride him, especially a girl. Furthermore, it would be impossible for Miss Danforth to ride since there was no lady's saddle available.

Much too sleepy to argue, and knowing he'd discover Abigail's predilection for riding astride soon enough, Maude rolled over, pulled the covers over her head, and thus declared their interview at an end.

Believing Miss Cunningham's assessment of the situation to be accurate, Jacqueline repaired to her room to complete her toilette while Kinkade headed for the pantry for a much needed cup of coffee.

Even though his friends had taken Maude's word as sooth, Morgan did not consider himself so gullible. He returned to the observation deck. In spite of his disbelief, having no better theory to replace it, he gazed into the distance in all directions except town as he slowly descended the steps. When he reached the ground, he doubted his senses, thinking them based upon hope, but nonetheless he thought he could detect a tiny speck in the distance growing larger, as if it were coming closer.

Having nothing better to do, he kept his eyes on the speck, and as it did indeed grow larger, and closer, his jaw dropped. There was no mistaking his horse—or the feathered plume on a riding hat.

Then, swiftly, there was no mistaking that the figure on Belvedere was Miss Danforth. And she was riding astride!

Belvedere was running straight out, as if his life depended upon doing his best for her.

Unable to believe his eyes, or the onslaught of unaccustomed emotions, Morgan's face still bore an expression of stunned disbelief as she rode Belvedere to a mud-splattering stop before him. Never before had he seen Belvedere try so hard. Nor had he ever seen, or heard of, a girl riding astride. He'd heard rumors that it could ruin them for marriage, but was uncertain how.

Exhilarated by her ride, Abigail's smile was radiant as she said, teasing, "Where were you, slugabed?"

"How dare you take my horse!" he exclaimed. "I was worried sick about him." Realizing that what he'd said did not even come close to what he was feeling, he blushed furiously as he swiftly added, "And you, of course."

"I had planned to ask you," she responded, smiling now at his awkwardness, "but you weren't around."

"Well, he's shot for the day." Taking him by the bridle, Morgan stroked Belvedere's nose.

"There is no race scheduled." Abigail shrugged.

Morgan scowled. Unable to voice his concern for her, he said instead, "At the pace you were going, he could have caught his hoof in a hole." He glared up at her. "Then where would your precious plan be?"

Abigail sighed. "You're right, of course. But we must have a match when I get Crosspatches back." Once again, she smiled, this time holding out her hands toward him. "Now, if you would please hand me down, I would appreciate it most kindly."

As he caught her in his arms, he was surprised at how small and dainty she was; she had been such a formidable presence upon the horse. As he lowered her gently to the ground, his heart was beating so fast he thought it might show through his jacket.

"Pray, do not be cross with me." Abigail gazed up into his eyes. "I am sorry," she continued. "I meant no harm. It's just that I could not bear being cooped up any longer."

Loathe to let her go, Morgan wanted nothing so much in the whole world at that moment than to smother her dear face with kisses.

With a snort and stamp of his hoof, Belvedere nudged Abigail on the shoulder, nearly unseating her hat.

"Hey!" Morgan exclaimed with a laugh, grabbing his bridle.

"Jacqueline tells me you like poetry," Abigail said as they walked the horse toward the ramp.

"Just verses, ma'am," he said with a shrug. "Nothing fancy."

"But if you are so fond of verses, why were you so quiet at dinner?" she asked, genuinely puzzled. "I know I mentioned Tennyson."

"Where I come from, when you come in from mending fences or a hard day punching cows, you're hungry. You eat and talk afterward. Sometime long into the night, there being nothing else to do but spin yarns. Tell stories. Make up rhymes."

"So you are not reciting another's poetry, but creating your own?" Abigail was impressed.

Morgan stopped as they reached the ramp. "I reckon I've never met a girl like you, Miss Danforth." Morgan's smile warmed her heart. "You ride like a man. Have ambitions like a man."

"Do you find me manly?" Abigail gazed up at him with a worried frown.

"Oh, no, Miss Danforth!" he exclaimed. "You are

the prettiest, the daintiest, girl I've ever met." He continued earnestly, "It's just that you're also the bravest, and the smartest, too."

It was Abigail's turn to blush.

Unable to look her in the eye, he nonchalantly patted Belvedere on the neck as he said, "You should carry a gun."

Surprised, she gazed directly at him. "A gun?"

With a most solemn expression, he returned her gaze. "You don't seem to realize you could be in danger, any more than you seemed to know you were in danger when you rode Belvedere just now."

Abigail thought for a moment before responding, "Would you instruct me in its use?"

Realizing he'd now have good cause to see her privately, Morgan's smile was enormous as he tipped his hat in salute before leading Belvedere up the ramp. He could scarcely believe his own cleverness.

Curly tried every remedy known to man to cure a hangover. Nothing worked. Food wouldn't stay down, much less the highly touted raw eggs. More whiskey just put him to sleep. And forget girls. They always ended up saying something stupid, and when he tried to slap some sense into them, either they'd blubber and run out on him, or they'd fall down unconscious and he'd be the one to walk out in disgust. After a few days, he accepted his headache as permanent and set about to discover the exact amount of liquor it took to make it bearable without passing out.

Even when thus anesthetized, the thought of riding a horse, and the jostling of his head it would entail, made him shudder. But time was running out. Sooner or later there'd be a poster out on him. More than one person at Nelson's had heard of his and Sally's plans. His name was bound to be mentioned when her body was found with another man's, even if nobody had seen him enter the saloon. Driven by the knowledge that the gold would buy him escape and a new life, and maybe even relief from his headache if he could just get to California and find the right doctor, he retrieved his horse from the livery. With a supply of medicinal whiskey in his saddlebags, he set out for the graveyard.

Approaching the spot, his piercing gaze raked the landscape with intent to kill anything that observed his passage. He slid from his horse and, unpacking a hand shovel, hacked and dug at the earth until he'd uncovered the sack. Wanting to make a more even burden in his saddlebags by distributing the gold, he hacked at the canvas with his hunting knife, but it would not yield. He shot the lock off.

The texture of the brick as he grabbed it inside the sack registered first. Before he held it close to his aching eyes, he knew it wasn't gold. He also knew that the rest of the bars in the sack would also be bricks, but he dumped them all out to prove it.

The pounding in his head nearly brought him to his knees. Unpacking a bottle from his saddlebags, he drank deeply and leaned against his horse, moaning, until the pain subsided. Replacing the bottle, he clamped his jaw tightly to keep from howling like a mad man as he mounted and spurred his horse toward the Baxters'.

Chapter Twelve

Polecat and Mulehead were no longer speaking by the time they rode into Dodge again. Or walked into Dodge; Mulehead's mount had lost a shoe and was limping too badly to be ridden, especially by a man of Mulehead's girth. Polecat had flat-out refused to trade horses, and the silence between them was deep and grim by the time they reached the stables where they had left the stolen horses. It was past midnight. Mulehead was starving, and his arm was about to drop off from carrying the lantern high to mark their trail.

But they were in luck. The stableboy, not yet in his teens and small for his age, had been left in charge as guard while the stable owner had taken a rare night off to be with his sick wife. Exhausted from his chores, the boy had curled up by the still-warm fire to sleep.

Tying his lame horse at the railing, Mulehead poked his head into the livery, quickly sized up the situation, and ran back to his still-mounted partner, frantically signaling at him to stay quiet. Assuring him that he was no longer angry, after a brief, whispered discussion wherein a plan was made, Polecat dismounted.

Tying his mount beside Mulehead's, the smaller man

stealthily entered the livery. Mulehead watched over the sleeping child, prepared to smother him should he awaken, while Polecat snuck past him to explore the nether regions of the stables. In the third stall he discovered the Arabian.

Unfortunately, the Arabian recognized him and whinnied a greeting. Sweat began to drip from Polecat's armpits as he opened the stall gate and, stroking the horse's nose, stilled him before the boy awoke. Swiftly retrieving a bridle and slipping it onto the small horse, he led it past the sleeping stableboy, tying it next to their mounts on the street. To Mulehead's wordless question about Crosspatches, he gave an impatient shrug.

On a second trip past the boy, with Mulehead hovering nearby, he found the thoroughbred in the nethermost stall. Crosspatches had not been exercised since he'd been traded and, recognizing Polecat, went with him willingly.

The men quickly switched saddles and, leaving their old mounts tied at the railing, led Crosspatches and the Arabian out of earshot before mounting to ride off as fast as light from the lantern would allow.

"Now, now, Henry." Mrs. Dawson stood beside Hank's bed and peered at him. "Don't you fret none."

"My leg—" Hank moaned, clutching the covers to his chin.

Bending over him, she tugged gently at the sheet with her gnarled hands. "Lemme see, son." Though her voice creaked with age, her tone was firm. "What did you do?"

"Nothin'." He gulped, steeling himself against a flare-up of the pain when she peeled back the bandage.

"You don't set off such pain by doin' nothin'," she said, glancing at his face suspiciously before carefully peeling back the poultice. Gently pressing the healthy tissue surrounding the wound, she said, "You leg looks fine." She replaced the poultice. "It'll be a mite sore for a while yet, but it's healin'. So, fess up," she continued with a twinkle in her eye as she pulled the covers back up to his chin. "What did you do?"

"I tried to stand up," he said sheepishly.

"What fer?" She frowned again. "You shoulda called me. I'd fetch you anything you want."

Glancing toward the night jar by the door, he managed a blush. "I'd rather not say."

"Oh, for land's sake." She laughed as she followed his glance. "I plumb forgot. I left the slop jar clear over on the other side of the room, I did." Her step was quick as she went to retrieve it and slide it under the bed. "Reckon I was on my way to put it where it belonged when I heard the marshal ridin' up."

"Marshal?" Sheer terror set Hank's heart to pounding so loud, he prayed Mrs. Dawson could not hear it, or the panic in his voice.

"Well, don't this beat all?" Her smile was broad enough to reveal her gums. "Here we are jawin' away to beat all."

Hank managed a weak grin.

Still standing, she bent over to feel his forehead. "Ummmmm. Your head is cool. Fever's down for the first time since I found you." She looked him over. "You must be hungry."

"I could eat," he said eagerly, forcing himself not to ask about the marshal.

"You oughtta stay off that leg a tad longer." She started for the door. "Maybe you can come to the table for breakfast. I'll bring your supper on a tray."

But it was Mr. Dawson who returned with his meal. "Mrs. Dawson tells me you're talkin' now, son," he said, careful not to spill anything on the tray as he closed the door with his elbow before crossing over to the bed.

"Guess I kinda been outta my head," Hank said cautiously. He'd had very little to do with Mr. Dawson and wasn't sure how the old man felt about harboring a stranger.

"I reckon you know by now that Mrs. Dawson thinks you remind her of our son." As soon as the old man placed the tray on the bedside table, he shoved his glasses, which had slipped down his nose, back in place.

"That so?" Hank replied. The old woman had been spoon-feeding him soup, or gruel, for days, and his mouth had been watering in anticipation of his first real food to chew. But his appetite vanished as Mr. Dawson peered down at him silently, his expression hidden behind his glasses.

After a few awkward moments, the old man slowly walked to the foot of the bed.

In a sudden panic under such silent scrutiny, Hank forgot his wound and, sitting up, swung his legs over the edge of the bed. He gasped as his injured leg reacted with pangs of alarm, but reached for the tray to put it across his lap with as much relish as he could muster. Concentrating upon appearing calm before the old man, he ignored the throbbing, which soon subsided.

Watching Hank eat, the old man said casually, "Mrs. Dawson says you'd have an explanation for them extra saddles you were packin'."

Hank chewed and swallowed a mouthful of pork chop before answering. "A man has to explain himself

156

in these parts, does he?'' Without lifting his gaze from his plate, he shrugged casually as he speared a hunk of potato.

"I don't mean nothin' by it, Henry.'' The old man looked toward the door. "It's jest that Marshal Tilghman has stopped over for the night and he's askin' all kinds a questions.''

Hank stilled his knife and fork in midair. "What's that got to do with me?'' he asked, glancing at Mr. Dawson, his gaze filled with boyish innocence.

"Well, now,'' the man said. "That's what I thought you and me could talk about.'' He paused. "Without disturbing Mrs. Dawson too much, if you catch my drift.''

"I ain't sure I do, sir.'' Hank returned his attention to cutting another mouthful of pork chop.

"Mrs. Dawson dotes on you, boy. She don't believe you would crack a flea, never mind kill a man. I don't want her faith disabused.''

His mouth so dry he could no longer chew, Hank grabbed the glass of milk. He swallowed half of it with apparent gusto before he spoke nonchalantly. "Marshal's lookin' for a killer?'' He barely glanced at Mr. Dawson before returning his attention to his plate.

"And for the men who took his horse.''

Hank shrugged. "What if I told you them saddles belonged to me?''

"I'd listen to how you happened to come by 'em.'' Mr. Dawson took the few steps to the dresser and, absent-mindedly stroking the crocheted dresser scarf with great tenderness, patiently waited for Hank to continue.

Hank had spent a goodly number of his waking hours in thinking up ways to explain away how he had Polecat's and Mulehead's saddles in his possession, if asked. He was not a talented yarn spinner and tried to put a casual sound on what he said by continuing to pretend to pay more attention to his plate than his words. "It's my pay," he said, carefully cutting the last of the meat from the bone.

"Your pay?" Mr. Dawson did not bother to hide the skepticism from his voice as he folded his arms and glared at Hank. "For what?"

"For honest work." Once again, Hank used his boyish, innocent expression.

"For who?"

"I'd rather not say."

"What would your reason be for not tellin'?" Arms still folded, the old man returned to the foot of the bed.

"Don't want to shame a man's name for runnin' outta money through no fault of his. I agreed to the deal. Though look what it got me." Hank waved his knife in the general direction of his injured shin.

The old man's voice grew cold. "Seems to me like it got you the affection of a mighty good woman, young man."

Hank put his knife and fork down and looked the old man square in the eye. "And don't think I ain't grateful, Mr. Dawson." He smiled in the easygoing way that had endeared him to Billy Bub.

Wanting to believe this stranger who looked not unlike his son, Mr. Dawson shook an admonishing finger at him. "You jest see to it that her faith ain't mislaid."

"Yes, sir," Hank said meekly.

The old man turned to leave.

Hank could restrain himself no longer. "What are you gonna tell the marshal, sir?" he asked, hoping he didn't sound anxious.

The old man stopped at the door. He turned and stared at Hank for a long moment before he spoke.

"More'n likely Mrs. Dawson has already told the marshal that her son is in bed with a bum leg." He opened the door and closed it softly behind him.

Shoving the tray onto the bedside table, Hank collapsed on the bed.

Mrs. Dawson soon reappeared with pie and coffee, and beamed at him while he ate it with feigned gusto. Taking his demolished tray with her, she retired, satisfied that he was on the road to recovery.

As soon as the house got quiet, Hank lit the kerosene lamp, setting it low so that anybody passing his door would think the room dark while it shed enough light to keep him from bumping into things. After an hour or so, he could make it all the way to the door and back to the bed without having to stop. He limped; but he could depend on his leg to support him, and the pain was tolerable.

All the while he worried about whether to wear his guns to the breakfast table. Being a guest, Tilghman would probably be unarmed. Besides, the marshal had a reputation for taking his man without gunplay. If, as the son of the house, he went to breakfast with his guns, the marshal might get suspicious. But if he left his guns in the bedroom, he'd be a sitting duck if the Dawsons had mentioned his extra saddles and the marshal took notice.

Exhausted from the physical and mental exercise, he slept through cock's crow. Mrs. Dawson had to shake him awake.

The long night had been interminable, and Abigail had slept little. After much deliberation, she had decided not to presume upon Mr. Dade to continue to race Belvedere past their agreed-upon deadline of this day that had at last dawned, even though, given his burgeoning feelings for her, he'd be sure to acquiesce willingly enough. Crosspatches and the Arabian were not inanimate objects that would remain in good condition indefinitely, with efforts to exercise their recovery linked only to the pursuer's tenacity, and not to the passage of time. Given the foul weather and uncertain care they might have received, it would be miracle enough had the animals survived thus far.

Also looming large was the matter of Miss Cunningham and the need to move on to San Francisco. Abigail had given her word and had no heart to break it again.

Unable to sleep, she summoned Jacqueline at first light and, swearing her to secrecy, got dressed for the morning's events. Thrusting her arm into the coat trimmed with martens' skins that Jacqueline held outstretched, she buttoned the tight-fitting bodice. She stooped to check the angle of her huge hat, decorated with matching martens' skins and heads, as best she could in the tiny dressing table mirror. She did not notice that her color was high and her dark eyes alight with the anticipation that she would soon know if her plan had worked.

"The weather, she does not rain yet for the President's Day, miss," Jacqueline said. "The streets, maybe they will not be so full of the mud like the last—"

"Oh, pray, still your prattling, Jacqueline!" Abigail interrupted, snatching the handkerchief Jacqueline held out and stuffing it in her reticule. "You may go back to bed now if you wish," she said impatiently as she drew on her skin-tight gloves.

"Yes, miss." Jacqueline longed for the courage to defy custom and ask Abigail if she was going some-

160

where by herself before the rest of the household was fully awake. Or if anything was amiss. But her mistress had been in much ill humor of late, and she did not wish to be the cause of a flare-up. She paused at the door, hoping for a hint, but Abigail whirled to face her with an expression that said clearly that she was about to be scolded for tarrying. She dashed out before Abigail had need to speak.

The moment the door clicked shut, Abigail lifted her skirts to kneel and reach under the bed to pull out a valise that Jacqueline believed to be for storage. Rummaging underneath the summer scarves and understandings, she withdrew the derringer that Morgan had purchased for her and, slipping it into her muff, shoved the valise into place.

On the pretext of tending Belvedere, she had managed to gain some time alone with Morgan to practice its use. A man of the West, to his mind, guns were worn as naturally as boots, not for shooting people as the pulps would lead an easterner to believe, but for protection against snakes and other unfriendly varmints. Which is not to say he did not understand, and honor, Abigail's desire to keep her acquisition a secret from her traveling companions.

He had rigged a bull's-eye at one end of the horse car. Accuracy was not easy to achieve with a derringer even while standing on firm ground; in a moving railway car, it was impossible. But she had practiced incessantly and could sometimes hit the target, and occasionally, the center. She had done much better with bottles on a fence, but arranging to be alone with him in the countryside had proved so complicated that they had done it only once.

Just being alone with him had proved complicated as well. In the moving railway car, he had good reason to hold her by the waist to steady her aim. But, much to her surprise, the pleasure she had experienced while thus leaning upon his strength had extended far beyond pride in being able to occasionally hit the target.

And being alone with him on that bone-chilling day outside had proved so complicated that she still had not sorted out her emotions. He had cheered her success at striking three bottles in a row with unfeigned delight, sweeping her off her feet, spinning her around in his enthusiasm. When he had gently put her down, he had searched her face hungrily. For an instant, they had been so close their breath had mingled. Cheeks aflame with feelings she could not name, she had swiftly pulled away from his embrace, using her success as an excuse to cut her practice, and their time alone, short.

While certainly not a sharpshooter now, she was pleased with her progress. Should she meet the horse thieves, she would not be helpless. This, after all, was America, not London where even the criminal seldom carried a gun. Her experience with the Pinkertons and Marshal Tilghman had taught her that help from lawmen was undependable at best, but to arm Kinkade and thus place a paid servant in jeopardy was unthinkable. As the miles had passed and her skill had grown, so had her quandary. Would she actually be able to pull the trigger with the intent to kill another human being?

Abigail drew a deep breath as she opened the door to her stateroom, reassuring herself for one final time that no one could tell what was weighing so heavily in her muff. Tiptoeing past Maude's room, she let herself out onto the observation deck.

A veritable tangle of buckboards, wagons, and buggies were already beginning to assemble on the edge of the railway yard. Skirts lifted to the daring height of booted ankle, she made her way across the nearby field as spectators for the morning's baseball game were gathering. As she hurried past long, bunting-draped tables, ladies were already beginning to unpack their prize-winning corn relishes, pickles, and fruit preserves, all to be consumed with fresh breads and innumerable versions of potato salads and cole slaws. Her own table of cakes and chocolate delicacies would have much competition this time.

Reaching the wooden sidewalks at last, she lowered her skirts and slowed to a more ladylike pace past the stragglers and occasional groups of men standing around. Although engrossed in discussing the merits of the splendid horseflesh on display and their wagerings, every man noticed the richly dressed lady's progress and speculated in hushed tones after she had passed, whether or not she was that eccentric one from the East who was responsible for all the posters. None dared to accost her to ask.

Knowing she was being watched, Abigail took great care not to show any emotion; but her heart thumped wildly, and she had to bite her lip to keep from shouting for joy when she spotted the unmistakable shape of an English thoroughbred hitched to the railing in front of the restaurant. The white patch on his nose was gone, his coat was scruffy and unnaturally dark, but there was no mistaking Crosspatches. Thrilled by her discovery, she dared hope that the Arabian would be nearby. Although she scanned the street as far as she could see, he was nowhere to be seen. But the absence of the Arabian could not diminish her delight.

Shoving her hand deep into her muff, she grasped the derringer. And shivered. While feigning a disdain-

163

ful interest in each horse as she passed it, she observed the clusters of men that might contain the thief. Forcing herself to stroll slowly, with an insouciance she was far from feeling what with her heart in her throat, she approached her beloved horse.

Chapter Thirteen

"Come on, son, it's past time to wake up." Mrs.
Dawson bent over Hank's sleeping form and shook his
shoulder gently. "It's safe now. The others are finished
with breakfast and gone. It's jest the marshal and Mr.
Dawson now. See if you cain't walk this morning."

Awakened from a deep, but worried sleep, Hank
surfaced slowly. Angered at being thus disturbed, he
was about to brush away the offending hand on his
shoulder when the soreness in his leg reminded him of
his precarious situation. Instantly on guard, he mum-
bled an incoherent growl while stretching mightily. By
the time he opened his eyes, his temper was under control, and he could grin at her toothless, beaming face.
"I'll try," he said gruffly.

"Hot water's in the pitcher," she said, leaving him
to make himself presentable.

After much deliberation, he had finally decided to
leave his holster over the hook on the bedroom door
and to wear his gun in the belt of his pants. Freshly
brushed and pressed, his jacket fit so loosely from the
weight he'd lost that it concealed the weapon. Limping
slightly, a lump of nervousness in his throat, he closed

165

the door to his room and let his nose guide him to the kitchen.

Mr. Dawson remained seated at the head of the large oblong table while introducing him to Tilghman, who rose far enough from his chair to reach across and shake his hand. Hank took a chair opposite Tilghman and, reaching for the pitcher of milk, poured himself a glassful. Grease was beginning to congeal on empty platters that had held chops, sausages and bacon. Empty chairs as well as serving dishes were scattered about, all attesting to a meal recently completed.

"Looks like I overslept a mite," Hank said sheepishly, relieved he'd not had to face those ranch hands who were not on holiday, pretending a familiarity he did not possess. The old biddy had known what she was doing when she'd let him sleep.

Happily flitting about the kitchen with an energy that belied her years, Mrs. Dawson forced another cup of coffee on the marshal, all the while speculating on the doings in town for Washington's Birthday.

Although breakfast passed without incident, Hank's stomach was in knots from too much food eaten in fright. The meal finished at long last, he sighed with relief as the marshal and Dawson got up from the table. Still seated, he held out his hand to bid the marshal good-bye.

With a friendly smile, Tilghman refused to take it. "I'd sure enough appreciate it if I could have a few minutes of your time before I get on my way," he said, indicating with a nod toward Mrs. Dawson, who was standing at the sink and could not see, that he wanted only Mr. Dawson and Hank to join him in the parlor.

Mrs. Dawson whirled around. "I'll bring some fresh coffee," she said firmly, drying her hands on her apron.

"You tend to your dishes, Mrs. Dawson." Her husband scowled at her as Hank slowly rose from the table, favoring his leg.

"I won't take long, Mrs. Dawson," Tilghman added. "No need for more coffee." Casually retrieving his holster and gun from the peg in the hall, he buckled it around his waist as he strolled into the parlor after Hank and Mr. Dawson.

Mrs. Dawson hurried to the kitchen door. "Then I'll jest join you all and set a spell."

Ignoring the clear signals that she was not wanted, she followed the men into the parlor. With her toothless jaws clamped tightly, she settled herself on the sofa. For once, she did not pick up her basket of crocheting.

Mr. Dawson eased himself into his favorite armchair while Hank slumped into the antimacassared armchair opposite. With his hand in easy reach of his gun which was hidden beneath his jacket, he stuck his injured leg out, wishing it would stop throbbing so he could concentrate better, and tried to look at home.

Tilghman remained standing by the fire.

"Well, Marshal?" Mrs. Dawson broke the silence.

"I'm hard-pressed to know how to ask you this, Mr. Dawson," Tilghman said. " 'Specially when your hospitality has been so warm."

"What is it, Marshal?" Mr. Dawson asked. "You want to stay a few days? Rest Up?"

Hank froze.

"No, sir," Tilghman said. "But I got to talkin' with some of your men. It was not my intent to pry, mind you, but just passing the time, and one of them allowed as how your son died some years back."

Hand beneath his jacket, Hank slowly began to ease the gun from his belt while Tilghman's gaze was on the Dawsons.

"That's true, Marshal," Mrs. Dawson said. "I'm wonderin' what—"

"I was under the impression that Hank, here, was your son. In bed with a bum leg, you said?"

"Cain't a person have more'n one son, Marshal?" Mrs. Dawson glanced slyly at her husband.

"Why, sure, Mrs. Dawson." Tilghman smiled. "Five and eight sons isn't an uncommon occurrence if a family is lucky."

"Then why—"

"This man, now he's only your hired hand, I know, and not likely to know more about your family than you, but he told me that you found Henry. That he was unconscious when you brought him home and that you've been nursing him ever since." Tilghman kept glancing from the Dawsons to Hank. "He says Henry's a stranger to him."

"Who told you that?" Mrs. Dawson cried angrily. "I'll run him off this place. I'll—"

"Now, be still, Mrs. Dawson." Her husband held his hand out to quiet her. "Let the marshal finish."

"He told me about some extra saddles that Henry was packin'," Tilghman said.

Hank could stand the suspense no longer. Without warning, hoping surprise would save him, he pushed himself to his feet, his gun aimed at the marshal's heart. "Reach!" he cried. His leg sent out shock waves of pain, and his voice quavered with nerves as he tried to hold his aim steady, adding, "Or you're a dead man!"

Mrs. Dawson leapt from the couch, placing herself between Hank and Tilghman. "Henry!" she cried, raising her clasped hands in a pleading gesture. "Please don't shoot him, son!"

"I ain't your son!" Hank shoved her down on the couch and pointed the gun at her.

"No!" Mr. Dawson cried. With an agility that surprised them all, he sprang from his chair and threw himself across his wife's body.

"No need to get riled," Tilghman said in a soothing tone. He had noted Hank's sudden loss of color and the quaver in his voice, but a gun fired by accident was just as deadly as one fired with intent. He kept his hands spread wide, away from his holster. "I jest want to ask you a few questions," he said calmly.

"Oh, please, son," Mrs. Dawson cried, trying to shove her husband off. "Put down that gun!"

"He ain't our Henry!" Mr. Dawson growled, losing his patience as he held her down.

She twisted her head so that she could see the lawman. "You said they didn't git no gold!" she cried.

"He was part of the gang what robbed the train, Mrs. Dawson!" her husband said. "That he didn't git nothin' is more the Pinkerton's doin' than his!"

"They killed a man, ma'am," Tilghman said quietly, looking Hank straight in the eye. "And stole Miss Danforth's and my horses."

"I didn't kill nobody, Marshal," Hank said, stepping back a pace so that he could cover all three with his gun. "Curly did."

"You heard him, Marshal," Mrs. Dawson said eagerly. "He didn't shoot nobody. That Curly fellow did. He didn't steal your horses neither."

"I suspected he was just a tag-along, Mrs. Dawson," Tilghman said, keeping his eyes on Hank. "That's why I risked waiting the night to take him." Hands still wide-spread, he asked, "Where is Curly?"

"I don't know." Hank was bewildered by the turn their conversation was taking. But as long as the marshal made no move for his gun, he figured he might as well answer. His leg hurt and he wanted to sit down.

Maybe the lawman did just want to know where Curly was. Maybe he would just leave here and go looking for him. He drew a deep breath and said, "When Maw Baxter found out he'd shot a man, she threw him out."

"You got any ideas about where he'd go?" the marshal asked, taking care to keep his tone even.

Hank shook his head. "We had a watch around the Baxters' place in case he showed up again."

Mr. Dawson eased himself to a sitting position beside his wife. Securing her hair pins, she glared at him as he sat up.

"Why would he risk going back to the Baxters'?"

" 'Cause he didn't know that his canvas sack was full of bricks when he left. If he thought the Baxters cheated him, he'd want revenge."

"You can put away your gun now, son," Mrs. Dawson said, straightening her rumpled clothes. "Cain't he, Marshal?"

"Why should I?" Hank's aim had begun to wobble as they talked. He straightened himself and held the gun more firmly.

"You don't want the law hounding you from now to kingdom come." She looked up at Tilghman. "He's answered all your questions, hasn't he, Marshal? You'd let him go. Wouldn't you?"

The marshal looked at Hank. "Maybe."

"What do you want him to do?" She, too, looked at Hank. "He'll do anything, won't you, son?"

Hank shrugged. "What do you want me to do, Marshal?"

"Tell me where the Baxters' spread is."

"It's a day or so's ride. I cain't describe it to you, Marshal." Hank shook his head. "It's hid so good, you gotta be led to it the first time or two."

"Then take me there."

170

"They won't be too happy to see me, Marshal," Hank said. " 'Specially if I'm bringing the law on my tail."

"Don't do it, son. It's too risky," Mrs. Dawson said. "Besides, it's too soon for you to be ridin' with that leg."

Mr. Dawson stood and looked down at his wife. "If he ain't got gumption enough to risk his skin, then he don't deserve to go free!" he said heatedly.

Mrs. Dawson glared at her husband, but could not deny the justice of his remark. Turning to the marshal, she asked, "If he led you there, at great risk, mind, would you let him go free?"

"If, as a result of his leadin' me there, I capture Curly and the horse thieves, I reckon I'd owe him somethin'," the marshal said.

"Well, son?" Mrs. Dawson looked at Hank.

Hank shrugged and lowered his gun.

Mrs. Dawson stood and faced Tilghman. "If'n anything happens to my boy, Marshal, I won't ever forgive you."

Tilghman nodded. "Then let's get ready to ride." He started for the hallway.

Grabbing Hank by the sleeve, Mrs. Dawson halted his departure. "This is your home now, son."

Hank nodded wordlessly at the old lady, unable to understand her affection. He did, however, understand all too well the dark expression on the old man's face.

Dawson turned on his heel and stomped out of the parlor, through the kitchen, slamming the back door on his way out.

Tilghman caught up to him on the back steps.

Dawson paused before going down the stairs. With a quick glance at the lawman, he said quietly, "If that boy don't come back, it's all right by me, Marshal."

Taking out a kerchief from his back pocket, he wiped his brow, then his mouth, before continuing with a shake of his head. "He held a gun on Mrs. Dawson—"

"I don't think you need to worry about Hank's coming back," Tilghman said softly.

"I'm pleased to hear it, Marshal." He started down the steps.

Tilghman followed. "I'd take it kindly if you'd sell me a packhorse," he said as they reached the yard and headed for the barn. "I'll be wanting to take those saddles with us."

"Consider it done," Dawson replied, turning toward the lawman with a frown. "But what for, if you don't mind my askin'. Cain't we store 'em for you till this is over?"

"A man's saddle is his home, Mr. Dawson," Tilghman replied. "I can use 'em for bait."

Abigail stood directly in front of the horse at the hitching post. Adjusting the martens' skins draped around her shoulders, she glanced at the people milling about the sidewalk and street before taking a handkerchief from her reticule. Satisfied that no one was paying attention to her, she spat upon it and rubbed it on the horse's nose where a white patch should be.

Recognizing her, Crosspatches neighed a greeting. Although she rubbed briskly, his nose remained dark, but a telltale smudge of dye stained her handkerchief. Not wanting to excite him further, she refrained from patting him and swiftly returned the evidence to her purse. Just as she snapped it shut, a huge man hurried out of the restaurant, wiping his moustache on his sleeve.

"What are you doing to my horse?" Towering over Abigail, Mulehead kept his voice hushed. From his vantage point by the window, he had watched the fashionably dressed young lady as she had approached his horse. He had looked for her companion, but to his amazement, she had seemed to be alone. Just in case, he continued to scan the street as he spoke.

Startled by his sudden appearance, Abigail shoved her hand into the muff to grab the derringer as she asked, "You say this is your horse?"

"Yes, ma'am, he sure 'nuff is." His chest expanded with pride.

"In that case, sir, I arrest you," Abigail withdrew the gun.

Mulehead's smile was hidden by his moustache. "Not with that little bitty toy, you don't." Before she could take aim, he had put his huge hand over hers and squeezed.

Abigail gasped with pain. To avoid having her knuckles broken, she relinquished the weapon. "Unhand me!" She stamped her foot. "Or I shall scream."

"I reckon I'd have to shoot you, little miss, if you did that." Mulehead held her arm fast to his side while he palmed the gun.

He spoke with such calm assurance that Abigail did not doubt his sincerity, and she suddenly realized that she was in grave danger. She swallowed, hard, trying to still her mounting panic.

Mulehead was far from calm. Now that he had hold of an obviously refined, delicate lady, he hadn't the vaguest idea what to do with her, and Polecat was still upstairs in their hotel room. Polecat relished sleeping on a real bed between clean sheets much the same as Mulehead enjoyed food. Planning to awaken just in time for the race, he had remained in bed when Mulehead had left for breakfast. In desperate need of Polecat's advice, Mulehead tucked Abigail's arm firmly in his, pocketed the derringer, and started for the hotel.

Embarrassed by the ease with which he had disarmed her, outraged at being so ignominiously dragged along, and frightened, Abigail tried to summon her father's imperious manner as she demanded, "Where are you taking me?"

Her manner had no effect as he replied, "I got me a partner." His voice was gruff with a fierceness he was far from feeling. Truth to tell, he was grateful that she followed so meekly, not realizing that his sheer size robbed her of any choice. Had she screamed, he had no idea what he would have done.

It did not occur to Abigail to scream, knowing that he could maim her in any number of ways before help arrived.

"We'll jest see what Polecat has to say," Mulehead muttered, dragging her several doorways down the wooden sidewalk, into the hotel. He released her aching arm only so that she could precede him up the narrow wooden stairs, there being no clerk behind the desk to challenge them.

Nor was there anyone in the second-story hallway that Abigail could appeal to for help. She was distraught by the time they burst into Polecat's room.

Expecting to find Polecat up and washed, Mulehead had not bothered to knock. It was a mistake.

Hidden by Mulehead's body as he tied her securely to a chair, leaving her muff and reticule in her lap, Abigail could not see Polecat while he dressed, but she heard plenty as he called upon the behavior of bizarre creatures with mismatched body parts to describe and embellish upon the low esteem in which he held Mulehead's ancestry, poker playing, intelligence, disposition, luck, and ability to cause the trouble they were already in, never mind this latest mess he'd made by bringing a lady to their room wearin' more critters on her hat than they could trap in a season.

"What was I supposed to do!" Mulehead cried when, fully clothed with holster in place, Polecat paused for a breath. "Let her shoot me and take the horse?"

"You'd be better off, fer all I care!" Polecat exclaimed.

Bound tightly to the chair, helpless, Abigail struggled against her bonds. Knowing she had but herself to blame for her precarious situation, she fought against a mounting panic to find her voice.

Jacqueline's face was in flames as she stood before an angry Miss Cunningham. Hands nervously twisting behind her back, head bowed, she dared not lift her gaze from the carpet in the parlor of the railroad car.

"But how could you let your mistress leave unattended?" Maude paced back to her chair by the window before turning toward Kinkade and Morgan, who stood at attention by the dining table. She raked them with her fierce gray-eyed gaze.

Hat in his hands, turning it nervously by the brim, Morgan said uneasily, "She did ride Belvedere alone."

"This is different, young man," Maude replied, her manner stern. "As we have already ascertained, Belvedere is quite safe in his stall."

Morgan cleared his throat. "Pray, do not scold Jacqueline, Miss Cunningham," he said. "It is my fault that Miss Danforth left the car on her own."

"Nonsense!" Maude exclaimed. "However valuable you may have proven yourself to be, Mr. Dade, you are not a permanent part of Miss Danforth's en-

175

tourage. I cannot hold you responsible for her actions."

"But you do not understand, Miss Cunningham. I am sworn to Miss Danforth," he said earnestly. "I should never let her out of my sight."

Eyes wide, jaw slack with astonishment, Jacqueline gazed at him in wonderment.

Kinkade gasped.

Maude tried to maintain her composure as she slowly sank into her chair. "How can that be, sir?" she asked when she'd caught her breath. "Miss Danforth has said nothing to me."

"Oh, she doesn't know," he said. "I have not told her. I had not wanted to pressure her for an answer until this day had passed. But I plan to ask for her hand whether she finds her horse or not."

With a knowing glance at one another, Jacqueline and Kinkade visibly relaxed.

Maude refrained from laughing outright as she asked, "Do you actually expect Miss Danforth to live on a ranch?"

"She rides like the wind—"

"My dear young man," Maude interrupted scornfully, "most women of Miss Danforth's class ride exceedingly well."

"Astride?"

"Well no," Maude admitted reluctantly. "But Miss Danforth has plans for her life," she continued. "You do not know her in the least well."

"I beg to correct you, Miss Cunningham." Morgan drew himself to his full height. "I have gotten to know Miss Danforth quite well enough to know that she is the wittiest, bravest, most daring girl I have ever met. She has engaged my affections most passionately in the time we have spent together—"

Shocked to the core, Maude stood. "Are you trying to tell me you have spent time alone with Miss Danforth?" She glared at Jacqueline and Kinkade for confirmation.

Each looked at the other in open-mouthed horror before hanging their heads in shame.

Morgan blushed furiously. Unable to reveal Abigail's secret possession of the gun, he could say no more.

Kinkade ached to biff him upon the nose for compromising his mistress, but knew he never would. It might cost him his job, since marriage now seemed inevitable.

Maude was the first to recover. "We still have the problem of Miss Danforth's whereabouts," she said resolutely. "You," she said, pointing at the men, "go at once into town and search for her." Turning to Jacqueline, she said, "Fetch your hat and mantle. You will come with me."

As they left to do her bidding, Maude strode to her stateroom to gather her wraps. As she buttoned her plain black overcoat, she tried to focus upon the immediate problem of finding Miss Danforth.

But the knowledge that her young friend, with her dream of being the world's first consulting detective, was now doomed to marry the handsome young rancher loomed too large to ignore. Yet with her virtue compromised beyond repair, she would have no choice. Maude sighed heavily, trying to hold her tears at bay while donning her hat as, once again, her hopes of avenging Charlie's death dimmed.

Chapter Fourteen

"Gentlemen!" Abigail exclaimed when Polecat caught his breath. Fuming at herself for having allowed her emotions to cloud her powers of observation, she added impatiently, "Pray, be still, if you please!"

Open-mouthed with astonishment at her imperious tone, both men turned to stare at the expensively dressed young lady tied to the chair.

Polecat's tirade had given Abigail a chance to collect herself, and she had begun listening intently to the manner in which the wiry little man spoke as well as his words. Their quarrel seemed an old one. Although her captor was a large man, and weather-beaten, he was round of face and middle, betraying an overfondness for food. She surmised that his name meant something stubborn.

"Gentlemen," she repeated more softly, now that she had their attention. "Perhaps I just might have a solution to your problem."

"You ain't no solution, beg pardon, miss." Polecat removed his hat and held it to his breast. Bowing slightly, he continued, "You are the problem!"

Abigail realized that she must look, and probably

sounded, ridiculous, considering her helpless plight. Her muff had fallen to the floor, and her hat felt dangerously off balance; but she nonetheless said with earnest sincerity, "I shall be pleased to call off the lawmen who are looking for you."

Polecat and Mulehead exchanged veiled glances. They did not think her ridiculous. Worry that they might spend their last days in jail had done much to fray their friendship. Polecat was the first to speak. "Now, how in tarnation do you suppose you're gonna do that, Miss—ah—?"

"Danforth," Abigail said. With a winsome glance and smile, she indicated her piteous condition. "I would offer you my hand, sir, but as you can see I am unable."

Once again, the men exchanged glances. "She was carrying a gun," Mulehead said, stroking his moustache. Neither man made a move toward her.

Abigail fought against a mounting panic at their blank-eyed refusal to untie her. With a fast-dwindling self-assurance, she said, "I wonder if you gentlemen know that the other horse you—ah—confiscated belongs to Marshal Tilghman."

"Bill Tilghman?" Polecat threw his hat onto the back of the bedside chair and glared at Mulehead. "The marshal will be on our trail till we're in the ground fattenin' worms fer fish bait!"

"You got nobody but yourself to cuss at, and you know that's the truth," Mulehead said, frowning.

"By thunder's blue blazes, it warn't me!" Polecat said, shaking a finger under his partner's nose. "That three-handed dealer plucked you cleaner than Sunday's chicken." He shook his head sorrowfully. "You got luck like a horse can fly."

"I had me three aces that last hand!" Mulehead exclaimed.

"Hah! Right when all five of his cards was wearing the same complexion!"

Mulehead sighed. "That man could sure 'nough outhold a warehouse," he said, his voice full of awe.

"Gentlemen!" Abigail interrupted again, heartsick at the implications of their conversation. Before Polecat could speak again, she asked, "Am I to assume that you lost the marshal's horse in a poker game?"

Polecat shook his head sorrowfully. "The sun will rise on judgement day 'fore Mulehead strikes it rich playin' poker," he said, his voice full of disgust.

Duly noting the stubborn name, Abigail quelled her dismay as she continued with an enthusiasm she was far from feeling. "The marshal is mighty eager to get his horse back. It was to have become his Foundation Sire."

"That little old runty horse?" Mulehead was not impressed.

"Is he fast?" Abigail asked.

Polecat snorted. "Does a tornado spin?"

"Then perhaps you can understand why the marshal would be grateful for his return."

Again, the men exchanged silent glances.

Completely disheartened, Abigail asked, "How long ago did you lose him?"

"Last night," Mulehead said.

Hopes rising again, she said, "Could I prevail upon you gentlemen to take me to him?" Abigail smiled persuasively. "The marshal would be most grateful for his recovery."

"Grateful?" Polecat squinted at her suspiciously. "How grateful?"

"Oh, I'd say grateful enough not to arrest the man

who—ah—borrowed the horse because of circumstances beyond his control. And who only kept him because he did not know the true owner. And who returned him, at once, when he found out."

"How can you do that?" Mulehead asked.

Out of sight behind her back, Abigail crossed her fingers. "Marshal Tilghman and I are quite good friends." She tried not to blush while telling the fib.

"So you're sayin' if'n we was to give you them two horses, we could go free?" Polecat asked. "Nobody'd be chasin' after us?"

"You have indeed described the situation, Mr. Polecat." Abigail smiled. "Furthermore, it would benefit you both if you could effectuate such return quite soon. If I do not return shortly, my companions are sure to set up a hue and cry."

"Shucks, Polecat." Mulehead stared at the toe of his boot. "We ain't doin' so good." He ran a hand through his hair as he said mournfully, "No horses, no gold, and no saddles."

Polecat folded his arms across his chest and glared down at Abigail. "No, nothin' doin'."

"No jail," Abigail replied firmly. "No Marshal Tilghman on your trail."

"The pot jest ain't sweet enough, miss." Mulehead shook his head.

"What if I were to buy you two new mounts?"

Mulehead was about to accept when Polecat held out his hand to stop him. "Now, maybe if you was to git back our saddles fer us, too?"

"Where might they be?" Abigail asked.

"The Baxters'," Polecat answered.

"We can show you how to git there," Mulehead volunteered eagerly.

181

"Then all it will take is a handshake to seal our bargain, gentlemen."

"Untie her, you addle-headed nincompoop!" Polecat cried.

Mulehead hurried to do his bidding.

As soon as the rope fell away, Abigail stood. Although her gloves had saved her wrists from any real damage, her hand still ached from Mulehead's having wrested her gun away. Polecat's grip was surprisingly strong, and she winced as he shook her hand. She then went straightaway to the mirrored dresser to secure her hat. Confident that it was at its most becoming angle, she turned and said, "Now, if you gentlemen will join me, let us retrieve those horses."

Mulehead handed her muff to her while Polecat hurried to open the door. Bending close to her ear so that Polecat could not hear, he whispered, "I sure hope you can git our saddles back, little miss, or it'll spell the end betwixt Polecat and me."

As Abigail smiled at him reassuringly, it occurred to her that if she had shot and killed him, she would never have found the marshal's horse.

Morgan Dade was beside himself with worry and frustration. Banished from active participation in the hunt for Miss Danforth, he had brushed and curried Belvedere until the horse had grown restive under his ministrations. The stall was spotless, all tack gleamed, his saddle and boots shone, and his silks were in perfect order. There was nothing left to do but fret—and pray that Abigail would return unharmed.

While she had readied herself to search for Abigail in the city, Maude had realized that someone should stay behind in the event that Abigail returned while they were gone. Although she was loathe to have Abigail return only to be alone with the young man, she much preferred it over having Morgan creating an unseemly scene in public upon discovering Abigail's whereabouts. Nor would they exactly be alone; Maude had made sure that there would be numerous porters about, both in and outside the cars.

The sun was high by the time the three began their search. Arranging to meet at the far end of town to exchange information, Maude and Jacqueline had taken one side of the street, and Kinkade the other. The cheers of the crowd proclaimed the baseball game well under way by the time they finally met. None had news of Abigail.

Two gold pieces secured the return of the Arabian. Although there had been a tense moment wherein the hung over cowpoke had suggested holding Abigail for ransom, she had persuaded Polecat and Mulehead that their interests were better served by returning the horses.

Retrieving Crosspatches from in front of the restaurant, they avoided the vicinity of the grandstand where the speechifying had commenced and went around the back way to retrieve the Arabian from the livery. Engrossed in the oratory, few heads turned to notice them, and they managed to reach the vicinity fo the horse car without incident.

Morgan flew down the ramp when they drew close. "Miss Danforth!" he exclaimed, his face aglow with joy at her safe return. So intent was he upon reaching her, that he did not notice the two men, or the horses, until she gestured toward them. He stopped in midstride. "Is that—"

"Ah, Mr. Dade!" she cried. "I am so glad you're still here. Pray, see to the horses' every need."

Taking the reins of the two horses from Polecat and Mulehead, Morgan turned his back on them to face Abigail. "Did you capture those two men single-handed, with just that tiny derringer?" he whispered, eyes agleam with admiration.

Too embarrassed to explain what had really happened, Abigail bowed her head, trying to think of a clever retort.

"You are stupendous, Miss Danforth!" Mistaking her silence for modesty, Morgan lost his heart entirely. He was about to express his feelings when she abruptly turned away.

"This way, gentlemen," Abigail said. Blushing furiously from Morgan's unearned praise and disturbing gaze, she indicated to Polecat and Mulehead that they were to follow her.

Vowing to speak his heart the moment he could see her alone, Morgan watched her disappear into the private varnish, before leading the horses up the ramp.

It took not a little urging on Abigail's part to get Polecat and Mulehead to sit at the table in the parlor. The porters brought coffee, and settled at last, Abigail questioned them at length about the Baxter gang and the whereabouts of their hideout. From their descriptions of the gang members, she had deduced that Curly must have been the one to pull the trigger on Osgood, when she heard the door slam as Kinkade entered the corridor. They could hear his voice calling as he ran toward the parlor. "Miss Danforth!" he cried, "where are you?"

Motioning to Polecat and Mulehead to remain seated, she rose and went toward the curtain. "I am

184

in here, Kinkade," she called to him. "Kindly refrain from shouting."

"Oh, Miss Danforth," Kinkade said, entering the parlor. "Thank heaven you are—" Noticing Polecat and Mulehead, who stared back at him with alarm, he paused. "Who are they—?" Realizing it was not his place to question his mistress, he interrupted himself. "I mean, pardon me, miss, but we have been looking—"

"These are our culprits, Kinkade," Abigail interrupted. "The men we've been looking for. Crosspatches and the Arabian are safe with Mr. Dade."

"Congratulations, miss!" Kinkade beamed. "Jolly good show, if I may say!"

Once again, Abigail blushed at the undeserved praise. "Now, pray fetch Miss Cunningham." She waved him away. "We have much left to do."

He no sooner turned to obey, when Maude, with Jacqueline in tow, appeared at the curtained doorway. "Where have you been?" Maude demanded. Looking directly at Abigail, who blocked her view of the table, Maude did not notice the two seated men. "How dare you go off alone like that and—"

Abigail stood aside and, with a sweeping gesture of her arm, revealed Polecat and Mulehead, who smiled at Maude sheepishly.

"It's them!" Maude exclaimed. "He's the one!" she said, pointing her finger at Polecat. "I'd know him anywhere." She looked around the parlor. "Where is the sheriff?"

Polecat and Mulehead exchanged glances of alarm.

"There is no need for a sheriff, Miss Cunningham," Abigail said.

Unbuttoning her coat, Maude removed it and,

handing it to Jacqueline, said, "How did you capture them, pray tell?"

Not wishing to miss a word of Abigail's story by leaving to hang the coat, Jacqueline stood next to Kinkade near the entrance with Maude's coat over her arm.

Abigail's cheeks were on fire with embarrassment. The ignominious manner in which she had been overpowered far outweighed any triumph she might have felt at having recovered the horses. Holding her head high, she replied, "Without bloodshed."

Mulehead cleared his throat. Fishing into his pocket, he brought out the derringer and placed it on the table. "Here's your gun back, miss."

"You used a gun?" Hand to her heart, Maude sank into the chair by the window.

Once again, embarrassment silenced Abigail as she picked up the gun.

"Where did you get a gun?" Maude asked.

"We will discuss that later, if you please." Determined not to be bullied by her companion even though she knew she was in the wrong, Abigail turned her back on Maude and moved to the desk. "We have plans to make."

Unwilling to call Abigail to task in front of the servants or the disreputable strangers, Maude said, "I'll not forget to have our discussion, Miss Danforth." Her tone was ominous. "Now what plans do you have, pray, besides calling in the sheriff to lock these bandits away."

"Oh, I am not going to have them put in jail," Abigail said firmly as she placed the gun in the desk drawer and shut it.

"What?" Maude sat forward.

"The reason they both came with me so peacefully

186

is that I promised to try and recover their saddles and horses for them."

"You made a pact with those—those—thieves?" Maude could scarcely contain her distaste.

"They can lead me to Osgood's killer."

"May I remind you, Miss Danforth, that we went on this expedition to recover the horses, not to solve Mr. Osgood's murder!"

"We did agree to return Marshal Tilghman's horse to him, as I recall." Seating herself at the desk, Abigail cast a sly glance at Maude. "Since we have had no word of the capture of Osgood's killer, I would assume the marshal is still on his trail. If we merely returned the Arabian to Chandler, I doubt that we would find him there."

Maude thought a moment before speaking. "These men know where the killer is?"

"Not quite," Abigail said.

Mulehead cleared his throat. "We know where they went to divide the gold."

"But they didn't get any gold," Maude replied.

"They didn't git no gold!" Mulehead exclaimed.

Polecat slapped his knee. "Curly's gonna be madder than a fresh-made steer!" He laughed.

"I beg your pardon?" Maude glared at him.

Polecat blushed and did not reply.

"It's a place to start, Miss Cunningham," Abigail said. "And it is where Polecat and Mulehead will find their horses and saddles."

"Polecat and Mulehead?"

Raising themselves slightly from their chairs, the two men bowed toward Maude. "Pleased to meet you, ma'am," they chorused.

Maude ignored the introduction. "And presumably the killer also resides at this place?" she asked.

"If'n he didn't blast them Baxters into Paradise and burn leather for the other side of China!" Polecat exclaimed.

Maude glared her disapproval at his disgraceful slang.

"We'll just have to see for ourselves, won't we?" Abigail replied. "You must reroute us to Cameron Junction at once, Miss Cunningham."

"With this holiday in effect all over the county, it is unlikely I'll be able to effect such a transfer until morning."

"Good enough," Abigail replied. "We will drop Mr. Dade off at Kansas City so that he can return home with his father's horse."

Jacqueline covered her mouth with her hand to conceal a grin.

Kinkade frowned at her.

Unwilling to mention Mr. Dade's announced intentions in front of the drifters, Maude glared at the servants and ignored Abigail's remark. "And when we reach Cameron Junction?" she asked. "What then?"

"We will hire horses for Polecat, Mulehead, and Kinkade. I will ride Crosspatches. The four of us will seek out the Baxters."

"What about me?" Maude asked.

"You can remain with the car and begin its restoration. Jacqueline will stay with you. We'll leave the Arabian in safety at a reliable livery."

"No, you don't!" Maude exclaimed. "You'll not embark upon such a dangerous enterprise without me!"

Realizing that she could easily find a way to leave Maude behind when the time came, Abigail graciously acquiesced.

" 'Scuse me, miss," Mulehead said.

"What is it?" Abigail asked.

"Afore we leave, please ma'am, can I have one a them chocolate eclairs?"

In her plain dressing gown of dark flannel and hair in two braids for sleeping, Maude tapped on Abigail's door.

Jacqueline let her in.

"Pray, may I see Miss Danforth alone?" Maude asked.

"That's all right, Jacqueline." Seated at the dressing table, Abigail held out her hand for the hairbrush. "We were nearly finished. You may leave."

"Yes, miss." Handing her mistress the brush, Jacqueline swiftly left the room, closing the door behind her.

"Do sit down, Miss Cunningham." Assuming Maude had come to hear the details of her success, Abigail completed the end of her braid and turned to face her with a smile.

As Maude settled herself upon the bedside chair, she said, "I have something serious to discuss with you, Miss Danforth." Her countenance was severe.

Abigail's smile vanished. "Whatever is the matter?"

"Mr. Dade is planning to ask for your hand."

Abigail blushed furiously. "I had no idea—"

"And it is well he is doing the honorable thing!"

"Honorable?" Abigail drew back with an expression of hauteur; then the memory of that bitter cold day came flooding back, and all color drained from her face.

"How many times were you alone together!" Maude demanded.

"But he was teaching me how to shoot, Miss Cunningham," Abigail said faintly.

"He nonetheless compromised you most shame-fully."

"So that's it!" Abigail stood and paced the few steps to the door before turning to glare at Maude. "The only thing that concerns you is that he and I were alone!" she said heatedly.

"You know that an unmarried girl should always be accompanied by someone in public!"

"I'll wager that you are not in the least concerned for my safety. I do not hear you scold me for capturing Mulehead and Polecat single-handedly!"

"Don't you know by now how important it is to protect your reputation?"

"Ah ha! Just as I thought!" Abigail paced back to the dressing table. "My reputation! I was kidnapped. I could have been killed. But no. All you care about is my good name!"

"You know as well as I that your reputation must remain unblemished if you are to attract a worthy husband."

"It is insulting to be accompanied in public as though I were too simple-minded to find my way alone just so some man will consider me unsullied enough to marry!"

"It's the way things have always been, Miss Danforth," Maude said with a shrug. "And in all likelihood, the way they always will be."

"Being continually chaperoned places more value upon my chastity than my intelligence. Or health. Or good humor."

"Miss Danforth!"

Abigail sat and faced Maude. "I have no wish to explore the mysteries of the marriage bed without benefit of matrimony, Miss Cunningham, but I do resent having my worth as a human being judged solely upon my ability to remain pure!''

"Your father entrusted your care to me." Maude was adamant. "And your staff. It is I, and they, who will suffer his ire if something amiss should happen to you. And now it would seem as if you have compromised yourself beyond repair."

"I would have thought that you, of all people, would be more lenient toward my having some freedom."

"It is because I have suffered much that I feel constrained to reprimand you, my dear," Maude replied softly, her eyes full of sympathy.

Abigail paused. "Life does hold its small ironies, does it not?" She sighed heavily before continuing, "That which I desire most in the world closely resembles that which I most despise."

"Oh?" Maude frowned.

"Don't you see?" Abigail reached out to touch Maude's hand. "I do care a great deal about my reputation." Her smile was ironic. "Not as a chaste woman, but as a successful detective!"

"Alas," Maude replied, patting Abigail's hand. "I fear Mr. Dade will not allow you to pursue a career."

Abigail withdrew her hand and sat tall. "But what if Mr. Dade were to join us upon our adventures?" she asked.

Maude's eyes were wide with astonishment as she said, "Do you really believe he would?"

Abigail's gaze was solemn. "I must wait to discover that answer until I have returned the Arabian to Marshal Tilghman."

Chapter Fifteen

"Well I'll be danged if'n you din't grow some more Billy Bub." Sampson laughed. "I thought you was supposed to be in that bedroom there bein' sick."

With a mighty yawn, Billy shuffled over to the table and sat. For the first time in his life, he needed a real shave. His clothes hung loose, and his sleeves and pant legs were shorter than ever.

"Stop your cussin', Sampson," Maw said as she put a bowl of hot oatmeal in front of Billy Bub.

Without looking at either of them, Billy doused the steaming cereal with sugar and drowned it in heavy cream before digging in.

"Cat got your tongue, boy?"

"Leave him be, Sampson," Maw said as she handed him a plate stacked with flapjacks. "It's his first time outta bed. Cain't you see he's still poorly?"

Sampson syruped and started in on his flapjacks.

The man and boy ate in silence.

"More oatmeal, son?" Maw asked, when Billy Bub scraped the bottom of his bowl.

He shook his head no.

Removing the bowl, Maw replaced it with a plate of

flapjacks stacked higher than Sampson's had been. Billy poked a spoonful of butter between each one before drenching them with syrup. Alternating mouthfuls of bacon with the flapjacks, he washed them down with two glasses of milk.

"Boy, you eat like a half-starved Indian," Sampson said with disgust as Billy cleaned his plate before he could finish his own.

Billy Bub opened his mouth as if to answer, but brought up a kettle-rattling belch instead.

Sampson grinned in spite of himself.

Maw turned her back so that they wouldn't catch her smile.

"Where's Boss?" Billy Bub asked, stirring sugar into his coffee.

"Gone after Polecat and Mulehead," Sampson said.

"Do I recollect you tellin' me that Hank flew the coop?" Billy asked before taking a swig of his coffee.

"Mercy, son, that was long about two weeks ago," Maw said, taking her seat with a mug of coffee.

"Any word on him?"

"Nary a sign," Sampson said. "Boss come back to report he'd disappeared like some magic trick."

"Yeah," Maw said. "Appears to me like somebody oughtta seen him packin' all them saddles."

"Or a livery shoulda bought one," Sampson said. "He cain't be travelin' all that fast to've disappeared so quick."

"Shhhhh!" Maw held up her hand and whispered, "Is that the dog?"

In the silence, they could hear the dog greeting somebody, or chasing a squirrel.

Sampson drew his gun and ran for the window on the far side of the door.

Maw fetched the shotgun and went for the other window.

"What's the matter?" Billy Bub said. "It's jest the hound."

"Hush, boy!" Sampson growled. "Git back in bed so's you won't git hurt."

Billy stood, but he had to steady himself by holding on to the back of his chair. "Not till you tell me what's happenin'."

"We ain't heard from Curly yet, son." Maw waved at him to go back into the bedroom.

"Maybe it's Boss," Billy said.

"Maybe so," Sampson said, peering out of the window from the side. "Or it could be Polecat and Mulehead."

"Din't you say Hank had their saddles?" Billy asked, scratching his head.

"They don't know that!"

Tapping his head and dropping his jaw, Billy imitated a dunce. "Where's Boss's shotgun?"

"You couldn't lift it, never mind fire it, shape you're in," Sampson said. "Now git like Maw said!"

"Aw, come one Sampson," His strength returning, Billy let go of the chair and started over to the big man. "Let me have your other gun." He held his hands out. "You know I'm good."

"Don't you do it, Sampson," Maw cried.

"Get out of the way, boy!" Sampson pushed him away as Maw went to the door.

Billy stood his ground out of the large man's reach. "Then lemme stand by and reload for you."

"Oh, all right," Sampson said, peering out of the window. "But keep your head out of harm's way."

Billy Bub eased himself down to squat at Sampson's

194

feet as Maw opened the door a crack. "Who's there!"
she shouted.

"It's me, Maw Baxter! Hank!" Hiding by the side
of the porch, out of range of the windows, Hank
shouted over the dog's yapping.

"What do want!" Sampson shouted in return.

"I know you're holdin' a gun on me," Hank said.
"Don't shoot. I jest want to talk."

"After what you did?" Maw's voice was muffled,
but clear. "Runnin' off like that with them saddles,
you 'spect to jest sashay back in here like nothin'?"

Hank glanced back at Tilghman, who was crouched
behind him. Tilghman motioned for him to keep talking.

"I brought the saddles back."

"Let me see 'em!" Maw shouted.

"Promise you won't shoot?"

"You show me them saddles or we don't talk!"

While the dog continued barking at Tilghman, Hank
fetched the pack horse and, with his spare hand in plain
sight away from his holster, led it to the front door of
the cabin. "See!"

Maw opened the door a crack. With Sampson covering her, she stuck her head out and peered at the
horse. "Where might your mount be?"

"Back thataways so's he won't git shot at." Hank
motioned to the woods.

"Take that horse and them saddles to the barn.
Don't want them settin' out front for anybody to see."

"Then what?" Hank asked.

"Come on in, boy," she said, slamming the door
behind her.

"Miz Baxter!" Hank shouted over the dog's continued barking when he returned from the barn.

"I said to come in!" she shouted back.

"I got somebody with me!"

"Who might that be?" Sampson shouted.

"Lemme tell you that when we git inside!"

"You both better have your hands in the sky when you hit that porch."

Tilghman had remained crouched by the side of the house. He had tried to quiet the hound to no avail and motioned for Hank to come close so that he could be heard without yelling. "I'm not going in that house till I know how many's in there."

"They ain't killers, Marshal."

"You get their number first."

Hand shrugged as he mounted the steps. "Hey, Miz Baxter!"

"Now what do you want?"

"Who you got inside?"

"What's it to ya?"

"I don't wanna go walkin' into no trap," Hank replied.

"You're the one what come back, boy."

"Yeah!" Sampson shouted. "Make your move. You comin' in or not."

Hank looked helplessly at the marshal. "Promise not to shoot?" he shouted.

"I ain't promisin' you nothin' if you rile me, boy!" Maw said. "Now git inside 'fore I have to shoot that dog to shut him up."

Hank shrugged. "Best I can do, Marshal."

"Okay," Tilghman said. "Let's go."

With their hands raised high and the dog yapping at Tilghman's heels, Hank and the lawman walked across the porch.

Billy Bub got to his feet and, weak from the unaccustomed exertion, slid into his place at the table as Hank and the stranger entered. Motioning for Sampson to remain by the window and keep the drop on the two men, Maw stood her ground near the stove, shotgun at her side.

"Keep your hands where we can see 'em," Maw said. "Now, jest who is it you've brought to call, Hank."

"I'm Bill Tilghman, ma'am," he said, removing his white Stetson.

Maw looked him up and down. "Not Marshal Bill Tilghman?"

"Used to be marshal, ma'am." He smiled. "Right now, I'm retired."

Horrified, Sampson aimed his gun at Hank. "What do you think you're doin' bringin' the law down on us!"

"Hesh your mouth!" Maw said, wiping her hands on her apron as she walked toward the marshal. "Why not? We ain't got nothin' to hide." She shook hands with Tilghman and motioned for him to take a seat at the table. " 'Sides, he says he's retired."

Tilghman removed his hat, but remained standing. "I do have a few questions on my mind I figured you might help me with, Miz Baxter."

"Put that hardware away, Sampson, 'fore you hurt somebody," Maw said as she returned to the stove. "You had breakfast, Marshal?"

"Yes, ma'am."

"Well, take your coats off, men, and set a spell. I'll git you some coffee. Go on, Hank. You, too."

Tilghman put his hat on the peg by the door and found a place at the table.

Ruffling Billy's hair, Hank sat beside him. "This here is Billy Bub, Marshal. Looks kinda peaked. You been sick?"

"Had the grippe."

"And that there is Sampson."

Tilghman held his hand out, and Sampson reluctantly reached across the table and shook it.

After pouring their coffee, Maw pulled up a chair and joined them. "So what can we do for you, Marshal?"

"There was a shooting connected with a train robbery a while back, Mrs. Baxter."

"What would that have to do with us?" she asked innocently.

"Let me assure you, I am not interested in the robbery," Tilghman said hastily. "The bandits did not take any gold. But I am interested in finding the killer of my friend, Mr. Osgood, and the men who stole my horse."

"That was your horse, Marshal?" Billy asked.

"You git back in that bed where you belong, Billy Bub!"

"But, Maw!"

"Move!"

Reluctantly, Billy left the table and, scuffing the toes of his boots, walked toward the room that served as sleeping quarters.

"Like I said, Marshal," Maw continued when he'd shut the door, "what's that got to do with us?"

"Not a whole lot as far as the law's concerned, ma'am."

"You didn't drag Hank all the way out here for nothin', Marshal," Maw said.

"What I'm tryin' to say is that I'm not interested in pursuin' any interest you might have had in the robbery itself." He held his hand up to forestall Maw's interruption. "And by that, I'm not sayin' that you had any interest in it at all."

"You sure can beat around a bush, Marshal."
Sampson shook his head.

"That's enough outta you, Sampson," Maw said.
"Marshal Tilghman is makin' right good sense to me."

"Thank you, ma'am," Tilghman raised his cup in
salute and, collecting his thoughts, sipped at the coffee.
Placing the mug on the table, he glanced at Hank.
"Hank here tells me that it was Curly who actually
pulled the trigger and killed Mr. Osgood."

"Don't you say a word, Sampson," Maw said.
"This could be a fancy trap."

"It's no trap, Mrs. Baxter," Tilghman said reassuringly. "I want Curly for the killing of Mr. Osgood.
That's all."

"And the men who stole your horse?" she asked.

Tilghman nodded and smiled. "Yes. And the men
who stole my horse."

"And Hank here told you we'd know somethin'
about how you could trail all of them rascals?" Maw
said, glaring at Hank.

"You gotta understand, Maw," Hank said. "The
marshal promised he wouldn't put me in jail if'n I'd
help him. He'll promise you the same thing. If you
help, too. Won't you, Marshal?"

Maw turned her stare toward the marshal.

"I got no real power to promise such things, Mrs.
Baxter. However, nobody knows, but me, who I talk
to. Or what we talk about." He shrugged. "I'm not
after people who've done no real harm. I'm mighty
grateful for any help I can get to capture a killer. Or
the thief who stole my horse."

"What if'n we told you we agreed with Hank. That
it was Curly what killed that man," Sampson said.
"What then?"

"I'd be mighty grateful for your testimony, Sampson," Tilghman responded. "And I'd ask you if you knew where this Curly might be?"

"We jump every time that hound barks for want of knowing that, Marshal," Maw said.

"You mind tellin' me why?"

"Soon as I found out he'd shot a man, I threw him out," Maw replied. "Now, if'n we did have anything to do with robbin' that train, and I ain't sayin' we did, it woulda took us some time to find out there weren't no gold. I mean Curly coulda been long gone with his share, thinkin' he was rich."

"I think I'm beginning to understand," Tilghman said.

"Curly's the kind who'd git real mad if'n he thought he was cheated," Maw continued. "He'd want revenge."

"Yeah, we've been expecting him to come back any day," Sampson said.

"And the men who stole my horse?"

"Didn't Hank tell you?"

"I'd like to hear your story."

Maw cupped her hand to her mouth and shouted, "Billy Bub!"

"Yes'm?" Billy stuck his head out of the door so fast that Maw and Tilghman exchanged amused glances. "Tell the marshal what you saw," Maw said.

"What I saw when, Maw?" Billy said, stepping into the room.

"Stop playin' dumb, Billy!"

"You mean about Polecat and Mulehead?"

"Hurry up, boy!" Maw said ominously.

Making the most of his moment in the limelight, using his hands and whistling his sound effects, Billy described Polecat and Mulehead's exodus from the freight car. One of the horses he described was unmistakeably Tilghman's Arabian.

"Do you know where they were headed?" Tilghman asked.

"Them horses was goin' so fast, Polecat and Mulehead was jest tryin' to stay put."

"We been waitin' for 'em to show up here, same as Curly, Marshal," Maw said.

"We thought they'd be callin' for their saddles." Sampson glared at Hank. "Till Hank took 'em."

"I brought 'em back, didn't I?" Hank said defensively.

"Somethin' tells me you found yourself in a corner where you didn't have a whole lot of choice," Maw said.

Tilghman held his hand up to stop their quarrel. "As long as you're waitin' around for all these people to show, do you folks mind if I wait, too?" he asked.

"Why not, Marshal?" Maw said, glaring at Hank. "When any one of 'em gits here, they ain't gonna be too happy. Be glad for the extra gun."

"Not so quick, Maw," Sampson said. "Whose side are you on, Marshal?"

"Let's just say I'd like to see all three of them get a fair trial."

"And what about us?" Sampson asked.

"I've got no reason to want you in jail, 'specially since you're bein' so helpful in bringin the real killer to justice."

Sampson shrugged and looked at Maw. "Then stay," he said as the dog began barking again.

Sampson shoved his chair back and scurried to the window.

Billy rushed to Sampson's side.

Hank dove for the other window.

Maw ran back to the stove and picked up the shotgun.

Crouching, Tilghman hurried to the side of the door, gun drawn.

"Who's there?" Maw shouted when they heard footsteps on the porch.

"It's me!"

Everyone, except Tilghman, relaxed when they recognized Boss's voice.

"Well, don't hang around out there scarin' us all half to death!" Maw shouted, leaning the shotgun against the wall again. "Come in!"

Sampson, Billy, and Hank moved to the table.

Tilghman holstered his gun, but remained standing near the door.

Boss entered and, removing his hat and jacket, hung them on the peg before he turned and saw Hank. "What dragged you in?"

"Meet Marshal Tilghman, son," Maw said. "This is my boy, Marshal," she said proudly. "Folks call him Boss."

Tilghman held out his hand.

Boss looked at the lawman's hand without extending his own. "What are they doing here?" He glared at Maw, frowning. Boss was bone tired. Thwarted at every turn, nothing had gone right since that stupid robbery, and Maw had never let up blaming him for everything.

"The marshal here is lookin' for Curly," Maw said as though speaking to a dunce.

"Curly?" Boss looked at them all vacantly.

"Come on, son," Maw said. "He knows we didn't do nothin'. He's jest after the killer on that train robbery."

"He's after Polecat and Mulehead, too," Billy said. "They stole his horse."

"What is the marshal doin' here lookin' for them?" Boss asked with growing impatience.

"I can answer that, Mr. Baxter," Tilghman said. "I understand that you all are waiting for the return of the same men that I also wish to see. Since our interests lie in the same direction, I figured I could wait for them also. Only difference is, when they appear, I'd like to escort them to jail."

"Well, you figured wrong!" Drawing his gun, Boss motioned for Sampson to do the same. "You better reach, Marshal."

"What are you doin', son?" Maw cried, shocked. "You heard the man."

"He's lyin' to you," Boss said, puzzled that they had been taken in. "He wants to put us all in jail!"

"That ain't so!" Hank said.

Boss's voice was harsh. "You want me to believe a turncoat like you?"

"It's true, Baxter," Tilghman said. Alarmed by this swift turn of events, he raised his hands to show that he did not mean to draw. But in that moment, obeying a signal from Boss, Sampson relieved him of his gun.

"If'n you think I'm gonna trust some lawman who only wants to make himself look good, you're crazy, Marshal," Boss said as he took Tilghman's gun from Sampson and stuck it in his belt. "You, too, Maw!"

"But, son," Maw cried. "The marshal can help us when Curly shows up. Hank, too."

"You got Sampson and me," Boss said. "What more do you need?"

"And me," Billy said.

"Me, too," Hank said, not looking at Tilghman.

"You're makin' a big mistake, Baxter," Tilghman said. "You, too, Hank."

"You're the one what made the mistake, Marshal," Boss said. "Fetch some rope, Billy. We'll have to tie him up till we figure out what to do with him."

While Boss kept his gun aimed at Tilghman, Sampson took the rope from Billy and tied Tilghman's hands behind his back.

Outnumbered, and with Boss's gun aimed straight at his gut, Tilghman did not resist. He did, however, keep his wrists far apart and flexed so that the rope could not be tied too snug.

"Don't tie him in here!" Maw said as Billy pulled a chair toward Tilghman. Secretly pleased that her son was finally showing some gumption again, even though she thought him wrong-headed, she added, "How do you 'spect me to feed you with him starin' at us? Put him in the bedroom."

Boss stayed in the doorway, keeping his gun aimed at the lawman while Hank, Tilghman, and Sampson went single-file past the unmade bed to reach the chair on the far side of the tiny room.

Hands already tied behind his back, Tilghman sat himself in the chair. "I trusted you, Hank," he said as Hank stooped to wrap the rope around his boot and the chair. "So did Mrs. Dawson."

"Shut up!" Hank said. Standing, he removed his kerchief. He rolled it in a knot and gagged Tilghman while Boss nodded his approval.

Satisfied that Tilghman was firmly bound to the chair, the men returned to the kitchen.

"What are you gonna do with Tilghman, son?" Maw asked.

"We're gonna hafta kill him, Maw," Boss said,

more to get her goat then thinking to actually do the deed.

"You cain't do that, son!" Maw gasped. "The law will be after us till kingdom come!"

"They won't never find us," Boss said, still half-teasing. "How could they?"

"But the Dawsons will know!" Hank cried.

"Who might they be?" Maw asked.

"The people who took care of me when my leg was banged up. The marshal found me there."

"How are they gonna find out?" Boss asked.

"Yeah," Sampson said. "You gonna tell 'em?"

"No. Who me?" Hank tried to show a smile to both men at the same time. White with fear at the idea of killing so famous a lawman, he realized his own life was not worth dirt unless he could make Boss believe him. "Never!" One hand on his heart, he raised the other skyward. "Never!"

"I know what." Boss placed his arm around Hank's shoulders like a long-lost buddy. "We'll just let you do the killin'." He liked the idea so much that it suddenly became a real possibility, and he turned toward his mother for approval. "That way we know he'll never tell."

Maw scowled at him. "You know how I feel about killin', son." But there was no heat in her protest.

In the bedroom, the marshal struggled against his bonds in vain.

Chapter Sixteen

Curly dismounted in the woods that surrounded the Baxters' cabin. Determined not to have his arrival announced by a yapping hound, he secured his horse. Knowing the dog's fondness for raw meat, he had bought a box of Sure Death Rat Killer and had laced it through half the carcass of a rabbit. Taking care to scrub his hands in the stream, he had eaten the other half of the rabbit, roasted, the night before for his supper.

Taking the poisoned rabbit from his saddlebags, careful to crack no twigs in his progress, he crept stealthily toward the cabin.

Weary from its recent greeting of Hank and Tilghman, head resting on its forepaws, the hound lay sleeping on its rags on the porch.

Curly stayed hidden in the underbrush that surrounded the yard. Selecting a stick, he thrashed a bush as though squirrels were chasing each other.

The dog was instantly alert.

Curly repeated the sound.

The dog stood, its head cocked.

Again, Curly rattled the bush.

Growling deep in its throat, but not barking, the dog lunged from the porch and raced toward the sound

Curly timed his toss so that the rabbit landed a few feet directly in front of the dog's path. Drawing his gun with the intent to kill the dog if it did not grab the bait—no matter the noise it made—he held his breath and watched.

The dog braked to a stop and, tail wagging, sniffed the bait. There had been no scraps from breakfast yet. The hound made up for its neglect by gnawing and gulping the unexpected bonus. Before he finished the last bite, the convulsions began.

Holstering his gun, Curly sat on his haunches and, with a sour grin at the success of his plan, watched the entire agonizing process. Though the dog foamed at the mouth and staggered in the agony of its death throes, it made no noise loud enough to alarm the household.

When he was certain the dog was dead, Curly grabbed the carcass by the tail and dragged it into the underbrush. Crouching, he worked his way to the barn, hoping to figure out how many men were inside the cabin by counting the number of horses.

Much to his surprise, he found enough horseflesh packed in the barn for a whole new gang to be organizing for another try at a train. Three were ready to ride. One horse had two saddles on its back! His head was pounding so hard, it took him a few minutes to remember that the saddles belonged to Polecat and Mulehead. He checked the stalls to see if their mounts were still there. They were.

His head ached too much to put a story to why their saddles should be on a horse that didn't belong to either one of them. Reaching for the flask in his jacket, he took a long pull. When the throbbing eased somewhat, he decided to rush the house in spite of the number of men who were probably already there. It would be simple enough to kill one or two and take others hostage to keep the rest in line.

If Polecat and Mulehead were among them, so much the better. They'd be easy to terrorize. And he could always threaten to shoot Maw if they didn't fork over his share of real gold. He might shoot the old biddy anyhow. Teach her a lesson for throwing him out. Teach them all.

"That there's the place, little miss," Mulehead said, grinning at Abigail, his voice filled with all the pride of an explorer discovering a riverhead as he pointed toward the rocky overhang. Dismounting, he fished in his saddlebags for the coffeepot. "I'll have the java goin' lickety split."

Polecat dismounted from his new horse and, taking the reins to Mulehead's horse and Crosspatches when Abigail had dismounted, led them to a spot of grass.

"I'll tell the others," Abigail said, her gaze fondly following her beloved horse. Dressed in the same blue velvet, split-skirted riding habit and the matching plumed hat that she had worn the morning Osgood had been killed, she walked back to join Kinkade and Morgan, who had fallen behind.

Watching Abigail's departure, Polecat grabbed an armful of branches for the fire and hurried to Mulehead's side. "I'll be a horn-swaggled hoppy toad!" he exclaimed, dumping the wood near the burnt spot where they'd built their last fire. "I ain't never seen the like!"

"What are you jawin' at now?" Mulehead said with a puzzled frown.

"The Petticoat Terror of the Plains never rode like that!"

"What brought Belle Starr to mind?" Mulehead asked, wondering why Polecat was underfoot. He'd never before been so helpful with firewood.

Polecat cracked a branch and handed it to Mulehead. "Maybe Belle's looks could skin goat, but even she rode Venus side saddle. Like a lady."

"What's the matter, Polecat? You don't like the little miss ridin' astride?"

"No, you blubberhead, I don't!" Polecat exclaimed. " 'Tain't fittin'! Her bein' a dainty lady and all."

"Shhhhh!" Mulehead whispered as Abigail approached. "Don't you open your trap. You and me could be spendin' the rest of our days as jail bait if'n it warn't for her bein' so nice."

Both men froze at the sound of gunfire. Noticing their reaction, Abigail hurried toward them. "Pray, do not be concerned," she called. "Mr. Dade is giving Kinkade some last minute instructions in the use of firearms." Both Kinkade and Maude had been so insistent that he learn to shoot that she had relented.

Mulehead relaxed. "Go fetch them biscuits from my saddlebags, will ya Polecat?"

Touching his hat brim as he passed Abigail, Polecat muttered, " 'Tain't fittin'."

Abigail did not hear his comment. "How far are we from the Baxters' now?" she asked Mulehead when she had climbed into the cleft in the rocks.

Mulehead stood as the flames caught. "An hour or so, depending how fast we ride."

"Kinkade is beginning to look like he has always carried a gun," she said sadly, holding her gloved hands toward the fire. She may have been outnumbered when it came to allowing him to learn, but it did not assuage her guilt, nor her feelings of unease at having her servant gain skill in the act of killing. "Mr. Dade is a good teacher," she continued with a heavy sigh.

"I hope he don't have to use it, miss."

"So do I!" she exclaimed. "It would be a terrible burden to carry should he injure or kill someone."

"If'n you don't mind my askin'," Mulehead said, setting up the coffeepot on the tripod. "What's that Miz Cunningham gonna say 'bout you sneakin' away like that while she was sleepin'."

"I don't think she is going to be too pleased." Abigail smiled. "Especially since I gave in to Mr. Dade's importuning and allowed him to come along."

"If'n I left Polecat behind like that, I reckon it'd be the end of us." He shook his head in wonderment. "Must be different with you women folk."

"It would appear that Mr. Polecat has forgiven you for taking me to your room."

"You heard for yourself how close it come."

They fell silent when Polecat returned, and when the coffee had boiled, Mulehead banged two tin mugs together to call Morgan and Kinkade.

"I say, Kinkade!" Morgan exclaimed as the tin cups sounded in the distance. "You are getting ever so much better. You almost knocked that branch off the tree."

Knowing he'd missed the branch by a mile, Kinkade was not pleased by the flattery and wondered what the young man wanted as he holstered his gun.

It was not long in coming. "I wonder if I might ask you something?" Morgan's manner was so casual, it deepened Kinkade's suspicions.

"You may ask," Kinkade responded, starting for the rocky overhang. "I don't know if I'll have an answer for you."

Morgan hung back. "Do you know why Miss Danforth refuses to see me?" he asked plaintively.

Not privy to his mistress's thoughts in this particular matter, yet disliking to admit he wasn't in the know, Kinkade shrugged noncommittally as he kept on walking.

Morgan hurried to catch up. "Do you think she loves me?" he asked eagerly.

"Oh, sir," Kinkade said, sincerely hoping that she did not. He had no wish to settle in Kansas. "I'm sure I would not want to speak Miss Danforth's heart."

"But she has not seen me since she recovered the horse, although I have implored her for an interview." Morgan kept pace with Kinkade's brisk stride. "She seems to be avoiding me."

"That was but a short time ago, and there has been much—"

"But when I try to ride beside her now, she pulls away, or puts one of those drifters in between us."

Not knowing what to say, Kinkade shrugged again.

"Ah, but she did consent for me to come along to the Baxters'!" Morgan exclaimed happily. More to himself than to Kinkade as they drew close to the others, he said, "That must mean something." Realizing that he was just now missing an opportunity to be with her in the overhang, he left Kinkade behind as he scrambled up the incline.

Kinkade felt awkward about taking refreshment at the same place as his mistress, and when Mulehead handed him his cup, he strayed off to the side. He hadn't had a chance to sip the scalding liquid before he spotted two horses approaching at a gallop. "Miss Danforth!" he cried before the others saw them approach. "I do believe I see Miss Cunningham and Miss Bordeaux!" he exclaimed, pointing his finger.

"What?" Abigail looked in the direction that Kinkade indicated, only too pleased for an excuse to escape once again from Morgan. Her feelings were too unsettled, and she was not yet ready to respond to him should he plead his case. "How can that be?" she asked, hurrying to Kinkade's side.

"Morgan!" Kinkade shouted, placing his mug on a rock. "Uh, I mean, Mr. Dade, sir. Let's go help the ladies dismount."

Polecat and Mulehead stayed put in the overhang while the two men hurried toward the riders, with Abigail following close behind. "Well at least they's ridin' sideways like proper ladies," Polecat muttered as they watched Maude and Jacqueline draw close.

"What are you doing here?" Abigail cried when Maude pulled up beside her.

"I knew you would try to leave me behind just when things were getting interesting, so I prepared myself to be ready to leave whenever you did," Maude responded breathlessly.

Helping her dismount, Morgan set Maude down gently and, with a longing look at Abigail, took the reins of her horse to lead it to the others.

"How did you find us?" Abigail asked.

"We were not so far behind that we could not follow your trail," Maude replied, straightening the bodice of her riding costume. "And why, pray tell, did you see fit to abandon me?"

"My only concern was for your safety!" Abigail protested.

Maude raised an inquiring eyebrow.

Having been unsure of Maude's abilities as a horse-woman, Abigail had been concerned about her keeping up.

Maude looked at her askance. "If your concern for

212

my safety is so great that you would deceive me, then perhaps you can understand how I feel about yours?"

"*Touché!*" Holding her skirt wide, Abigail bowed a deep apology.

"You are not angry that I am here?" Maude asked.

Abigail's grin was infectious. "You are not angry that I tried to leave you behind?"

"Since you did not succeed, Miss Danforth. . . ." Maude held open her arms, inviting a rare embrace which Abigail did not refuse.

Amazed, Mulehead watched the two laughing women approach arm in arm. He poured a mug of coffee for Maude.

Meanwhile, Kinkade had reached Jacqueline. His hands almost encircled her tiny waist as she slid from the Arabian. It took all his self-control to release her when her feet touched the ground. Hovering over her, he kept his back toward the other so that he'd not be overheard. "You foolish girl!" he exclaimed, beside himself with worry. "Why did you do this!"

"Oh, *Monsieur* Kinkade." She looked up at him gravely. "Pray do not scold. I am so very sorry I am here. Miss Cunningham forces me—!"

"You should have refused!" Knowing full well that to refuse was impossible merely added to his concern.

"If only it is possible!" She took a few steps and stumbled. He grasped her arm. *"Sacre blue! Mon derrière!"* she cried.

"You must go back!"

"You know I cannot!" She leaned heavily on his arm. "But how can I go on?" she cried. *"Mon Dieu!* I hate the horse!"

"There, there," he said, longing to take her into his arms and comfort her, but able merely to pat her hand.

"I packed some tea. Perhaps you will feel better after a cup."

"What shall I do if Miss Danforth marries Mr. Dade and we live on a ranch?" Tears welled in her eyes.

Color drained from Kinkade's face. "Has she given her consent?"

Jacqueline shook her head. "She has told me nothing." Jacqueline shrugged eloquently. "At night and morning I am quiet so that she can speak, but Miss Danforth is quiet, too. And all the times we change her clothes, she frowns and seems to worry, but she says nothing."

"Mr. Dade tells me he has had no opportunity to ask for her hand."

"I do not know what Miss Danforth will say when he does." Jacqueline sighed. "And I do not know what I shall do if she says yes."

When Abigail and Maude reached the fire, Abigail turned to watch Jacqueline and Kinkade approach. Her smile was ironic as she surveyed her entourage and thought, *Not one female, but three; two train robbers, a major domo by trade, and a rancher.* Not a little concerned about the danger she might be leading them into, she muttered, "I'd say we are a most uncommon posse."

Chapter Seventeen

Gun drawn, Curly crouched. Placing his boot cautiously on each tread so that it would not creak, he mounted the stairs to the porch. Still crouched, he tiptoed to the door. As his heartbeat increased, so did the hammer blows to his skull. Grabbing the latch string, he yanked the door open. "Freeze!" he shouted.

Seated around the kitchen table, Boss, Sampson, Hank, and Billy Bub each snapped his head around to face the door. In open-mouthed shock, they stared at their worst nightmare come true framed in the doorway.

Maw was standing at the stove, right where Curly had expected her to be. Aiming his gun at her belly, he shouted, "Touch your guns and she's dead!"

Instantly, the men showed their empty hands above the table.

Thankful for the long skirts that concealed the trembling of her limbs, Maw cleared her throat. "Why, if'n it ain't Curly." Her voice was a squeak, but she managed a smile.

"Now, Curly," Boss said. While keeping his hands

in plain sight, he started to stand. "Don't do nothin' you're gonna be sorry for."

"Sit!" Curly commanded, keeping Maw covered while slamming the door shut with his boot heel.

Boss sat abruptly.

"We been wonderin' when you'd show up." Sampson grinned nervously. With a casual shrug in Hank's direction, he added, "Haven't we, Hank?"

"Yeah." Hank gulped. "We was jest sayin' we was wonderin' when Curly was gonna show."

Eyeing each man as he spoke, Billy Bub's Adam's apple bobbed up and down, but he could muster no words.

Curly squinted his eyes against the pounding in his head. "Anybody moves and the old biddy gits it in the gut!" he cried, thrusting his gun toward her.

"Careful, there, Curly." Boss glanced at his mother. His laugh was shaky. "That thing might go off."

"You be mighty careful when you drop your guns!" Curly's voice was hoarse; the look in his eyes, wild. "One at a time!" he shouted at Sampson and Hank, who had also started to rise when Boss had gotten to his feet to remove his holster.

"Okay, okay," Boss said soothingly, reaching for the buckle to his holster. "Don't git so excited."

"I ain't excited!" Curly yelled. "Don't you rile me!"

Slipping his gunbelt from around his waist, Boss dropped it to the floor.

Sampson, then Hank, slowly followed suit.

"Why didn't the dog bark?" Billy found his voice when Hank's holster hit the floor.

Curly ignored him.

"I told you, we shoulda had a lookout." Maw glared at her son.

"Shut up!" Curly screamed, which set his head to pounding worse than ever.

Maw gasped and swiftly put her hands high in the air, unaware that she still held a spoon.

Curly kept his eye on Maw while he indicated he was talking to Billy with a nod of his head. "Shove them gunbelts over here real easy like, boy."

Billy rose slowly from his chair to obey, too terrified to ask about the dog again.

Curly said nothing while Billy carefully stacked all of the holsters by the door. When the boy regained his seat at the table, Curly said, "Now, I'm gonna ask this question just once." His voice was ice.

Knowing only too well what the question was, but terrified what Curly would do when he heard the answer, the men all stared at the floor.

Curly took his eye off Mrs. Baxter long enough to look at each man in turn as he said slowly, "Where is my gold?"

Maw spoke up. "We don't have no gold," she said, lowering her arm to place the spoon on the stove and fetch the coffeepot.

"Don't touch that!" Curly snarled, aching to reach in his pocket for the flask.

Maw swiftly raised her hands again.

"Don't lie to me!" Curly shouted.

"She ain't lyin', Curly," Sampson said, his voice cracking. Embarrassed, unable to look Curly in the eye, he coughed before continuing earnestly. "We didn't git no gold neither."

"You expect me to believe that?" Curly sneered.

"It's the truth," Boss said. Still holding his hands in the air, he nodded in the general direction of the backyard. "You can check by the woodpile. All them bricks piled up is the same as your'n."

"Honest, Curly." Hank held his empty hands out toward Curly. "There weren't no gold."

"The Pinkertons salted the train," Sampson said.

"You're lying!" Curly still held the gun on Maw. "Where's them drifters, Polecat and Mulehead?"

"We don't know," Maw replied.

"Why are their saddles out there on one horse?" Curly asked.

Boss looked at the others before he spoke. "Hank here jest brought 'em back."

"Did they git the gold?" Curly asked in disbelief.

"There weren't none to git." Boss placed his trembling hand on his heart. "Honest."

"Don't be mad, Curly," Billy pleaded.

"Yeah," Sampson said. "Put that gun away 'fore somebody gits hurt."

"Posse gave up lookin' for us a long time ago," Maw said.

Sampson spoke. "Yeah, Pinkertons never was interested in catchin' us."

"Marshal Tilghman is lookin' for Curly!" Billy chimed in.

Boss started for Billy, his hand raised to swat him.

"Whoa!" Curly shouted.

Boss froze in mid-stride.

"Marshal Tilghman, eh?" Curly said with a smirk, aiming the gun at Billy's heart. "How do you know?"

Billy's Adam's apple worked furiously as he glanced helplessly at Boss, Sampson, and Hank before any words would come. "He was here," he began.

Crouching slightly, switching his aim again to Maw's midsection, Curly eyed each man. "What did you tell him?"

"We didn't know where you was!" Maw cried.

"He don't want jest me, you know!" Curly said. "All of you robbed that train!"

"That's what I told 'em," Boss said, looking at the others for confirmation. "That's why we tied him up in the next room."

"What!" Curly exclaimed, which set his head to pounding worse than ever.

Billy eagerly explained, "Boss got the drop on the marshal, and we tied him up in there 'cause Maw didn't want—"

"You expect me to believe you got Marshal Bill Tilghman tied up in the next room?" Curly said in disbelief.

"We was jest tryin' to figure out what to do with him when you come in," Boss said.

The others nodded in agreement.

"This I gotta see for myself." Slowly, Curly circled the table, keeping his gun on Maw. "First man makes a move near them guns, I kill her, got that?"

The men all muttered promises that they wouldn't move.

Curly's eyes never strayed from the old woman until he shoved the bedroom door open with his boot and, still facing into the kitchen, his gun still pointed directly at her, he quickly turned his head to peer into the bedroom.

On the far side of the bed, a man was bound hand and foot to a chair. But he was so far away, and so huddled over, he could have been anybody. "You Marshal Tilghman?" Curly asked.

Tilghman was exhausted from his struggles and no nearer to being free. And thoroughly embarrassed by his predicament. He had no idea who Curly was. Hoping against hope that the man was friendly, he grunted through the gag and nodded his head.

219

Shutting the door, Curly looked at Boss with new respect. "Well, I'll be!" he exclaimed, relaxing his aim at Maw. "Who'd a thought you'd of had the nerve!"

"I don't want to go to jail any more'n you do, Curly." Boss slowly began to lower his hands, testing Curly's change in demeanor.

"How'd the marshal find this place?" Curly asked.

Hoping to draw Curly's attention away from his mother, Boss said, "Hank brought Tilghman here to trail you."

Still seated at the table, Hank's eyes grew wide, his jaw slack with fear.

Curly stiffened. He turned his gaze from Maw to glare at Hank.

"What did you go and tell him that for?" Hank cried, his voice shrill.

"Stand up, you bastard!" Curly snarled.

Trembling hands raised high, too scared to speak, but pleading with Boss and Sampson for help with his eyes, Hank rose from the table and backed away a few steps.

Boss watched Curly's face.

"Is it true?" Curly asked, his voice icy. For the first time since he had slammed into the room, except for the brief moment he had aimed it at Billy, Curly had taken his gun off Maw. He pointed it directly at Hank's heart.

"I couldn't help it!" Hank's voice broke.

"You cain't shoot an unarmed man!" Maw cried. Although she dared to speak, she kept her quivering hands in the air. "That's jest plain murder!"

"Hush, Maw!" Boss exclaimed, grateful for having Curly aim his gun at Hank instead of her. He did not care what happened to Hank.

220

"Wait, Curly," Sampson said. "Hank couldn't help hisself!"

"I can explain, Curly!" Hank cried.

"He snuck outta here in the middle of the night," Boss said contemptuously. "He stole Polecat's and Mulehead's saddles!"

"I didn't mean no harm!" Hank said frantically. I jest needed me some kinda pay for the time I put in. You felt the same way, Curly—"

"You went and got yourself caught!" Boss interrupted. Facing Curly, he continued, "Then the turncoat went and brought the law down on us!"

"Don't say that, son!" Maw cried. "You want to git Hank killed?"

"Shut up, Maw!" Boss shouted.

She glared back at him, a bewildered expression on her face.

"It wasn't that way at all!" Sampson protested. "The marshal didn't want—" Suddenly realizing that he'd be in deep trouble with Curly if he finished his sentence, Sampson's voice trailed off.

"Go on!" Curly shouted. "What did the marshal want?"

"He was after you, Curly," Boss said with a sly glance at Sampson.

Sampson's conspiratorial nod of agreement was almost imperceptible.

Boss continued, "So Hank brought him here to start lookin'."

"You double-crossing snake!" Curly cocked the hammer.

"No!" Maw screamed. "No!"

"You cain't jest shoot him!" Billy cried. "He don't have a gun!"

Clasping his hands together, Hank fell to his knees.

Abject terror numbed the pain from his shin. "Please, don't kill me, Curly. Don't—"

Sampson and Boss looked away, unable to hide their disgust at Hank's cowardice.

The explosion echoed throughout the cabin.

At the sound of gunfire, Tilghman struggled even harder against his bonds. From the moment his captors had left the room, he'd tried every trick he knew to get free. Nothing had worked. His wrists were raw and bleeding. But infinitely more serious than a few scratches was his difficulty with breathing. He'd yanked his head around so often in an effort to free himself from the gag that the inside had begun to unroll and a corner of the kerchief threatened to strangle him.

He'd had to learn to keep his frustration in check, for when his thrashing became too frenzied, the chair tilted dangerously. His boots were more tightly tangled in the chair legs than when he had begun. But the sound of gunfire overcame his caution. For one awful moment he teetered on one chair leg. With no free arm to wave to regain his balance, he crashed to the floor.

No one in the other room heard Tilghman's fall.

They watched, horrified, as Hank fell backward, a shocked expression on his face. His head struck the floor with a sickening thud. A widening red blotch stained his shirt as the stench of gunpowder and urine filled the room.

"You killed him!" Maw screeched. "You killed him! You killed him!"

"Shut her up!" Curly screamed at Boss. "Or she'll be next!"

Her chest heaving, Maw put both hands to her mouth to try and control herself.

Taking his hands away from his ears, Billy started for her.

222

"Stay put, kid!" Curly waved the gun at him.

Unable to stop staring at Hank's body, Billy inched himself back to the table and sat. "What did you go and do that for?" he asked; his voice creaked.

"Serves the traitor right," Boss said, trying to erase the terror in Hank's voice that still rang in his ears.

"How can you say that!" Maw yelled at him. "Hank didn't deserve killin'! You as good as pulled the trigger yourself!" She sobbed, dabbing at her eyes with her apron.

Boss winced at her words.

"Shut up, old woman," Curly snarled. "I'm jest waitin' for an excuse to shoot you!"

Forcing himself to remain calm, Boss asked, "What do we do now?"

"Prove you're with me!" Curly said.

"How?" Boss gulped.

With a tilt of his head, Curly indicated the bedroom. "Kill the marshal," he said with a cold smile.

"You cain't do that, Boss!" Sampson exclaimed. "He's helpless. You cain't shoot a man tied to a chair like that!"

"They'd never stop huntin' for you!" Maw said.

Desperate to survive, and only too glad that Curly was no longer focused on his mother, Boss managed a thin smile. "Wasn't we all settin' here, gettin' ready to do away with the marshal when Curly comes bustin' in?" he asked.

Sampson, Billy and Maw all reluctantly admitted that Boss was right.

Curly longed for a drink to still the throbbing in his head.

"What's the difference of me doin' it 'cause I think it's right and Curly tellin' me to?" Boss asked reasonably.

223

Curly removed the flask from his pocket while he kept his gun aimed at Maw.

" 'Cause I never said it was right!" Maw cried. "I thought we'd talk, peaceful like, and when your head cooled some, you'd see it didn't make no sense to dry gulch the marshal." She shook her head. "Ain't none of us ever killed nobody afore. Didn't you see how them Pinkertons didn't even bother to come alookin' for us?"

Curly twisted the cap off with his teeth and took a swig.

Boss opened his mouth to respond, but Maw continued before he could speak. "You kill that lawman and you dig your own grave. You won't live for a trial neither. They'd string you up—"

"Shut your mouth, you old biddy!" Curly yelled when the whiskey had burned its way down and he could speak.

"I'm gonna do what Curly says, Maw."

Mrs. Baxter put her hands on her hips and glared fiercely at her son. "If you do this dastardly deed, don't you never call me Maw agin," she said. "You'll be no son of mine."

Carefully watching Curly take his drink while also watching his elder engaged in dispute, Billy had slowly shifted himself from chair to chair until he was now in the chair closest to the door—and the pile of holsters. Curly's attention—and his gun—was focused on Maw as Billy eased himself as far off the edge of the seat as he could without falling, hand outstretched for Sampson's gun.

Facing Curly, as well as Billy, and watching the boy's slow progress, Maw had tried to ignore his maneuvering while she'd been arguing to give him time.

But, desperate for rescue, her eyes flickered for an instant in his direction to check his progress.

Sensitive to his target's every reaction, Curly did not miss Maw's glance. He crouched and, spinning on the toes of his boots, caught sight of Billy just as he was grasping the handle of Sampson's gun. Instinctively, Curly pulled the trigger.

Shocked by the overwhelming pain as the bullet splintered his wrist, Billy shrieked.

Writhing on the bedroom floor, Tilghman struggled against his bonds in vain.

"Don't kill him!" Maw screamed. "Don't kill him! Tears streamed down her face as she sobbed, "Please God, don't kill him!"

"Shut up, you old fool!" Curly whirled around to point the gun at her again.

Maw covered her mouth with both hands to try and stop herself from crying.

Holding his bleeding wrist with his good hand, Billy rolled on the floor, his eyes shut, howling.

Hands still clasped to her mouth, Maw started toward him.

"Move one more step and you're dead," Curly said.

Crying openly, Maw retreated to the stove.

Eyes squeezed shut, Billy continued to howl.

Boss and Sampson remained frozen at the table, careful to keep their hands in plain sight.

Gasping for breath, Billy opened his eyes. Seeing the wreck of his wrist and his hand dangling at a grotesque angle, he fainted.

"You saw him!" Curly said, glaring at each in turn. "I had to shoot him. He was goin' for a gun."

Sampson and Boss exchanged glances. "Sure you did," Sampson recovered first, nodding his head in agreement.

"He'll be all right," Boss said reassuringly. "We can git him to a doctor and git that arm patched good as new."

"We ain't doin' nothin' of the kind," Curly said. "I'm gonna keep this gun pointin' at your Maw's gut. If'n Sampson even looks funny, she gits it. Understand?"

Sampson and Boss nodded.

Mrs. Baxter stared at Curly, transfixed with horror.

"Now, I'll tell you what I'm gonna do," Curly said.

Sampson and Boss exchanged silent glances at the menace in Curly's tone.

"I'm gonna go over there real easy like and fetch your gun, Boss," he continued, indicating the heap of holsters. "Know what I'm gonna do next?"

Boss shook his head.

"Well, I'll tell you," Curly said with a sneer. "I'm gonna carry your gun to the bedroom door. You, Boss, gonna open that door. Then I'm gonna hand you your gun, and you're gonna shoot the marshal."

Maw gasped. "You cain't!" she cried.

"It's you or him, Maw," Boss said, his voice bleak.

"Then you'll be as wanted as me," Curly said with a smirk. "We'll hightail it to California together."

"I ain't goin' nowhere," Maw said. "I'm too old to be on the lam. This is my home and I'm stayin'."

"Suit yourself," Curly said, moving slowly toward the door. Circling around Billy's body, his aim never wavered from Maw, even as he stopped and pulled Boss's gun from its holster. Motioning for Boss to get out of his chair and meet him at the bedroom door, he made his way back across the room.

No one spoke as Boss took his position at the bedroom door.

Curly had his hand on the door to shove it open when there was a banging on the front door.

Everyone froze.

They all looked to Curly for instructions.

Curly motioned with his gun for Boss to answer.

"Who is it?" Boss hollered.

"Abigail Danforth!" a young lady's voice replied. "I'd like a word with Mrs. Baxter, if you please."

Chapter Eighteen

Shaking his head in admiration at Abigail's spunk as she mounted the steps to the cabin with all the self-assurance of a neighbor paying a call, Mulehead nudged his horse toward the barn. Polecat followed close behind.

Standing by their horses in the yard so as not to crowd the porch, the others were watching Abigail's progress too intently to notice Polecat and Mulehead's whereabouts.

Keeping their horses to the side of the barn in plain sight of the others, they dismounted and, squinting to adjust their eyes to the dim light, entered the barn. Mulehead spotted the packhorse first. "Ain't them our saddles!" he exclaimed.

"Wonder who's the scalawag what put 'em both on one horse." Polecat said, hurrying toward the packhorse.

"What do you care?"

"I care if'n anything is missin' from my saddlebags!"

Mulehead headed for the stalls.

Polecat unbuckled his saddlebags and rooted around

until he found the kerchief. Pulling it out, he glanced at Mulehead's retreating back before touching the cloth to his cheek. With great reverence, he unfolded it. Gazing fondly at the golden locket, he opened it and sighed. With a swift glance in Mulehead's direction, he clicked it shut and brushed it with his lips before rewrapping it and installing it in his saddlebags.

"Ooee, Polecat!" Mulehead called from the stalls. "Our ole horses is still here!"

"Shhhhh!" Polecat whispered. "You tryin' to spook a stampede?"

Mulehead came back toward Polecat. "Let's go see how that little lady is doin'."

"How come?" Polecat took hold of the bridle of the packhorse. "She's got that Kinkade feller to back her up. And that lovesick cowboy. She don't need the likes of us'n. Let's saddle up."

"Naw, Polecat, now. I don't feel right jest ridin' off like that."

"Who said we was gonna ride?" Polecat began leading the packhorse back toward the stalls. "We'll jest git ourselves ready for when she finds out what direction to take."

"Come to think on it," Mulehead said as he and Polecat pulled their saddles free and heaved them onto the backs of their old mounts. "Do we gotta follow along with Miss Danforth while she hunts Curly down?"

"I don't recollect where we said we would," Polecat said with a shrug.

"I don't remember promisin' nothin'," Mulehead agreed.

"Don't you reckon we done what she asked?"

"Like you said"—Mulehead pulled the cinch tight—"if'n we see they don't need us, we'll be ready to ride."

Holding their horses by the bridles, Polecat and Mulehead walked them to the barn door. With a glance toward the cabin and then at one another in silent agreement that they were not needed, they led their horses outside, past the two they'd ridden in on, and around to the far side of the barn. Still on foot, they did not get deep into the woods before coming across Curly's horse tied to a tree.

"Now, why would a body leave their horse way out here?" Mulehead unbuckled the bulging saddlebags and looked inside. "He's packin' enough whiskey to stock the Long Branch in Dodge."

"You 'spect it's Curly?"

"Yep." Mulehead hurriedly buckled the flap. "I recollect his saddle."

"But how come he left it out here 'steada tyin' up at the railin'?" Polecat scratched his chin. "Or in the barn?"

"If'n he was bein' this sneaky, he cain't be up to no good." Mulehead looked toward the house. "We cain't desert the little miss now."

"We ain't desertin' her, bug brain! Curly is who she's come to find! She ain't got no use fer us at all now."

Mulehead looked longingly at Curly's bulging saddlebags. "You reckon he'd miss jest one bottle?"

"I'd sooner have a mama grizz thin' we had ahold of her pup."

Mulehead shrugged and mounted his horse.

"We been put to enough grief, with nothin' to show fer it." Polecat urged his horse to a slow walk.

"That ain't all true." Mulehead kneed his horse to catch up. "I got me somethin' I'll never forget."

"What's that?"

"I tasted me a chocolate eclair!"

* * *

At the sound of Abigail's voice, Curly nodded to Sampson to go to the window and see who was there.

Sampson parted the curtain slightly and peered through the crack. "Lord-a-mercy," he whispered. "The yard's full of a crowd."

"Where's that hound dog?" Boss asked.

Curly ignored Boss's question. "Stop foolin' around, Sampson," he said ominously. "Whadda you see!"

"There's two men on horses over by the barn. And two more men—well, one of 'em seems right young—standin' in the yard."

"I thought that posse gave up," Boss said.

" 'Tain't no posse." Sampson smiled. "There's two more women out there, besides the one at the door."

"Women?" Maw started toward Sampson.

"You stay put!" Curly waved the gun at her.

Maw retreated.

"The two men still on their horses look to be Polecat and Mulehead," Sampson said. "Yep, that's who they are," he continued after a pause. "They're headin' for the barn."

"What are they doin' here?" Curly asked.

"After their saddles," Maw whispered. "We shoulda brought 'em into the kitchen. Now if'n they ain't jest gonna go and walk away with 'em." She was disgusted and did not bother to hide it.

"Shhhh!" Sampson waved his hand at Maw to be still. "A real tiny lady jest come up and sat on the porch steps like she cain't hardly walk."

As Jacqueline sat gingerly on the steps, Abigail could hear mumbling from inside the house and wondered what was keeping someone from answering. She knocked on the door again.

"You suppose they're lookin' fer me?" Curly asked, gesturing for Maw to answer the door.

"Jest a minute!" Maw hollered. "I'm a comin'!"

"They don't look like they's goin' away any time soon," Sampson said. "Maw'd better open the door."

"You git them bodies in the other room," Curly said. "Move!"

Sampson left his post at the window. Stooping over Billy, he winced at the sight of boy's smashed wrist. Hoping the kid would stay unconscious and out of pain and, more importantly, silent, he carefully placed what was left of his hand on Billy's chest and, scooping the boy up, carried him into the bedroom, where he placed him gently on the bed.

Grunting with effort, Boss dragged Hank's body by the boots to where it was just out of sight behind the door. Returning to the kitchen, he said, "You cain't cover us and that whole crowd all by yourself, Curly."

Curly hesitated but a moment. "Jest you remember," he said, handing Boss his gun. "You do anything funny, I swear I'll kill your maw." His head pounded so hard, he could barely think.

"I'm on your side, Curly," Boss said, going for his holster by the door. "Always have been."

"What about me, Curly?" Sampson said. "I don't wanna go to jail neither."

"Git your piece, Sampson." Curly motioned for Sampson to pick up his holster.

Sampson did not need urging a second time. Buckling on his gunbelt, he took his place by the window. Boss stood at the other.

Curly sat at the table. Concealing his gun underneath, he kept it aimed at Maw as she went to the door.

When Maw opened the door a crack, Abigail got a whiff of gunpowder. She stepped back a pace.

"What do you want?" Naturally suspicious of strangers, Maw's manner was unfriendly.

"Are you Mrs. Baxter?"

"What's it to you?"

"My name is Miss Danforth," Abigail continued as though the woman had answered her politely.

Maw just stared at her, not missing one stitch of Abigail's fashionable riding habit, right down to her matching blue gloves and boots.

Wondering if the woman's churlishness was her normal bad manners, Abigail decided not to risk her ire by inquiring about Curly directly. Certain that she had beaten Tilghman to the Baxters' hideout, she asked instead, "I was wondering if perhaps you had seen Marshal Tilghman lately."

"I ain't seen nobody," Maw said. "Lemme ask my son." She shut the door. Eyes wide with fright, she looked at Curly.

"Go git the marshal." Curly motioned to Boss and Sampson. "He'll be our ticket outta here."

"We'd need us a week of Sundays to untie that mess, Curly," Sampson whispered.

"Yeah," Boss added, keeping his voice low. "He's so upside down tangled in that chair, ain't nothin' gonna git him loose."

"Then git her inside, away from the others," Curly said. "We'll take her hostage."

Opening the door again, Maw asked, "Won't you come in, Miss Danforth?"

"No thank you." Abigail remained standing a few paces away from the door. Their many delays in answering her knock had made her uneasy. She felt safer in the open where her friends could see her. "I appreciate your offer of hospitality, but there are too many of us.''

"Jest you.'' Maw forced a smile as she opened the door a little wider.

"I really cannot,'' Abigail insisted, fully alert that something was amiss. "We must leave soon if we are to get back into town before dark. If you will kindly tell me whether you've seen the marshal, then we will be on our way.''

Maw shut the door again.

"We'll have to make a break for it,'' Curly said. Standing, he moved toward the door, and Maw.

"But didn't you hear her say they'd be goin'?'' Sampson protested.

"She's lyin','' Curly said. "How'd she know to ask about the marshal less'n she knew he was here?''

"Ain't nobody out there fit to stop us,'' Boss said. "But if they was to ride off and hide to ambush us, it'd be a different story. I say we git.''

"I'll take that tall horse tied by the porch,'' Curly said.

"Polecat's and Mulehead's horses are ready to ride by the barn, and they ain't gonna shoot at nobody. There's even a lady's sidesaddle for Maw,'' Sampson said. "All we gotta do is rush them two dudes and that lady. Even if they are armed, I betcha they cain't hit nothin'.''

"I ain't goin' nowhere!'' Maw protested.

"Oh, yes, you are,'' Curly snarled. Grabbing her by the wrist, he twisted it behind her back.

In spite of herself, Maw gasped with pain and yelped.

"Don't you hurt her!'' Boss cried.

"I won't,'' Curly said, "long as she gits me outta here.''

Alarmed by this further delay while waiting for the

woman to reappear, Abigail took the precaution of withdrawing the derringer and concealing it in the folds of her skirt.

Maw opened the door as Curly stood behind her, twisting her arm, using her as a shield.

Alarmed by the tortured look on the woman's face, Abigail crouched, aiming her gun at them.

Shocked that Abigail had the drop on him, not knowing whether to shoot her or Maw first, Curly panicked. He shoved Maw at Abigail.

Maw stumbled toward Abigail, completely off balance.

Trying to get a clear shot at Curly, Abigail did not dodge in time. The large woman crashed into her. As they tumbled to the floor, Maw landed on top of Abigail, spoiling her aim.

Sitting on the steps, Jacqueline heard the commotion behind her. She stood and turned in time to see Maw crashing into Abigail. "Miss Danforth!" she cried. She started up the steps, hands outstretched to catch her mistress.

Boss and Sampson rushed from behind Curly. Jumping over the two women on the floor, they leapt off the side of the porch and ran toward the barn and the saddled horses.

At the sight of two armed men running directly toward Maude, Kinkade grabbed her and shoved her to the ground, falling on top of her to shield her from harm.

Mouth agape at the onrushing men, Morgan drew his gun.

Thwarted in his attempt to take either Maw or Abigail as hostage, Curly ran past them and grabbed Jacqueline's outstretched wrist.

Maw struggled to get up, but an excruciating pain

in her hip would not allow it. She slumped over Abigail, pinning her. Hoping that if the marshal were set free, he might capture Curly before he had run off with her son, she said in a loud whisper, "The marshal is here."

"He is?" Flabbergasted, and disappointed, that the marshal had gotten here before her, and not seeing him anywhere, Abigail asked in disbelief, "Where is he?"

"Tied up in the bedroom."

"And in need of rescue!" Abigail exclaimed, her disappointment changing to pure delight. Sliding from underneath Maw, she crawled toward the cabin door.

With great caution, she crossed the kitchen toward the only door. Gun in hand, she shoved it open. For one awful moment she thought that the dead body sprawled on the floor was Tilghman. Then she heard the grunts and thumping from the other side of the bed. There appeared to be another dead body on the bed, and she shuddered as she wondered how the marshal had been able to survive such carnage.

As Abigail bent over Tilghman, the amazed expression in the lawman's eyes would have been of immense satisfaction had she not been in such a rush to free him. He ceased struggling, his face red with embarrassment at having her discover him in such a helpless predicament.

Kneeling in back of him, she placed the gun on the floor while removing his gag. "How did you find this place so quickly?" she asked when, at length, the last knot parted.

Working his jaw before he spoke, he said, "My usual methods." His voice was not much more than a croak from being so dry. "How did *you* find it?" he asked, too astonished by her appearance to be grateful.

"I have my methods," Abigail said cooly. Yet, even

236

as she freed his wrists, she blushed at the memory of being helpless in Mulehead's grasp. Standing, she said, "You may untie the rest yourself." Retrieving her gun, she ran for the door, eager to redeem herself by taking an active part in capturing Curly.

"Wait, Miss Danforth!" Tilghman cried as he tugged and pulled at the ropes that still bound him firmly to the chair. "Do not be so rash as to chase after that killer without me!"

When she reached the doorway, she paused and looked back at the struggling lawman. "By the by," she said sweetly. "I have recovered Crosspatches and your Arabian." Her smile was wicked. "Now I must hurry after Curly before his head start is too great."

"Stop!" Tilghman called after her. "Curly is extremely dangerous!" He worked frantically to untangle himself.

Knowing Tilghman to be safe, Abigail ignored his importunings and raced back to the porch. She reached the doorway just in time to see Curly mount Crosspatches. He held the reins to the Arabian, trailing a precariously seated Jacqueline.

Jacqueline screamed with terror. Her hands were bound to the pommel. One slip, and she'd be dragged to a horrible death.

Chapter Nineteen

Maude could not breathe. Flat on the ground, with Kinkade on top of her, only her long hat-pins had kept her hat from flying off. Her gloves had saved her hands from too bad a scratching, but she blushed to wonder to what heights her skirts had flown and prayed that her ankles had not been exposed. She wished for nothing more than to scold Kinkade soundly, if only she could speak. But as bullets exploded overhead and tore holes in the ground nearby, she swiftly changed her mind, realizing that Kinkade had no doubt saved her life. Head down, she watched, amazed, as Kinkade gained his feet and sped toward the barn to head off the two huge men racing for Polecat's and Mulehead's mounts.

Boss and Sampson dared not shoot at Kinkade again for fear of hitting their means of escape. The dudes were proving harder to hit than they had thought. And the kid had actually shot back, nearly winging Sampson.

Reaching the horses first, Kinkade grabbed the reins to Polecat's mount, then fell to the ground, whereupon he wrapped the reins around the back legs of Mule-head's horse.

Yelling curses at Kinkade that would have blistered Mrs. Baxter's ears, Boss and Sampson scurried into the barn while Kinkade hobbled their mounts.

From his knees, Morgan had gotten off two shots that were wide of their mark.

Maude started to get up.

"You stay there!" Kinkade hollered at her as he scrambled to his feet.

Open-mouthed, Maude stared at him.

"Oh, Miss Cunningham," Kinkade began to apologize for speaking to his betters in such an unforgivable manner. "I mean, if it please—"

"Hurry, Kinkade!" Morgan cried, dashing to the side of the barn. "Or they will escape!"

Giving up all hope of redeeming himself with Miss Cunningham, Kinkade joined Morgan, who was crouched beside the barn door.

Maude got to her feet and, lifting her skirts, dashed toward them.

Inside, Boss and Sampson found Tilghman's and Hank's saddled horses. Thinking only of escape, they grabbed the reins and had their boots in the stirrups when Kinkade and Morgan rushed through the door. "Drop your guns!" Morgan shouted.

"Okay! Okay!" Boss said. "Don't shoot." Caught in his awkward, half-mounted position, he dropped his gun and slid from the horse.

Sampson followed suit.

"Back away from the guns!" Morgan said.

Hands high, Boss and Sampson exchanged glances, trying to gauge their chances of rushing them.

Kinkade's fierce expression brooked no disagreement. "Away from those guns!"

239

The two men backed up.

"I would be much obliged if you would be so kind as to retrieve their weapons, Miss Cunningham," Kinkade said, aiming his gun at Boss while Morgan kept Sampson covered.

Not by so much as a flicker of an eyelash did Maude betray how proud she was of Kinkade as she complied with his request.

By the time Abigail reached the porch, there was no one in sight to join her in the chase after Curly and Jacqueline. Fuming at herself for spending so much time freeing Tilghman, she despaired of ever catching up with Crosspatches on one of the rented mounts.

Kinkade's horse had seemed more lively than Morgan's. Not wanting to waste time by fetching it and leading it back to the porch to mount, she took a deep breath, got a running start down the steps and vaulted herself across the saddle. Startled, the horse was in motion before she'd gotten her boot across its back and into the stirrup.

Urging the horse into its top speed, her heart sank. She knew she could never overtake Crosspatches. Still, she dodged through the trees and kept it headed toward Jacqueline's ever-diminishing cries.

Shocked by the cruel gouging of Curly's spurs, Crosspatches obediently lengthened his stride. He'd never before had so much as a mayfly's touch for chastisement. Now hornets stung him fore and aft. He ran faster. They stung him again.

Spurring him to greater effort, Curly lashed Crosspatches across both flanks.

The sting of the whip was the final indignity. For the first time in his life, Crosspatches put his ears back and, upon taking his next stride, sank both hind hooves into the ground. Thrusting his mighty chest upward, he pawed the air with his front legs. Neighing his anger and fright, he swerved in midair. Stiff-legged, he landed with enough force to dislodge a saddle. Instantly, he whirled in the opposite direction.

Again, he reared.

He had no need to rear twice.

Curly had not bothered to lengthen the stirrups to accommodate his longer legs. Boots thus free, he fell clear.

Coming down the second time, riderless, shaking his mane and snorting, Crosspatches pranced in a small circle then, still prancing, reversed direction.

Jacqueline had begun to free herself the moment Curly had turned away to mount Crosspatches. The rope was thick, her wrists tiny, and when he'd tightened the half-hitch in haste, he'd left some play in the knot. She had hoped her horse would slow Crosspatches. She had kept screaming to telegraph her whereabouts and had managed to remain in her precarious seat long after her wrists were free.

The moment Crosspatches reared, she jumped. Landing on her feet, her momentum forced her to roll onto her hip and slide. Her hands were saved by the palms of her gloves, which were scraped away in the fall. Her chin, having no such protection, was badly scratched and her bonnet was knocked askew.

Frantic to discover the whereabouts of her captor before he spotted her, she raised her head to look around, biting her lip to keep from crying out.

Curly had regained his feet. Hat lost, his angelic curls were a stark contrast to his rage-contorted face.

A few yards beyond Curly, Crosspatches continued to prance.

The Arabian, which had been yanked to a halt when Crosspatches landed the second time, was still roped to his saddle.

Enraged with Crosspatches, nearly blind with the pain in his head, Curly forgot his human hostage. Thinking to ride her mount, he drew his gun. "I'll kill you for that!" he yelled, running toward Crosspatches. "I'll kill you!"

Crosspatches danced out of reach.

"No!" Jacqueline screamed. "No! Don't shoot!"

Crouching, Curly turned and fired at the sound of her voice.

Jacqueline ducked the moment she saw him turn. The bullet whizzed over her head. Hugging the ground, she felt the vibration of an approaching horse and, remaining flat, prayed that the rider was friendly. "Help!" she screamed. "Help! This way!"

Urging her mount toward the cries, Abigail drew the derringer and rode into sight just as Curly grabbed Crosspatches' bridle, readying himself to shoot the horse. She reined her horse to a halt. "Stop!" she cried. "Or I'll shoot!"

Curly spun and fired twice.

As she had shouted, Abigail had bent over, hugging the back of her mount. The instant Curly began to turn, she slid off.

Both shots missed her.

"Throw down your gun, I say," she cried from her kneeling position beside her mount. "Or I shall shoot you!" She no longer doubted that she could kill a man. This man.

Once again, Curly fired, hitting her mount's flank. It sped away, leaving Abigail exposed. Smiling, he pulled the trigger again, but it clicked on an empty chamber.

Hearing that his gun was empty, Abigail stood. "Drop it, I say."

"You're jest a greenhorn girl!" Curly tauted, reaching for bullets in his gunbelt. "You won't shoot me!"

Outrage at his endangering Jacqueline heated Abigail's blood. That he had nearly killed Crosspatches robbed her of reason. Steadying the derringer with both hands, she took careful aim at his chest. "I shall shoot you if you do not drop your weapon at once!"

"You cain't hit nothin' with that toy!" Curly laughed as he began to reload.

Abigail pulled the trigger.

The bullet splintered his kneecap.

Curly shrieked. Falling backward, he dropped his gun and grabbed his knee—and screamed.

Gun still in both hands, Abigail approached him.

"My knee!" Curly screamed. "My knee!" Looking at Abigail as she drew near, gun aimed at his head, he cried, "Don't shoot! Please, don't shoot!"

Jacqueline hurriedly limped toward them.

"Your chin is a sight," Abigail said, glancing briefly at her maid. "Are you all right?"

"Yes, miss. I untie my hands and jump."

"See his gun?"

Jacqueline nodded.

"Go around that way, if you please, and bring it to me."

As Jacqueline swiftly did her bidding, Abigail changed her position so that Jacqueline never came between her sights and Curly.

Eyes full of hatred, Curly glared at Abigail and cursed between sobs. Only his certainty that she would shoot him again kept him from lunging at Jacqueline as she retrieved his gun.

"Now untie the rope that's holding your horse to Crosspatches and tie his hands behind his back."

"If you please, miss," Jacqueline said, slightly raising the skirt to her riding costume. "My slip, she makes the better binding."

Abigail nodded her approval. Jacqueline turned her back to tear strips from her petticoat.

"Turn over!" Abigail commanded.

"My knee," Curly cried, holding his blood-soaked pants. "I cain't. My knee!"

"I care not a fig for your knee," Abigail said with an icy calm. "If you do not turn over at once, and remain perfectly still while my maid ties your hands, I shall shoot you in the stomach!"

Screaming and cursing, Curly turned.

"Hands together!" Abigail said. "Or I assure you I shall shoot you without the slightest regret."

Curly continued yelling and cursing, but he remained docile.

"Tie him tightly!" Abigail said.

"Yes, miss," Jacqueline replied. "I am the *sempstress*. I know the knots."

Securing Curly's hands to his belt, Jacqueline stood. Dizzy, she started to ask if Abigail had by chance brought the smelling salts when they both heard the sound of an approaching horse.

Before they had time to dive for cover, Tilghman rode up. "Are you all right?" he cried, leaping from his horse, gun drawn.

"There is your fugitive, Marshal." Abigail smiled sweetly, placing her derringer in the pocket of her skirt. "And in less than one month."

"I reckon I owe you an apology, Miss Danforth." Tilghman tipped his hat. "And a large debt of gratitude for saving my life."

His words of genuine praise instantly erased all trace of Abigail's resentment toward him. She blushed with pleasure.

Tilghman turned to Jacqueline. "And you?" He smiled. "How are you after your close call?"

Trying to copy her mistress's aplomb, Jacqueline began a curtsy. Suddenly realizing the peril she had narrowly escaped, dizziness overwhelmed her. She fainted.

Chapter Twenty

Abigail had disappeared from view on her chase after Curly and Jacqueline by the time Maw Baxter had dragged herself to the porch railing. Pulling herself up to her knees, she had discovered that her hip had not been broken, even though it hurt like the dickens. Limping, she had taken her place at the stove to boil water to cleanse Billy Bub's wound. She had no heart to partake in what was happening in the barn and prayed that her son would not be killed.

In due course, Boss and Sampson were led into the kitchen by their captors. A heated discussion had ensued regarding who should go after Abigail and Jacqueline, but the two women, and Tilghman, had returned with Curly before a decision had been reached.

Sedating him with some of Curly's whiskey, Maw bandaged and splinted Billy's arm for travel to the doctor in town. Then she cleansed and bound Curly's knee, though not with the same tenderness. She had made fresh coffee and heated some biscuits, insisting that they all refresh themselves before loading the injured, and Hank's body, into the buckboard. For once, no one had argued.

In the privacy of her stateroom in the railroad car, long after the others had retired, Abigail lay awake. Again and again, she relived the scene where Curly had his gun pointed at Crosspatches' head. Again and again, she felt the heat of blind rage pass through her—rage that fueled an urge to kill. And a gun had made it so easy. She shuddered at how close she'd come to killing another human being. Remembering how rage had contorted Curly's face, she touched her own.

Finally unable to resist satisfying her curiosity, she rose and, slipping into a dressing gown, lit the oil lamp on her dressing table. Peering into the mirror, she examined her familiar, youthful face with its straight nose, warm brown eyes and firm chin. Once again, she relived the incident. She felt the gun in her hand and the urge to kill. To her horror, her expression hardened and aged her features to those of a hateful stranger. Someone she would be afraid of. Someone she did not wish to know. Someone she did not want to become.

With a groan, she blew out the lamp, flung herself on the bed, and wept. When her tears were at long last spent, she reexamined her desire to devote her life to the infant science of detection. To solve mysteries, bring criminals to justice, and free the innocent remained a passion. But she could not bring herself to further pursue such a life at the expense of becoming a murderess herself. And, at last, she knew how she was going to respond to Mr. Dade's request for her hand.

* * *

"Oh, Miss Danforth," Morgan cried. "You cannot mean that." He sank into Maude's favorite chair by the window.

"Oh, but I do," Abigail responded sadly. "I assure you I am quite serious when I say I cannot marry you." Unable to bear his stricken expression, she gazed at her hands folded demurely in her lap.

Morgan leaned forward eagerly. "But I love you," he said.

Abigail glanced up briefly. "Could you stop wearing your gun, for me?"

Shocked, he drew back. "But Miss Danforth!" he exclaimed. "Whatever for? It is my right to wear a gun!"

"Not too long ago, it was also a right to own another human being," she replied.

"That's different!" he exclaimed. "Of course slavery was wrong!" Dismissing her comment with a wave of his hand, he continued, "I'd be lost without my gun."

"Curious," Abigail said, gazing at him directly. "I have discovered that I lose who I am, or who I wish to be, when I use one."

Morgan stood and paced to the desk. "What is so wrong about carrying a gun?"

Her expression grim, Abigail rearranged her already perfectly placed skirts. "I must admit to a certain amount of pride in hitting bottles on a fence, Mr. Dade." She shrugged. "But wanting to kill a man is—" she shuddered—"horrible. And having a gun in my hand would have made it so easy." She gazed at him earnestly. "I cannot tell you how grateful I am that I missed. As it is, he will be crippled for life."

"But you were in danger, Miss Danforth!" Morgan returned to Maude's chair and sat on the edge. Leaning close, he said earnestly, "Curly would have killed you had you not shot him first."

"On that point you are correct," Abigail stared out of the window. "I do not know what would have happened had I not shot him." She turned her gaze to Morgan. "I do know that I did not like myself afterward. And I am the one who must live with me, before I can live with another."

"But how can you pursue your desire to become a detective without carrying a weapon?"

Abigail shrugged. "Lawmen in England have always gone unarmed."

"But you might be killed!"

"That may be." Abigail stood to signal that their interview was at an end. Morgan was on his feet in an instant. "I shall have to be careful," she continued. "But although I relish putting a criminal behind bars, the idea of killing one is abhorrent to me."

As they reached the curtained doorway, he turned and looked down at her hungrily. "Oh, Miss Danforth, do you not love me, even a little? Won't you change your mind?" he cried.

She gazed up at him through her lashes. "Would you?" she asked gently.

He shook his head helplessly. "I don't know what to say."

Offering him her hand in a farewell gesture, she said, "Then I most respectfully suggest, sir, that we say good-bye."

* * *

Entering the private railroad car, Tilghman placed his white ten-gallon hat in Kinkade's outstretched hand. "And how is the plucky Jacqueline this morning?" he asked.

"Very well, sir," Kinkade replied, brushing aside the curtain to the parlor. "She's having a bit of a rest today."

Because of her mourning, Maude's entire wardrobe was black, but she had borrowed a heavily fringed white lace shawl from Abigail. Artfully draping and catching it with a brooch, she'd transformed a dowdy dress into a stylish gown. Pearls dangled from her ears. Standing, hand outstretched, she greeted Tilghman.

"If I understand your arrangement," he said with a bow toward Abigail, who was seated by the window, "you plan to write about the recovery of Crosspatches and the Arabian and the arrest of the Baxter Gang?"

"I do believe it will sufficiently enhance Miss Danforth's reputation to warrant publication," Maude replied with not a little pride.

"It adds very little to my own," he said sheepishly.

"Never fear, Marshal Tilghman," Maude said. "Respect for your prowess as a lawman will not be diminished." Seating herself in the chair opposite Abigail, she indicated that he make himself comfortable in the chair that Kinkade proffered, then dismissed Kinkade with a wave of her hand. "I will appreciate your informing me of the outcome of the trials so that I may add an epilogue."

Wishing to garner a tid bit of gossip with which to entice Jacqueline, Kinkade left the room, but remained within earshot.

"You might wish to write that Mrs. Dawson was deeply grieved by Hank's death." Tilghman sighed.

250

"She blames me, of course, even though Curly pulled the trigger."

"There is little doubt that Curly will be put away for life, is there, Marshal?" Abigail asked.

"He won't be our prisoner for long, ma'am," the Marshal replied. "He's wanted in Leavenworth for the murder of his lady friend and a possible rival. If he doesn't get the death penalty for Mr. Osgood and Hank, he'll hang for shooting Sally. Folks around here don't take kindly to the murder of women. Boss and Sampson will probably serve time. But they just might let Mrs. Baxter and Billy Bub go free."

"I hope so," Abigail said. "Had she not told me you were a prisoner, you might be tied to that chair still."

"And may I congratulate you on your fine shooting, Miss Danforth?" Tilghman said. "It is the writers from the East who have given us our reputation for winging a man." He glanced at Maude.

Maude smiled a rare smile that reached her gray eyes.

"In reality, we usually go for the kill if you must shoot," Tilghman continued. "Too dangerous to wound him. Might just make him crazy angry. But as I say, that was quite a shot. With a derringer, too."

"Thank you for the compliment, Marshal," Abigail responded. "But actually, I missed. I was aiming at his heart."

"Your modesty becomes you, Miss Danforth," the marshal replied. "I only wish you had not allowed Polecat and Mulehead to escape justice."

"I must confess I borrowed a page from Dr. Conan Doyle," Abigail said. "He has written that on occasion, more harm can be done by discovering the criminal than the criminal has done by his crime.''

"And you applied that philosophy to Polecat and Mulehead?'' Tilghman was astonished by her audacity.

"You need but converse with them to realize that they are not evil men,'' she replied cooly. "Their crime of stealing our horses was a matter more thrust upon them by necessity than something they had planned.''

"But they tried to rob you!'' Tilghman protested.

"I'll warrant they'll not try anything similar,'' Abigail said. "Furthermore, they took excellent care of Crosspatches and your Arabian. I shudder to think what would have happened had they fallen prey to Curly.''

"And they were lured into your trap, Miss Danforth,'' Maude said, her rare smile still in place. "Is that not the real reason you are so inclined to excuse them?''

Abigail blushed.

"And so you are now playing tricks with the laws of the West rather than your own conscience?'' Tilghman asked.

"That sounds like a paraphrase from one of Dr. Conan Doyle's stories!'' Maude exclaimed.

"We are not entirely unlettered in the West, Miss Cunningham,'' Tilghman said with a gracious smile.

"And you yourself have had so many adventures, Marshal,'' Maude said. "Why, I should introduce you to my publisher in New York!''

"I'd be delighted, Miss Cunningham. Perhaps we may meet again.''

"I most sincerely hope so,'' Maude replied shamelessly.

"May I offer you coffee, Marshal?" Abigail asked.

"No, thank you, Miss Danforth," he said, standing. "I just wanted to wish you a safe journey before my train came. I understand your connection will be here at noon?"

"Yes." Maude stood to escort him to the door. "We will finally be on our way to San Francisco."

Abigail smiled. "Where, at last, our adventure will begin, eh, Miss Cunningham?"